UNDERTOW

NEW YORK TIMES BESTSELLING AUTHOR

JANA DELEON

Safe Harbor

"All water has a perfect memory and is forever trying to get back to where it was." – Toni Morrison

CHAPTER ONE

PORTLAND, OREGON

JILL MORGAN—KATE Coleson to her readers—signed the book and gave 'Becki with an *I*' a big smile as she passed it back to her. The fortyish woman giggled and bounced, causing her ample chest to go on its own jaunt.

"Moooooommmmm," her probably preteen daughter whined. "You're embarrassing me."

Becki rolled her eyes at her daughter and fixed her brilliant smile on Jill. "Thank you so much, Kate! You're my favorite author, ever. You inspired me to write my own book."

Becki launched into her confused plot and descriptions of the thirty or so characters she had appearing in the first chapter because the reader needed to know everyone or they wouldn't 'get' the story. Jill just froze the smile on her face and thought about the book she was currently working on and the load of laundry she'd forgotten in the washing machine that morning.

"Hey, maybe we could meet for coffee sometime and you

could tell me what you think," Becki said, finally bringing her monologue to an end.

"Mom, stop bothering her," the daughter said. "No one wants to read your book, and I'm sure everyone asks her that. I want to be a singer, but I'm not going to harass Taylor Swift at her concert next month to help me."

Jill wanted to tell the daughter she was right about all of it, but that wasn't allowed. However, she was impressed with the young girl's situational awareness, logic, and character assessment, although she suspected Becki's opinion of her daughter's abilities wasn't as favorable, especially when the critical eye was focused on her.

"I'm sorry," Jill said. "I don't really have the bandwidth for that sort of thing. My schedule is very tight."

"Did I tell you I drove all the way from Seattle for this?" Becki persisted.

Jill nodded. At least twenty times already.

"This has totally made my year," Becki said.

"Enough, Mom! Take classes like everyone else. Now can we go?"

Jill held her smile in place as Becki finally allowed her frustrated daughter to pull her out of the bookstore. As soon as the door closed behind them, the store owner, Wanda, clicked the lock in place and flipped the Closed sign around.

"I'm closing early," Wanda said and leaned against the door with a sigh. "Why is it always the last one?"

"It's intentional. Then they don't have to rush off because there are more people waiting."

"So they think they have you captive." Wanda shook her head. "I like people. I'm good with people. You've seen me work a room. But sometimes... Anyway, I have wine breathing for us upstairs. And I might have those chocolate-covered strawberries you like so much."

"Will you marry me?"

Wanda laughed. "If only we were built that way. We'd make the perfect couple, although I'd be a bit of a cougar."

At thirty-three, Jill was at least a decade younger than Wanda, probably closer to two, but in addition to winning the good gene lottery, the older woman wasn't afraid to spend her store profits and alimony to keep people guessing.

Jill followed Wanda to her suite above the bookstore, headed into her half bath—which looked like something you'd find at the Ritz—and removed the wig of glossy short black waves. Her real light brown hair tumbled down her back, and she could practically feel her scalp breathing. She left the wig on the bathroom counter, then headed for the living room where she plopped down on an overstuffed white chair and gazed out the huge reflective glass window that looked over the street.

People milled up and down the sidewalks, taking in the sights, shopping, and restaurants in this artsy little area of town. Wanda had picked the location because of the quirky surroundings shortly after her divorce from husband number two. Husband number one had been a 'young and foolish' mistake that she'd had annulled almost as soon as they'd said 'I do' but number two had stuck for decades. She'd gotten a settlement large enough to pay for the building outright and remodel it to serve as both business and cool modern living quarters, and she still had some socked away for when she got 'too damned old to deal with people.'

"How's art class going?" Jill asked after she took a sip of the truly excellent wine along with a bite of one of the chocolate-covered strawberries.

Wanda sank into the chair next to her and sighed. "You know those pictures that mothers all over the country have on their refrigerators—the ones their kindergartners do?"

Jill nodded.

"Worse than that."

Jill grinned. "So take up something easier?"

"At this point, the only thing easier would be crayons and a coloring book."

"Always an option."

Wanda waved a hand in dismissal. "I've never been good at artsy things. It's a shame really, because I have an artist's spirit and I love being around that creative energy. But I accepted long ago that any time I step into artistic pursuits, it has to be at the hobby level only. And an extraordinarily bad hobby level at that. But I do find it relaxing, which I suppose is the point as I don't need to make money from it."

"Well, since most artists doing it to pay the bills no longer find it relaxing, that seems a fair enough trade-off."

Wanda smiled but Jill could tell it was a tiny bit forced. Her friend looked out the window and the corners of her well-Botoxed lips turned down a tiny bit. She tapped on the side of her wineglass with one long gold nail.

"What's wrong?" Jill asked.

Wanda's eyes widened a tiny bit, and then she shook her head. "I don't want to say."

Jill frowned as she stared at Wanda, who couldn't quite meet her eyes, then tensed.

"You got one of them," Jill said, her words not a question because she already knew the answer.

Wanda nodded. "The card was dropped through my mail slot. As soon as I saw the envelope and that it was addressed to you, I knew. It just felt creepy. I know it sounds stupid because a pink envelope shouldn't be scary, but it was."

It didn't sound stupid at all to Jill. She'd been terrified of pink envelopes for five years now.

"Did you open it?" she asked.

4

"Yes. I wasn't going to, but then I thought if I go hiking my loud mouth into the police station, all demanding and stuff, and find out it was from a normal fan, then they're going to take things even less serious than they do already."

Jill held in a sigh. It wasn't that the cops didn't take her stalker seriously. It was more that they couldn't do anything about him—mostly because no one knew who he was. And even if they could locate him, a restraining order was the extent of her options because he hadn't threatened her. Which was completely different from feeling threatened, which she absolutely did. The cops knew that too and didn't think the stalker's intentions were good either, but ultimately, their hands were tied by limited facts and an even more limited legal system.

"What did it say?" Jill asked.

Wanda tapped on her phone and passed it over to Jill. "I knew you'd want to know—well, not *want* to, but want to—anyway, I took a picture."

Jill looked down at the image of the card—the same card she'd gotten fifteen times, now sixteen—and felt her chest tighten. It was a simple white card with a red heart drawn on the front, made to look like crayon. It was also mass produced and available in every drugstore and retail center in the country. The inside was blank—when new—so that someone could personalize their message. The cards she received were always personalized using a red crayon to match the front. She flicked to the next image, knowing Wanda would have taken a shot of the inside.

MY HEART BLEEDS FOR YOU.
When will yours finally bleed for me?

. . .

SHE SUCKED IN A BREATH, trying to steady her racing heart. This message was so much worse than any she'd seen before. They'd always been about when she and the stalker were united as one. This...this felt like something else entirely. Had he finally tipped over the edge of threats and into preparing for action?

You're safe here.

She just needed to keep reminding herself of that. Wanda might be eccentric and artsy, but she was also wealthy and originally from Texas, which meant her security system was top-notch and she had a gun in the Gucci handbag on the coffee table in front of her.

"After I took those pictures, I put the card and the candy in a plastic bag and marched it right down to the police station myself," Wanda said. "Sat there for thirty minutes waiting on that Detective Ward, but I wasn't leaving until I showed him personally."

"What did he say?"

Wanda threw her hands in the air. "Same thing he always does—they'll run it for prints, but that you shouldn't get your hopes up."

"They're not likely to find any, given that the last fifteen were clean."

"When was the last one?"

"Three months ago at the book signing in Seattle."

"He's escalating," Wanda said quietly. "Less time in between and that message... It's not like the others. You know it, I know it, and that damned Detective Ward knows it."

Jill gave her a helpless shrug. "What can we do?"

Wanda sighed. "It's times like these I wish my grandpappy was still with us. He'd have you sitting in the middle of the street at 2:00 a.m. while he sat smiling on the roof with his sniper rifle just waiting for that cowardly pervert to show."

"You're saying your grandfather would use me as bait?"

"I'm saying he would *successfully* use you as bait. Dad always said Grandpappy was the only person who went to war in Korea and had fun."

"I'm not even sure what to say to that."

"No one else is either. Look, I want you to stay here tonight. The guest room is already made up. We can order takeout, drink more wine, and argue the merits of who has the cutest butt at the coffee shop."

"We've already had that argument and it's definitely Jason, but they're all way too young for us." Jill shook her head. "If the stalker has finally decided to make his move, this is the first place he'll look since he knows I signed here today. He could be down there on the street watching this place, or he could have been that guy I signed three books for—the one with the weird bushy eyebrows."

"Too obvious."

"Regardless, the last thing I want to do is put you in the middle of it."

Wanda frowned, but she knew Jill was right. "But you're so secluded where you are, and you have that long drive."

"It's only a couple hours, and I'll be there before dark. After that situation in college, I became a ghost. The house is in a trust and my information isn't available to anyone but my attorney. Same for utilities. And I don't go by my birth name or Kate there. No one has ever connected the three. If the stalker had, he would be sending these cards to my house instead of book signings, which are all listed on my website."

"I know but...all those trees, and no neighbors within screaming distance."

"I like secluded because then if my neighbors Airbnb— which everyone with a view seems to be doing these days—I don't have people constantly flowing around me. The wig and

7

the glamorous makeup have worked fabulously for Kate, and no one has connected her with Jill. I'm glad I started with them from the beginning of my career."

Wanda shook her head. "Sooner or later, as Jill, you're going to run across that person with a keen eye for faces and they're not going to matter."

She shrugged. "I already have a time or two. I just smile and say I get that a lot and move on. It's not like anyone can prove it. And before you start worrying about me leaving here, I'm putting the damned wig back on before I go, as always, and I'll take it and the makeup off before I get home. I'm very careful, Wanda. I've been careful for years."

"What if he follows you when you leave?"

"If I don't notice someone trailing me for two hours, then I'm dumber than the big-boobed girl in the opening scene of every horror movie and deserve to be killed."

Wanda pursed her lips. "That's not funny. I know from all those damned self-help books I read that your joking is a coping mechanism, but I also know you're scared because *I'm* scared and I'm not even you."

Jill reached over and squeezed Wanda's arm. "You're right. I *am* scared. But I'm also very careful. Staying here only makes things worse for you, and I have to go home at some point anyway."

"Unless we figure out that marriage thing. Then you could move in."

Jill smiled at her friend. The two of them had taken to each other the second they'd met four years before when Jill had done her first signing at Wanda's store. Ever since, they'd been thick as thieves. But Wanda also knew that Jill would never stay if she thought it put Wanda on the line.

"I don't think we've dated long enough for marriage," Jill said. "And we still haven't had the finances discussion."

"If we agree on no kids, then the finances are a lot easier." Wanda sighed. "I know you have to go home. Have to be in your space to create, and ultimately, staying here doesn't fix anything. But I need you to know that you're always welcome. Any time. Without warning. Whatever. Just remember if you turn up on Monday or Thursday, I have Pilates that night and I'm pretty sure my instructor was a prison warden. I drink heavily after class, so a bottle of wine in your overnight bag is always appreciated."

Jill smiled. "You're the best friend ever. You know that, right? And I promise I'll text you when I get home."

Wanda shook her head. "Someone can conk you over the head, use your face to open your phone, and send me a text so I don't send out the troops."

"Your faith in humanity is overwhelming."

"I read your books. I want FaceTime from your living room."

"I have an empty pizza box on my couch."

"No one is perfect."

———

WANDA WAVED at Jill as she drove away. It was only 5:00 p.m. and her friend had plenty of daylight to make the drive home, especially on a Saturday, which meant no commuter traffic to speak of. Wanda knew that Jill had the best in security systems in her home because Wanda had recommended the company who'd installed it. And everything Jill had said about her being impossible to track back to her address, even if someone did know her real name, was also true. But none of it stopped the overwhelming feeling of foreboding that swept through her.

Never one to give in to 'fancy' unless it was fancy dress, jewelry, or food, Wanda headed through the back door and into the building, then stood in the middle of the retail area, hands on her hips. Everything in there was still as perfect as she'd left it an hour ago. She had a full night ahead of her and absolutely nothing on her calendar. Even worse, now that Jill had mentioned pizza, Wanda was craving it, but figuring her Pilates instructor would be able to smell it on her two days later kept her from pulling out her phone and putting in an order.

She spent another five minutes wandering around the shop. Then after deciding there was absolutely nothing about her business that needed her attention, she finally gave in to a night of pizza and TV and headed for the stockroom that housed the stairs to her apartment. She pulled out her phone and hit the pizza place on speed dial—then reminded herself to never let her Pilates instructor see her phone. When she stepped into the stockroom, she saw movement out of the corner of her eye.

She only had a second to realize her mistake—she hadn't set her alarm as soon as she'd walked inside. All she managed was a scream before something struck her on the back of the head and everything went black.

CHAPTER TWO

Oregon Coast

JILL DROVE up the winding road to her house and frowned when she saw the familiar truck in the driveway. Jacob Thomas was a local handyman whom Jill had hired to help with basic maintenance things that she didn't want to tackle herself. It was a fairly long list, especially the landscaping, which Jill had made an attempt at but had mostly only succeeded in killing flowers. Jacob had seemed relieved when she'd told him she was going to find another hobby.

But she hadn't hired Jacob to do any work lately.

She spotted him in her side yard as she pulled into her garage. He lifted one gloved hand to wave and then turned back to the large tree limb he was attacking with a chain saw. She shook her head as she climbed out of her car. If Wanda knew there was a man with gloves and a chain saw in her yard, she'd have Jill on the next plane to someplace no one had ever heard of.

Jill forced her public smile back onto her face and crossed the yard. Jacob turned off the chain saw when he saw her coming and smiled back.

"Evening, Ms. Smith," Jacob said. "Sorry about the noise, but I won't be much longer."

"What are you doing exactly?"

"That tree was rotten. I've been keeping an eye on it for a while, afraid it needed to come down. When I was here putting those flowers in a couple weeks ago, I noticed the split on the side nearest to your house. We're supposed to have high winds tonight. Based on how easy my saw passed through it, I'm afraid it would have gone right into your dining room. I know you didn't ask me to do it, but I didn't want you to have a bigger problem come tomorrow morning. There's no charge."

Jill was fairly certain Jacob hadn't taken a breath the entire time he'd talked. He was always like that—either saying nothing or saying everything at once. Jill had recognized the signs of shyness when they'd first met to discuss the work she needed but had thought that they might decrease over time. So far, he'd been doing odd jobs at her home for two years and that hadn't happened. Jill was beginning to suspect Jacob's issues went deeper than being an introvert.

"I appreciate you taking care of that," she said. "And please bill me for whatever time that took. It looks like a big job, and I would have approved it. It's a shame to lose such an old tree, but I didn't love it enough to eat dinner with it."

He gave her a shy smile and nodded. "I'll get back to it then."

She turned around and headed into her house as he fired up the chain saw. The alarm system beeped at her as she walked inside. She turned it off, then stepped into the kitchen and grabbed a bottled water from her refrigerator before sitting at the counter and opening her laptop. She had stuff to prepare in the refrigerator, but she wasn't feeling it. Time to add another empty pizza box to her living room.

She accessed her account at the best pizza place in the area and ordered her standard pepperoni with extra cheese, then rang Wanda, who didn't answer. Jill followed up with a text, assuring her friend she was safe and sound, and then grabbed her water and headed out onto the back patio. She slid onto a patio chair and sighed as she watched the burst of color across the ocean. Her house sat high above the water, off a stretch of road with little development. The nearest homes on each side were several acres of dense woods away, and since she'd purchased that available acreage along with her home, it would remain that way.

'Jill Smith' was who she'd become after college, the result of a boyfriend who'd refused to accept their breakup. He'd gone from sad to clingy to threatening in a short amount of time, which had culminated with him breaking into her apartment and trying to rape her. And if she hadn't gotten out that first big scream before he gagged her, he would have succeeded. But that scream had her neighbor—who happened to be a retired cop—bursting through her door and leaving her attacker with no question as to who the bigger man was.

She'd been traumatized by not only what had happened but how close she'd come to things being far worse. Would he have stopped at rape? She honestly didn't know the answer but the more time that passed, the more she was inclined to believe that her neighbor had literally saved her life. Then he'd helped her preserve what bit of sanity she'd had left.

He put her in touch with a therapist and an attorney. The therapist addressed her nightmares and PTSD, and the attorney addressed her name change so that Jill Morgan could become Jill Smith and easily disappear into society. She'd been only weeks away from graduating, and the university and her professors had worked with her so that she could finish up her degree without returning to campus, something that left her breathless every time she attempted to step into a classroom that she'd shared with her ex-boyfriend.

Upon insistence by the cop neighbor, the university had gone even further and duplicated her records, issuing graduating credentials to both Jill Morgan and Jill Smith. 'There's no point in having worked her ass off for four years if she can't even use it,' had been his claim to the university president. So Jill Morgan/Smith had left Cornell University with a psychology degree and had moved across the country to Portland, where she'd accepted an entry-level job at an insurance company as a claims representative.

Not because it was at all what she'd educated herself for or what she wanted to be, but because no one would look for her there.

The psychology degree came in handy in the corporate world, and she quickly moved up in rank, making manager in only two years. By day, she kept claims flowing so that people had use of their insured property and by night, she wrote domestic thrillers. Her psychiatrist—whom she still did quarterly virtual check-ins with—had declared her selection of genre to be part therapeutic and part proof that she still wasn't healed, which Jill didn't necessarily agree with. What they both did agree on was that her authentic ability to capture the intensity, fear, and physical response to being a victim vaulted her storytelling talent into bestseller territory.

Four years later, when her second book showed up on the *New York Times* bestseller list and her publisher offered her a seven-figure advance for the third, she gave her notice at her insurance job and became a full-time novelist.

A year after that, she received her first pink envelope.

Every release had been more successful than the one before it, with three now optioned for movies. Her bank account had moved into stratosphere zones and even when she paid cash for her home with the incredible view, it still didn't seem real.

The wig was something she'd adopted from the beginning of her career, along with her pen name. She'd explained the situation to her editor—a hard-nosed businesswoman in her fifties but also the mother of a very beautiful daughter—and she'd immediately understood and supported her decision. She had also ensured that Jill's true identity had never been at risk for exposure. All paperwork was under her pen name and handled by her attorney. Her editor was the only person with the publishing company who knew Jill's real name.

In the early years, Jill managed to avoid public events altogether, but when the advances kept growing, the publisher became more insistent that Kate Coleson needed to get out among her readers. So Kate and her wig and glam makeup went on a small book-signing tour, and Jill Smith bought a secluded home off the Oregon coast that had been serving as a rental for several years. And her separate lives worked perfectly.

To the locals, she was a claims adjuster who worked from home. She figured keeping the same line of employment as before made it easier to answer any questions that might arise, even though Jill had discovered that most people had complaints about insurance companies but few questions. To explain the pricey home given a basic job, she also spread the story that she had inherited the home and land from a distant relative, hence the trust's name on the deed. That was assuming anyone was nosy enough to check, and she figured they probably were.

She was polite to everyone but kept to herself. You'd never find her at the gym or at any kind of club meeting, although she occasionally ventured out to grab a meal at a local restaurant and pick up her groceries, and delivery was part of her life. The local gossip circled back to her through Peggy, the ever-talkative clerk down at the local diner, so Jill knew that the theories on her life ranged from she was wanted by the Russian mob to she was hiding from an abusive ex-husband, the second being a little too close for comfort.

But regardless of her secretive nature, her polite demeanor, willingness to shop locally, and regular donations to local charities kept her in good standing and also prevented people from attempting to intrude on her solitude. And her fake identity— Jill Smith—was perfect. It allowed her to use her first name, which made responding to people automatic, and both were so common, it was easy to remain hidden in the deluge, especially as Jill Smith had no social media presence.

The doorbell brought her out of her trip down memory lane, and she realized that the chain saw noise was also gone. She hurried inside to claim her dinner, not sure whether or not she should be worried that she'd been so lost in thought that she hadn't noticed a chain saw no longer running. She gave the delivery guy a cash tip, as she always did, and the teen flashed his huge smile at her before hurrying off.

Jacob's truck was gone, which made sense as the sun had already set and there wasn't much light left, especially on the side of the house where the surrounding trees made things even darker with their shadows. She heard an owl call in the night and shivered even though it wasn't really cold. Suddenly unnerved, she closed the door, locked it, and set the alarm.

Someone was walking over her grave.

———————

At first, Jill thought the music was part of her dream, then she realized it was her phone and her spine tightened. She'd assigned the *Cops* theme ringtone to Detective Ward as a joke, although she was the only one in on it. She glanced at the time as she grabbed the phone from her nightstand, and a new wave of anxiety coursed through her. Six a.m. was way too early for a follow-up call about the card Wanda had delivered the day before. Six a.m. calls were as bad as 2:00 a.m. calls.

She popped upright and answered, now a little breathless.

"Ms. Coleson?" he said, and she sucked in a breath.

Using her pen name meant he was in front of other people and needed to protect her identity, which in the police department was known only by Ward and his captain. Something had happened. Something that required other people to be involved.

"What's wrong?" she asked.

"I'm at the hospital. Wanda Perkins has been attacked. She's stable but is still unconscious."

"Oh my God!" Jill jumped out of bed, fear coursing through her. "Attacked when? How? Did you catch him?"

"It happened yesterday evening. She'd just dialed a pizza place to order, and they heard her scream before the call dropped. The manager called it in, and a unit found her back door open and Ms. Perkins collapsed in the stockroom. She'd been struck on the back of the head, and she'd lost a good amount of blood already. The hospital got her stabilized quickly, but she still hasn't regained consciousness."

"Yesterday... Why am I just now hearing about this?"

"Because the unit that took the call didn't file their paperwork until early this morning, so the tickler to notify me wasn't seen until then. They called me as soon as they got the notification, and I met them at the hospital to get their story and talk to Ms. Perkins's doctor."

"What did he say? Is she going to be okay? Was anything stolen? She has some expensive art upstairs."

Jill's mind raced a million different directions. Was this her fault? Had the card stalker attacked Wanda, trying to get to Jill?

"You know what," she said. "I'll be there as soon as possible, and you can tell me everything then. Just text me the information."

"I don't think coming here is a great idea."

"She's my best friend, and since her being attacked might be because of me, it seems a shitty time to hide."

He sighed but knew better than to argue with her.

"Let me know when you get here," he said. "And I'll tell you where to find me."

Jill ran into her closet and threw on jeans, a T-shirt, and tennis shoes. She took a couple minutes to put on makeup, just to keep up the charade. Then she grabbed her larger handbag and transferred her wallet and pistol from her book-signing tote into it, then shoved her phone in, grabbed her car keys and her Kate Coleson wig, and hurried into the garage.

She made the drive to Portland at well over the speed limit and said a prayer of thanks that the traffic police weren't out and about. The last thing she needed was a delay in getting to her friend. The only stop she'd made was to pull over into an empty parking lot just outside of the city limits to don the wig. The entire drive had been an exercise in increased anxiety and guilt. What had happened? Why did he attack Wanda? Was she going to be okay? But the biggest question was the why.

And she was afraid she already knew the answer.

She texted Detective Ward as soon as she pulled into the hospital parking garage, and he told her to meet him in the ER lobby, which meant Wanda was still unconscious, because if she'd awakened, they could have looked her over and moved her to a room or even ICU. She jumped out of her car and practically ran into the hospital, scanning the text and arrows on the boards to locate the ER wing.

Detective Ward sat in the back corner of the lobby, holding a cup of coffee, which he set down immediately as he spotted her. He stood as she rushed over.

"Where is everyone?" she asked. "Why aren't there fifty cops in here trying to figure out what happened?"

He put his hands on her shoulders to steady her. "Because they're out looking for clues where they can make the most difference. And we needed to have this conversation in private, so I told them I'd take your statement since you're probably the last person who saw her."

"Except for the person who attacked her."

"Except for them, yes. Why don't you sit, and I can make some notes."

Jill ran a hand through her hair and blew out a breath before plopping down in a chair.

"First, how is Wanda?" she asked.

"There's been no change since she was brought in, but her vitals are strong. The doctor doesn't think there's any reason to believe she won't wake up and be fine. There's just a good bit of swelling and her body's protecting her right now. We have to wait until it's ready to give her back."

"That's a very pleasant way of describing a coma. I'm going to talk to you the next time I have to write one."

"I don't think people read your books for 'pleasant.'"

"No, but they do read them to see the bad guy taken down in the end. I need that to happen. Was anything stolen?"

"Wanda has to make the final determination on that, but my initial response is 'no.' Her purse was on the counter, and there was cash and a pistol in it. Neither were taken. And I'm sure those weren't the only items worth something in her apartment."

"Definitely not. The artwork is all original and some worth tens of thousands. And she has a Birkin bag."

He stared blankly at her.

"A purse worth about 50k."

He blinked. "A purse?"

"My point is, this wasn't a robbery, and she wasn't raped, so we both know this was about me. He knew I was signing in her store yesterday. That's why he left the note there."

"You think he was there for you."

"Do you have another explanation? I left through the back door. If he was watching the front of the store, he wouldn't have known that."

"But *he* left through the back door, and the front wasn't tampered with."

She blew out a breath of frustration. "Then I don't know the exact *how*, but I know the why and that's me. Because what I refuse to believe is that Wanda has incited anyone to the point of breaking into her home and trying to kill her. Everyone loves Wanda. Even her ex-husband still loves her, and he had to pay her a mint when they divorced. She's *that* person, you know?"

His expression softened and he nodded.

"What about her alarm?" Jill asked. "You said the pizza company called it in?"

"It wasn't set. It was disarmed around 5:00 p.m. and the call to the pizza place was about ten after."

"She disarmed it for me to leave. She'd armed it around

four when she closed up the bookstore and we went upstairs. I left a little after five. Why didn't she rearm it?"

"Detective Ward?" A man's voice sounded in the doorway, and Jill looked up and saw a doctor standing there. "Ms. Perkins has regained consciousness."

CHAPTER THREE

JILL JUMPED UP FROM HER CHAIR. "CAN I COME WITH YOU?"

"Are you Ms. Coleson?" the doctor asked. "If so, Ms. Perkins has been asking for you. You're welcome to come back if the detective is okay with it."

Detective Ward gave her a nod, and they followed the doctor down the hallway to a private room where he waved them inside then left them alone with Wanda. Relief coursed through Jill when she saw Wanda sitting upright, followed by intense anger at the huge bandage wrapped around her friend's head. She rushed over to the side of the bed and clasped Wanda's hand.

"Are you all right?" Jill asked.

Wanda squeezed her hand and nodded. "My head hurts worse than tax time...maybe even worse than the last year I was married to Phil, but I'll get over it."

Jill tried to laugh but was too choked up. Only Wanda could get attacked and make jokes after coming out of a coma.

"Can you remember what happened?" Detective Ward asked.

Wanda nodded, then winced. "I'll just stick to not moving

my head. Let's see, I'd just seen Jill off and had headed back inside my store."

"Through the back or front door?" Ward asked.

"The back. Jill was parked in the lot across the street. There's only one spot allocated to me directly behind the building, and Jill refuses to use it. Anyway, I walked back inside and stood inside the retail area for about five minutes, but since there wasn't anything to do, I decided to order pizza and have a night of television. I dialed the pizza place and started for the stairs in the stockroom when I saw a shadow off to my side. Then I heard footsteps, and as I screamed, something hit me on the back of the head so hard it felt like it exploded. I remember starting to fall, but I don't remember hitting the ground."

"Did you see the person who attacked you?"

"No. He was in the shadows and sort of behind me. I didn't have time to turn around."

"I didn't see any cameras in the stockroom."

"I only put them in the retail area, figuring that's where I would have problems." She sighed. "Every time I go cheap on something, I regret it."

"What about a general impression—height, weight?"

She frowned. "He was taller than me maybe by a couple inches, but it could have been more. I'm five foot seven and had on three-inch heels. I didn't get much of a look at him, but he wasn't a big guy—so not fat or overly muscled. But I got the impression he was in good shape. He moved so fast. I didn't have time to do anything."

"Is there any way he could have followed you inside after Jill left?"

"No. I only stepped outside a couple feet when she left— just enough to see her get safely across the street and drive off.

And I had a clear view of the back door from where I was standing in the retail area.

"Oh my God." Wanda sucked in a breath. "He was already inside."

Ward nodded. "He probably slipped in during the book signing. You said you have cameras in the retail area—I'm going to want the footage for yesterday."

"You think he was inside the store as well?" Wanda asked. "Surely not."

"You'd be surprised at the arrogance some criminals possess," Ward said. "Even if he wasn't inside yesterday, I would bet he has been at some point. Have you had problems with anyone lately?"

"No."

"Nothing at all? Even the smallest things can set a disturbed person off."

"There's nothing. My customers are a combination of locals, whom I know, and tourists who are there one day and gone the next. No one has even been rude lately, much less taken issue with me."

"What about your ex-husband?"

"Phil? Good Lord, no. Phil produces movies and has more money than God. Our split was amicable—well, as amicable as I wanted to be given that he was cheating. But Phil wanted the divorce as much as I did. Our marriage had run its course."

"Is Phil still paying you?"

"Yes, but he doesn't have to. Court-ordered alimony ended a few years ago. It's Phil's choice to continue with the payments."

Ward blinked. "Why would he do that?"

"Guilt, I'd guess. But that's his issue to work on. So until his therapist sorts that out, I'll keep cashing the checks. Being married to Phil was a metric ton of work. I consider it my pension plan."

"Okay, so the big question is still why this happened. I did a cursory check of your apartment and the obvious things to steal are still intact, including the cash and gun in your purse. Jill said your art is valuable and so is a handbag, but I didn't see empty space on the wall or gaps in your closet. Obviously, we'll need you to confirm, but is there anything you can think of that someone would take these risks to get their hands on?"

"Well, I suppose risk/reward is all relative, but if nothing's missing, then I don't have a clue. The valuables I have are readily apparent and easily accessible. It wouldn't take a minute to grab a painting and leave. And even if he was there for something else, why in the world would he leave cash and a gun behind? That makes no sense."

Jill looked down, unable to meet Wanda's eyes.

"Stop that," Wanda said, and Jill looked back up to see her friend staring right at her. "This has nothing to do with you."

"How can you say that when that card was delivered to the store?" Jill asked.

"Because if he was already inside, he could have come upstairs and killed us both after the signing," Wanda said.

"There's a pleasant thought," Jill said.

Wanda gave her a limp, dismissive wave. "You write this stuff every day. You know I'm right."

Detective Ward had been quiet during the exchange. Finally, he frowned, then spoke.

"Until we're certain what he was after, both of you have to be extra careful. Has the doctor said anything about when you might be released?"

"He's very vague," Wanda said. "Apparently if you're brought in unconscious, they don't like to commit to specifics like when you can go home."

"They have to make sure you're all right," Jill said. "And you're safer here than in your apartment."

"Really? You want to run numbers on how many people have died here versus my building?" Wanda sighed. "I'm sorry. I'm upset and my head is killing me. I just want that guy caught, and nothing can happen as long as I'm in here."

"Detective?" The doctor poked his head in the door. "Ms. Perkins needs to rest. You're welcome to come back this afternoon. That will give us time to run some more tests, and if everything looks good, we'll move her to a room."

"Doesn't sound restful to me," Wanda grumbled.

Jill leaned over and kissed her friend on the cheek. "I'll be back to check on you."

Before Wanda could utter a word of protest, Jill hurried out. She strode down the hallway and back to the lobby, then stopped, took a deep breath, and slowly blew it out. Wanda was the most vibrant, alive person Jill had ever met. Seeing her in that hospital bed, so pale, and with that fear in her eyes that hadn't been there before, had almost broken Jill.

Detective Ward walked through the double doors and into the lobby. "I talked with the doctor for a couple seconds. I think she's going to be fine. If her case is anything like the others I've seen, she'll probably only be in here for a day or two."

Jill nodded, wanting to believe him, but almost afraid to. Things sometimes went completely against the odds. She could only pray that this wasn't one of those times.

"I'm going to get a hotel room nearby," Jill said. "I can stay with her during the day and be on hand when she gets released. I don't want her going home alone."

Ward nodded, cluing in that there was no point in arguing. "The hotel at the end of the block has valet. And it would be a short walk on a crowded street if you wanted to go that route."

"Yes, thanks. That would be perfect. Is there anything I can do to help? Do you want me to go through the bookstore or her apartment?"

"No. You won't be able to spot things like Wanda could, and every person who enters could be compromising evidence."

"So sit and do nothing." Jill had spent enough time researching police procedure and investigative technique to know that she couldn't contribute, but it didn't stop her from wanting things to be different.

"I don't have to tell you to be careful, but I'm going to anyway. Be very careful. If this guy didn't get what he came for, there's a chance he'll come back. And since we don't know what he wanted, it's better to be more diligent with safety than less so."

———

Two days later, Jill helped a still-weak Wanda out of her car and into her bookstore. Detective Ward had met them in the parking lot, ready to go over everything with Wanda. Jill was on hand to remind Wanda to sit when she was tired because if Wanda had her way, she'd keep looking for a clue until she collapsed.

"I'm assuming you don't have any valuable books in the store—collector's item stuff?" Ward asked.

"No. Everything is shiny and new," Wanda said. "We have some signed editions, but the authors are still alive so they're not worth a lot yet."

"Okay, then," he said. "Let's start in your apartment. I want you to walk into each room and look around. Let that first initial feeling set in—is something off or does everything feel fine? Then start looking at the details, and if anything seems remotely different from the way you think you left it, tell me. It doesn't matter if you're wrong. This is just a starting point."

Wanda nodded.

They headed upstairs, and Wanda stepped into her living room and glanced around. Then she walked over to her favorite chair and sat, which made Jill happy. Just the walk up the stairs had left her friend winded, and she'd touched the side of her head twice already. Ward and Jill stood quietly as Wanda took in the room. Finally, she rose and shook her head.

"Nothing feels or looks off in here," she said.

"Then let's check out the other rooms," Ward said. "And please sit as often as you want. Take your time and let me know when you need a break."

They spent another hour in Wanda's apartment. Jill could tell Wanda was trying hard to find something—anything—that would indicate why this had happened, but when they'd circled back to the front door, Ward's notepad was still blank.

"I don't understand," Wanda said. "Why isn't anything missing?"

"The paintings are definitely the originals?" Ward asked.

"Yes. I read Jill's books. I know how the professionals will have a duplicate painted and replace the original so you don't realize it was stolen, but you saw me check the backs, right? On each one, I put a tiny ink mark using a color in the painting. No one would notice except me, and they're all there."

Ward nodded, satisfied. "Then let's go through the bookstore."

The bookstore seemed untouched as well. Even the signed copies of Jill's latest release were still stacked exactly as Wanda had left them. In the back room, Wanda walked them through her exact steps from entering the building to when she was struck.

"So he must have been in your office when you came back into the building," Ward said. "Let's check there next."

Wanda entered her office and looked around, but everything looked the same. She threw her hands in the air.

"Why can't I see anything?" she asked as she sank into her office chair. "I don't get any of this. Obviously that man knew how to break into the building. If he wanted something from my apartment, he could have taken it and left while we were at the signing. If he wanted something from downstairs, all he had to do was wait until I went back upstairs. If I'd set the alarm, it would have gone off, but he could have been halfway to Cleveland before cops responded."

She shot Ward an apologetic look. "No offense."

"None taken," he said. "And you're right about all of that. There are only three reasons I can think of that would explain it. The first is that attacking you was the objective."

"But—"

Wanda started to protest, but Ward held his hand up. "The second is that he wanted to put you out of commission to buy himself more time for whatever he was here to do. But he realized the pizza place had heard you scream before you dropped your phone, so he took off."

Jill frowned. She didn't like it, but so far, Ward was making a lot of sense.

"And the third reason?" Wanda asked.

"He panicked. You said you heard a noise and that's why you started to turn. He probably never intended to alert you to his presence, but once he did, he definitely didn't want you to get a good look at him."

"So he hit me before I could see him so that he could get away," Wanda said.

Ward nodded.

"But what if he didn't get what he came for?" she asked. "The building has been empty for days."

"With constant police patrol," Ward said. "Only a fool would have come back here so soon. Which means you have to be careful, because if he didn't accomplish what he came for, he might make another attempt."

Wanda leaned forward and put her elbows on her desk, then clutched her head. "When did my life get so complicated?"

She jostled the mouse with her elbow, and Jill saw her screen flash on. Wanda looked up as the bright light hit her face and frowned.

"What's wrong?" Jill asked.

"I didn't have this file open last time I used my computer," Wanda said. "I haven't had this file open in weeks."

Ward walked around and looked at the monitor. "What is it?"

Wanda's eyes widened and she sucked in a breath. "A mailing list for customers."

Ward's jaw flexed. "Is Jill's address on it?"

The blood rushed to Jill's head and she leaned back onto the credenza behind her. She already knew the answer.

"Yes," Wanda said. "I have to mail her stock sometimes, and this list is what I use to print postage. It's not under her name, of course, or Kate Coleson. I set it up as Angie's Nursery. A private joke between the two of us because Jill tends to avoid babies and can't keep a plant alive for more than a week."

"How long is the list?" Ward asked.

"Less than a hundred people. Amazon took away most of the mail-order print trade. The people on this list are mostly the ones who couldn't attend a signing but prepaid for an autographed copy. But he'd have to go through everyone on that list. Even if he looked up every address and saw that Angie's Nursery was a residential address, that doesn't mean that it couldn't be a home-based business. There's a ton of those these days."

Wanda's voice had increased in pitch and speed as she talked, and Jill knew her friend was on the verge of a grade-A panic attack. Unfortunately, Jill was halfway there herself and wasn't going to be any use to either of them.

"Oh my God," Wanda said. "If he was able to cross-reference this list with books shipped, then he'd know."

Ward stared at the two of them for several seconds, his expression grave. "I think we have to assume that it was Jill's address he was after. He probably didn't have time to cross-reference with the orders, but he's still got a working list of one hundred addresses. He'll start working his way through those—"

"And sooner or later, he'll get to me," Jill said. "But what I don't understand is why he didn't simply follow me when I left."

"He'd already left a note," Ward said. "You were on alert. How long would it have taken before you noticed him and called the cops?"

"Then why send the note at all? Why put me on notice?"

Ward frowned. "You're not going to like the answer—I don't think he could help himself. His obsession has begun to override logic."

Wanda looked absolutely stricken. "Oh my God, Jill, I am so sorry."

Jill shook her head. "I was here when we agreed on how you'd set the address up. We couldn't have known."

Ward nodded. "You've done everything possible to minimize your stalker's ability to locate you, but you're a public figure. There is no comprehensive answer to your problem. I know you've done your share of research and we've discussed the situation at length—"

The walls of Jill's carefully crafted life came crashing down around her. And all she could hear was Ward's words repeating in her head.

If he keeps at it, he'll eventually find you.

CHAPTER FOUR

JILL PULLED INTO HER DRIVEWAY BUT PARKED WITHOUT lifting the garage door. Detective Ward pulled in right behind her in his unmarked cruiser as she caught sight of Jacob planting some flowers in a bed around a wishing well in her side yard. She lifted her hand in a wave as she exited her car, and Jacob started walking toward her. He hesitated when he saw Ward step out of his car, then he continued but with a slightly wary expression.

"Hello, Ms. Smith," he said as he approached. "I hope it's all right that I started on the summer flowers. It's the ones you picked out. They were available a little sooner than we thought they'd be. I knocked on your door, but I guess you haven't been home."

"No. A friend in the city was ill and I went to help her out for a few days," Jill said.

Detective Ward stepped up, and Jacob looked slightly uneasy at his scrutiny.

"Colin," he said and extended his hand toward the other man. "An old friend of Jill's."

Jacob nodded and shook Ward's hand but didn't reply. Instead, he looked back at Jill.

"There was a man here late yesterday. He said he was doing a survey or something. I told him you weren't home, but he asked all kinds of questions."

Jill felt her back tighten.

"What kind of questions?" she asked.

"Like how old you were and if you had a husband and kids. I told him I just took care of the lawn. I didn't know anything about the people who live in the houses."

"That's smart of you," Jill said, forcing her voice to sound normal.

Jacob gave her a shy smile. "I figured if you wanted him to know that stuff, then you would tell him yourself when he came back."

"Did he mention when that might be?"

Jacob shook his head, then frowned.

"Is something wrong, Jacob?"

"I probably shouldn't say nothing, but I didn't like the way he looked."

"Why not?"

Jacob shrugged. "He wasn't dressed right. I've had those survey guys at my house before, and they're always wearing slacks and a button-up shirt. Got the businessman haircut. But this guy was wearing jeans and a T-shirt. Even had on a ball cap. And his beard needed trimming. I'll put shaving off for a couple days like the next guy, but if you're going to have a beard, you've got to keep it trimmed, otherwise, you look like a vagrant. Least, that's what my mom always said."

Jill forced a smile. "And moms are always right."

"Mine sure is. Well, I better get back to those flowers."

He gave Ward a glance before heading off.

"It was him," she said. "He's found me."

"We don't know that for certain, but I don't like the way it sounds. Does anyone here know your author identity?"

"No. I'm careful about it. When I'm Kate, I've always got my wig and the makeup. I put the wig on well before I drive up to an appearance and wear it and the makeup at least half the drive back just like I did today. Long enough to ensure I'm not being followed. I never wear it at home or around town."

Ward nodded his head toward Jacob's retreating figure. "What's his story?"

"Local guy. Highly recommended. Extremely reliable and conscientious."

"I make him nervous."

"You probably make a lot of people nervous. You're not exactly unimposing. But Jacob's shy. He barely looks at me when he talks, and he's been working here for years."

"I'll run him anyway."

Jill held in a sigh. She could point out that Jacob had just been in her yard with a chain saw a few days ago and hadn't killed her, but it wouldn't do any good. Ward was just doing his job. And if she had to guess, he probably felt a bit guilty over Wanda's attack, even though they both knew there was nothing he could have done to prevent it.

"I guess you should check inside," Jill said and started walking toward the front door.

Ward had insisted on following her to do a sweep of her home, which was why she'd parked in the driveway. Ward's orders—in case her stalker was lurking inside, ready to attack as soon as she was within striking distance. She unlocked the front door and pushed it open, then drew up short at the sight of the card inside her door. A wave of nausea swept through her, and she clutched the doorframe. The alarm buzzed so loudly in her head that she thought it would explode.

"Jill, the alarm." Ward's voice echoed in her mind, but she

couldn't focus on anything but the pink envelope in front of her.

She felt his hand squeeze her arm, and it broke her out of her trance. "The alarm!"

She stepped over the card and disarmed the system with only seconds to spare. Ward had moved to step inside but then stopped. She followed his gaze to the card on the ground.

"It was him," Jill whispered, and she staggered over to the couch and put her head between her knees, trying to catch her breath.

She heard the door close and lock but she couldn't look up. Not yet. Not while her world was falling apart. She forced herself to breathe, counting, in deep, out slowly, one, two, three, and slowly the nausea passed. Finally, she lifted her head and saw Ward squatting in front of her, his expression showing both anger and concern.

"You have to leave here for a while," he said.

"Ha. A while. He's been after me for five years—maybe even more for all I know. How long should I have to stay away from my own home?"

His jaw flexed and Jill knew he hated the situation, especially since he was the one who was supposed to provide solutions and the best he had was to run and hide, leaving her carefully crafted life behind.

"I can't leave," she said, trying to convince herself more than Ward. "Wanda is hurt. She's going to need help."

He looked her directly in the eyes. "Wanda is in more danger if you're around."

"Oh!" She covered her mouth with her hand and stared. How could she have been so stupid? She knew better. She lived in the minds of people like her stalker every day in her books.

"Do you have somewhere you can go?" he asked. "Somewhere no one will think to look for you?"

In the rush of uncertainty that had become her life, only one place came to mind.

"Yes," she said. "I can go home."

———

WANDA HUGGED Jill for the tenth time, squeezing her so hard she might have bruises tomorrow. Her friend wasn't a crier but Jill could see tears forming in her eyes when she released Jill and stepped back.

"I wish you were flying," Wanda said. "I know you can't tell me where you're going, but it's probably far away. Why do you insist on driving? A million things could go wrong."

"I can't fly. What if I'm recognized? And I'm sure he knows my fake identity by now and probably what I look like. And all it takes is one person low on cash and morality who works for the airlines to check for my name."

"That will only get him the city you land in. You could always rent a car and drive from there to somewhere else."

"It's too big a paper trail, and too many eyes on me."

"Then let me make some calls. Phil knows people who make him look poor. One of them is bound to have their own jet. I'll pay the tab."

Jill clutched her friend's shoulder. "Wanda, I love you and I understand what you're trying to do, but the easiest way for me to disappear is to drive. If Tom Cruise flew me there, I'd still need a car. And the last thing I want to do is put someone else in the line of fire. You could have been killed. I don't need you and some poor pilot on my conscience."

"But you're driving your own car," Wanda argued.

"Detective Ward is going to tail me for at least two hours. If anyone is following me, he'll get them. When I get to where I'm going, I'll put a temporary plate on the car and if anyone asks, I'll claim I just purchased it. But mostly, it will sit out of sight in a garage. This isn't a vacation. I'm going to get to a secure location and stay there."

"I don't understand why he hasn't been caught yet," she said and gave Ward an accusatory glance. "Your handyman was face-to-face with the guy."

"And he was wearing a ball cap and had a huge beard," Jill said. "Which was most likely fake. The police can't issue a BOLO for a tall white man with brown hair wearing jeans and a T-shirt."

Wanda pursed her lips. "I know you're doing what you think is right, but I don't have to like it, so I won't. In fact, I'll hate it. I hate everything about this. I don't know where you're going—I know, for your safety and mine—but I can't even talk to you."

"I'll check in with you weekly," Ward promised. "And any time you're worried, just give me a call."

"Why does he get to know?" Wanda asked. "This guy could find a broke, low-moraled cop just as easily as he could an airline employee."

"Jill's location won't be in any paperwork," Ward said. "My captain and I have already spoken about it. And we have a plan to keep you protected as well."

Wanda narrowed her eyes. "What plan?"

"For starters, your building will be under twenty-four-hour surveillance, as will Jill's home. If the stalker returns to either place, we'll get him. If there's been no movement in two days, we'll issue a press release stating that bestselling thriller author Kate Coleson is in protective custody due to a stalking incident. If anyone has information leading to the arrest of the person threatening Ms. Coleson, there's a $50,000 reward."

"Fifty thousand?" Wanda asked.

"I'm putting it up," Jill said. "I want this over with."

Wanda grasped Jill's hand. "You better not die on me."

"I'm not planning on it."

———

FIVE HOURS INTO HER DRIVE, Jill grabbed a protein bar and energy drink when she stopped for gas. It was a roughly forty-hour drive to Tempest Island, and she'd broken it up into four ten-hour days. If she ran into problems or needed more rest, it might run longer. Not that it mattered. The only person expecting her was the woman she'd rented her sanctuary from —a woman she trusted more than anyone in the world. And that woman already knew her arrival date was open.

Detective Ward had tailed her for almost three hours before calling her on her new prepaid cell phone and giving her the all clear. And even though she knew Ward had done his due diligence, she'd still felt uneasy at the thought of him turning around and heading back in the opposite direction. The overwhelming feeling of being totally alone was some-thing she craved most of the time, and her work required it. But now, she didn't feel alone—she felt lonely. And scared.

On the third morning of her journey, Ward called to tell her that her stalker had never shown and her captain was going to issue the press release. Jill prayed it had its intended result and protected Wanda from any future attacks. If her stalker wanted to take his chances with Detective Ward, Jill welcomed him to it. Ward was very professional and nice, but Jill didn't doubt for a moment that he was also lethal.

On the fourth day, she drove across the Florida state line and some of the tension left her shoulders. She'd seen the press release online the night before and hoped it worked. Her agent had been horrified with the turn of events but had wholly supported Jill in her disappearing act. She'd canceled all public appearances scheduled for the next month and would make a decision about the rest as things progressed...or didn't progress. Either way, her agent was in the same boat as Wanda —dependent on Ward to keep her as informed as he could risk. Ward had told her no email either, not even using a VPN.

It was late afternoon when the bridge to Tempest Island came into view and she couldn't help smiling. Even though her reason for coming back was an awful one, she refused to let it take away the joy at seeing her childhood home again. She sighed as she drove over the bridge and caught a glimpse of the sparkling waters of the Gulf. The Oregon coast was beautiful, but the water was a little too cold for her liking. She still took a dip on the warmest summer days, but nothing beat this stretch of powdery white sand and clear turquoise water.

She chided herself for not visiting sooner. It wasn't as though she had a clock to punch somewhere. But the truth was, she'd been out of touch a long time, and she felt guilty about inserting herself back into her previous life. Added to that, high school hadn't been without its issues, and she'd let old grievances fester so long that she'd built them up in her mind to the point she hadn't wanted to face them. And given the size of the island, you were forced to face everyone at some point.

But not this time.

This time, she'd be hidden away and the tormentors from her teen years would never even know she was there.

She turned into the marina and pulled to the last row. The woman standing on the dock looked almost the same as when she'd left the island. The blonde hair, trim figure, and ready smile sent Jill back to the childhood days she loved to remember. She barely got her car in Park before jumping out and running to hug the other woman.

Beatrice Shaw, or Aunt Bea to Jill, wasn't really her aunt,

but she'd always treated Jill like family. When Bea's sister and her husband died, Bea's niece Alayna had come to live with her. She was fifteen, the same age as Jill, and completely and utterly lost. Jill had taken an immediate liking to the smart, pretty girl, and they'd become thick as thieves in no time. When they'd first gone off to college, Jill and Alayna had stayed in touch, but as the demands of school and life increased, phone calls and email got fewer and fewer until eventually, Jill couldn't remember the last time they'd spoken.

Bea hugged Jill, almost as hard as Wanda had, and then pushed back to take a good look at her.

"You're too skinny," Bea said. "I don't know what it is with you young people that you think you need to be starving all the time. You can barely hang a shirt on Alayna and she still spends hours exercising every week. You'd think a chef would put on the pounds, but not that girl."

"I'm not big on exercising for the sake of it, although I do a lot of walking and thinking, but I will agree I don't eat well. I tend to graze on what I have in the house and order takeout in between. I used to have a few more pounds, but I think stress ate them away."

Bea sobered and nodded. "Stress will take it out of you, that's for sure. I want to hear what's going on, but let's grab your things and get out of here before someone spots you. I'll come back late tonight and get your car and put it inside my garage when there aren't so many eyes on things."

Jill opened the back of her SUV and Bea peered inside.

"You didn't bring much," she said.

Jill shrugged. "Don't need much to be a hermit, and you said there's a washer and dryer. I can do my job on my laptop, so aside from groceries, there's not much else I need."

Bea grabbed one of the two small suitcases and pulled it out of the SUV. "And you're well stocked on that. I got everything you asked for and threw in some selections of my own, especially in the alcohol department. But when you figure out something you need or run low on anything, you let me know and I'll get it for you."

Jill followed Bea onto the pier pulling the second suitcase and with her laptop bag and purse slung over her shoulder.

"I don't want to put you out any more than I already have," Jill said as they stepped onto Bea's boat.

"Don't even start," Bea said. "You're not putting me out and couldn't even if you tried."

Bea untied the boat from the dock and motioned to Jill to step into the tiny cabin area at the front of the boat. That way if Bea was spotted as she motored across the Sound, everyone would assume she was alone. And between the boaters, fishermen, paddleboarders, and general sunbathers, someone was certain to spot her.

Jill sat on the bench in the tiny cabin, sweat already running down her face. She hadn't even been here five minutes, and she already felt as if she'd been in the boxing ring with Tyson, and that made her smile. The boat increased in speed, and she braced herself as it bounced on the waves. The front of the boat was always a bumpier ride, but certain things couldn't be helped. Soon they'd be in the Gulf, and Bea would call for her to come out.

The burst of salt air that rushed across her skin when she stepped out of the cabin was incredible. Her skin tingled and her nose twitched as she took in all the familiar sights, sounds, and smells. The sun was still hanging on the horizon, and its rays looked like diamonds as they danced across the water. Gulls circled overhead and she cast her gaze to the water beneath them and spotted the pod of dolphins chasing their dinner.

Bea grinned as she looked over and slowed the boat. "That

pod has a couple of little ones. And so playful. You'll see them a lot. Their territory is around the lighthouse."

She increased speed, and Jill watched as the lighthouse sitting on a small bit of land and rock grew in size as they approached. It had always been beautiful, but now, with its new coat of bright white paint and black trim, it was breathtaking against the backdrop of clear blue sky.

"I still can't believe you bought it. I know you always said you wanted to, but I guess I figured it would never be for sale."

"Got decommissioned about eight years ago. Then the Island Authority sat on it for years, letting it deteriorate while they shoved paperwork at each other and had meetings about what to do with it. Since what I offered for it made up a budget shortfall they were trying to figure out how to cover, I was just in the right place at the right time."

"With a checkbook."

Bea laughed. "It always helps. Anyway, took me some time to get it remodeled but it's been ready for a while now. I just can't seem to pull the trigger on renting it. If Nelly knew about all of this, she would tell me I was holding it because you'd need it. I'm not sure I believe in that mystical crap, but I will say I'm glad it's available."

As they approached the dock, she cut the speed and eased the boat up to it. Jill tossed a tie rope over a piling and Bea killed the engine. Jill hopped out onto the dock and secured the front of the boat, then grabbed her luggage as Bea passed them up to her.

"I was going to leave my small boat here, but the dock is the only place to tie off and not much good in a storm. And I was afraid people would spot it and gums would start flapping. But I'm afraid that leaves you stranded and me serving as your waterway Uber, of sorts."

"I don't plan on leaving until this is over, so that's fine by me."

Bea nodded as they grabbed the luggage and started up the dock. "I don't like feeling trapped, and didn't want you to feel that way."

Jill gave the older woman a smile. "I don't feel trapped. I feel safe, which is exactly what I needed."

"Then let's go take a look at your hideaway."

As they walked, Jill took in the Private Property and No Trespassing signs that were posted on the dock. "You said you don't have a problem with day-trippers stopping here?"

"No. That's probably the only thing the Island Authority took seriously. This island was never available for public use, and they made sure everyone knew that. Anyone who missed the memo got a reminder by the Coast Guard. They run by several times a day. They know I own it now, and I told them I had a guest coming to stay a while. They won't bother you, but they won't let anyone else bother you either. You see someone docking here who doesn't belong, you call me and stay inside. I'll get them sent on their way."

At the end of the dock, they stepped onto a stone walkway that led to the lighthouse. The walkway was new and made of huge gray stones of varying shapes. It fit in perfectly with the untouched look of the tiny island. As they drew closer to the lighthouse, Jill saw the other signs of a human touch in the flowers that were planted close to the structure. The bright colors stood out against the white of the lighthouse as if they were backlit.

Bea unlocked the door and pushed it open, then waved Jill inside.

She stepped inside and took her first look at the place that would be her home for an indeterminate amount of time. The lighthouse part of the interior was the living room with bright white walls and contained a large blue-and-white-striped sofa and blue recliner placed to view a television mounted on the side wall. Rough scraped hardwood floors gave the room the perfect nautical feel. Behind the couch was an open entry to the building addition connected to the main structure. A new kitchen with navy cabinets, white quartz countertops, and navy-and-white sea-glass-tiled backsplash was so pretty and well thought out that Jill almost wished she liked to cook. In any event, the island counter would be a great place to sit with her coffee in the morning and gaze out the large window over the sink.

"Bathroom and laundry are in back of the kitchen," Bea said. "I couldn't figure out a way to squeeze out a bedroom down here without sacrificing the living area, but the couch folds out if you don't feel like climbing the stairs. Linens are in the laundry room."

Bea looked at the circular stairs. "Not going to be the best time hauling suitcases up there, but I give you points for making them small. You were thinking more than I was."

Jill poked her head into the bathroom/laundry room and saw that there was available storage in between the washer and dryer, which sat underneath a counter that ran the length of the wall behind them. Above was a rod for hanging clothes to dry but Jill had other ideas. The other side of the room contained the toilet, a vanity, and a small shower. The colors and tile were the same as the kitchen.

"You know what," she said as she looked back at Bea. "I don't think I'll take them upstairs. There's plenty of room to hang my clothes in the laundry room and this is where I'll shower anyway. And there's storage for the suitcases under the counter."

"That's smart. Then you're not always hiking up and down with clothes."

"And then you don't need to walk up those stairs."

Bea grinned. "That is definitely a bonus. There's a bed up there, of course, and a small desk and chair. Can't fit much more in there or you'll be ramming your knees into stuff every time you move. And it's not going to be a thrill if you have to go to the bathroom in the middle of the night, but I did have LED lights installed on the stairs, so you'll have good lighting. But be careful."

"Maybe I'll sleep half the night on the couch, then when I go to bed, I won't need the bathroom again until morning."

"I always said you were a smart one. Now grab us a couple waters out of that fridge and let's sit and you can explain to me what's going on. I have to say, when they said on the news that Kate Coleson had been taken into protective custody, my heart jumped into my throat even though you'd told me it was coming."

Jill grabbed the waters and they sat at the kitchen island. She took a big drink of the cold liquid, trying to decide where to start and finally deciding the beginning was probably best.

"So about five years ago, I got this card," she began.

Twenty minutes later, she'd hit all the high points—or she supposed they were better referred to as low points—of her life over the past five years, and backtracked even more to explain the college boyfriend situation and the name changes. Bea listened silently, her expression shifting from worry to anger and finally settling on a combination of both.

"I'm so sorry," Bea said. "No one should have to live with this. I know how hard it is. You know Alayna's back on the island, right?"

Jill nodded. Alayna's life had imploded so spectacularly that she'd been national news twice in the last couple years. And her old friend knew firsthand what it was like to be stalked.

Alayna's story had a happy ending, but she'd been extraordinarily lucky.

"It's a miracle that she's still with us," Bea said, her voice tightening. "I don't want you to go through anything like that. You and Alayna are like daughters to me. You did the right thing coming here. Jill Morgan disappeared from here years ago and Jill Smith never lived here. I've seen you on television with that wig and the heavy makeup. Even if someone you knew back then gets a look at you, they're going to see Jill Morgan, not Kate Coleson."

"I hope you're right. My life literally depends on it."

"Which is why I'm on board with your plan to stay put. But if you need anything, call me. You will never be a bother, so get that out of your mind. And if you get a feeling that something is off, call me. No matter the time, you pick up that phone."

"I can't disrupt your life over my sketchy feelings."

Bea leaned forward and narrowed her eyes. "Alayna knew someone was after her, even though there was no proof. Everyone but me kept telling her she was imagining it, but she knew. I believe you will too. So if you feel it, you call. Got it?"

"Got it. You've never told Alayna about me? Being Kate, I mean?"

Bea shook her head. "Not my story to tell, but if my opinion matters, I think you should. You've just walked away from your entire life. I know it's temporary, but having a friend will make all that easier, especially a friend who understands what you're dealing with and will do anything to protect your secrets."

Jill nodded. "I just didn't want to involve people, you know? After what happened to Wanda, I worry. I already feel guilty about involving you."

Bea reached over and squeezed her arm. "You're safe here. What about your parents? Are they still overseas?"

"Italy. Dad's going to die in uniform unless the Navy kicks him out. They know everything, of course, but they live on base and well..."

Bea frowned but just nodded rather than commenting.

Jill felt relief at not having to explain her somewhat tumultuous relationship with her parents. Bea had known her mother since they were teens—before she'd met Jill's father on the Naval base on the mainland. The older woman was well aware of how rigid and judgmental they could be, especially with their only child, who constantly came up short of their expectations.

Her father had expected a son and had been disappointed when he'd gotten a daughter. That disappointment turned into a permanent state of being when Jill's mother learned that due to complications with Jill's birth, she couldn't have more children. Her father would have considered divorce or adoption a failure, so he'd been 'stuck' with a female child, the alpha male he'd so desperately wanted snatched away from him.

Jill hadn't understood his indifference to her when she was young or her mother's willingness to cater to the cold, distant man she'd married. But as she grew older, she started to understand, even though she thought he was a horrible human being for feeling that way. Ultimately, he'd resigned himself to the fact that he would never have the biological son he wanted, so he shifted gears, pushing Jill to follow in his footsteps and become a fighter pilot—a feat that would be even more impressive because she was a woman and women were clearly inferior when it came to things like engines and war.

He'd never forgiven her for becoming an author. As far as her father was concerned, people were supposed to *do* exciting things, not write about them. Even her success hadn't moved the needle on his opinion and since her mother had abandoned having her own mind years ago, she had nothing to offer by way of support. When Jill had explained her current situation to them, she could practically hear the disapproval in their silence.

After all, if one's life was going to be threatened, it should be for a greater cause. Not over 'little' stories.

Bea stood up. "Well, if you can't think of anything else you need, I'm going to head out. I prefer not to boat after dark. Too many idiots out there doing it that have no business taking it on, especially since the majority are holding a beer."

"I'm good. I can't tell you how much I appreciate you, Aunt Bea. You've made an impossible situation as easy as it can be, and I'll be forever grateful."

Bea grabbed her in a hug. "Don't go getting all emotional on me." She turned Jill loose and headed for the door. "Remember what I said about needing anything. And I want you to eat those groceries, not just look at them. I'm not going to be satisfied until I get some weight on you. And some sunlight will do you good. There's a couple floats and such in the storage shed around back."

After Bea left, Jill put her hands on her hips and looked around. She should probably unpack, but she didn't feel like it. And really, what difference did it make if her bags were in the middle of the living room. It's not as if she would have visitors, and she had nothing but time. She pulled out her cell phone and sent Detective Ward a message that she'd arrived.

Now it was time to see the bedroom.

She headed up the stairs, circling around and around until her thighs ached a bit with the effort. When she got to the top, she opened the door and stepped inside. Then she let out a satisfied sigh.

It was simply gorgeous.

The same wood floors as downstairs but the walls here were a pale blue that matched the tints in the sea. The bed was whitewashed wood planks, and the comforter and pillows were striped with white and the same color blue as the walls. A single nightstand that matched the bed stood to one side. Windows were on the walls on each side of the bed, and on the side opposite the nightstand were a whitewashed desk and chair with blue cushions that matched the comforter.

Jill sat in the chair and looked out over the ocean. The window closest to the bed looked back toward the mainland, but this view was all sky and water. It was the perfect place to be creative or simply gaze and waste time. There was only one thing left to see, so she headed out of the bedroom and back onto the winding stairs. One more level rose above the bedroom—the walk at the top of the lighthouse. Only the room housing the staircase was enclosed. The rest of it was open to the elements, its steel railings the only thing separating you from a straight pitch down.

When she opened the door and stepped out, she couldn't help smiling. The only thing in front of her was another continent that she couldn't see. The last rays of sunlight danced over the water, and she felt a small burst of happiness. It didn't last—couldn't last the way things were—but it reaffirmed that she'd made the right decision coming here.

The locals always said Tempest Island was a magical place. She hoped they were right.

CHAPTER FIVE

ALAYNA SCOTT STARED AT HER CONTRACTOR, CHANCE, IN dismay. Surely he hadn't said what she thought he'd said, because there was no way he'd told her his plumber was in jail. Maybe she needed more coffee. It *was* early. That had to be it, right? The plumber couldn't be in jail because the plumbing was the holdup at her new restaurant right now. Without that work and subsequent inspection, nothing could move forward, and getting the restaurant open soon was critical. If she wasn't serving customers before the next Tempest Island city council meeting, Carlson Whitmore, city council president and her sworn enemy, would make sure it never happened.

"Your plumber is where?" she asked.

Chance gave her an apologetic look. "He got in a scuffle at a bar and the cops arrested him. It's not his first time drinking too much and throwing fists—not his second or third, actually —so his wife decided to leave him there for a while to let him learn his lesson."

Alayna threw her hands up. "Can we teach him after he finishes my plumbing? I can appreciate her situation, but she remained married to him after all the other times. Why did she have to pick now to stop enabling him?"

"I agree the timing isn't optimal."

"I suppose it would be wrong for us to bail him out."

"Have you met his wife? I suppose we could put up the bail, but then you're depending on him to meet the court's conditions. If he messes up—which I'm going to say is more likely than not—then that's ten thousand dollars we're out."

Alayna blinked. "Ten thousand? Good Lord, how many fights has this guy been in?"

"I think the real problem is he keeps winning, so people keep pressing charges."

"And you keep this guy employed, why exactly?"

"Technically, he's a contractor with his own business, not an employee. But the reason he's first on my plumber list is because he's as good a plumber as he is a fighter."

"Well, I wish he would pick one and stick to it. What about the number two plumber on your list?"

"Number two and all the way to the end are completely booked. I spent the entire morning trying to locate someone. There's not a plumber in a two-hundred-mile radius that isn't backlogged with their regular clients and hurricane repairs. I'm sorry, Alayna. I know this needs to happen."

Chance looked as miserable as she felt. The young man had a lot riding on this remodel as well. It would be the biggest and highest-profile job his company had handled, and he needed it to be a success.

"Can we fly someone in from out of state...somewhere that's not overwhelmed with hurricane repairs?"

"They'd have to be licensed in Florida or working as an apprentice for someone who *is* licensed in Florida."

"I don't suppose your guy can hire an apprentice from jail?"

"I have a feeling the inspector wouldn't buy it, especially

since Carlson's bank holds his mortgage. He won't break the law for Carlson, but he'll push us to the very edge of requirements."

Alayna threw her hands in the air. "So what do we do? Do we just call it quits now? Mark this whole thing down as a very expensive experiment that couldn't get off the ground because we needed a bigger bathroom? Good. God. The saying 'my business is in the toilet' is beyond accurate here."

"I'm going to keep trying. I've reached out to my father, and he's offered to call some of his friends in other areas of the state. Hopefully, they can find someone willing to get down here and finish this up..."

"But? Because there was totally a 'but' lilt in your voice with that last statement."

"But it's going to cost you. Travel expenses, per diem, an upcharge on the work itself. It could end up costing two to three times what you budgeted."

Alayna shrugged. "If I don't get this restaurant open, it will cost me a lot more than that."

"I'm really sorry. I don't know what else to say except that the plumber is off my list unless he gets some counseling and straightens himself out. And I'm not the only builder who's fed up with him. He put a lot of people in hot water with this one, and memories are long in small places."

"So are grudges. Just ask the Whitmores."

He winced. "I swear I'm doing everything I can. I don't like those people any more than you do."

She sighed. "I know you don't. And I know you're doing everything you can."

She just hoped it was enough.

JILL AWAKENED to sunlight streaming in from both windows. She'd considered closing the blinds when she'd gone to bed the night before but then figured there was no point. The room would be dark, and who the heck was going to see in when she was up that high? She'd assumed she'd have trouble sleeping and wouldn't be there long, so she was surprised when she checked her phone and saw that it was almost 9:00 a.m.

She threw the comforter back and stood up to stretch. Her muscles were still somewhat tense from the four days of driving, but the long night of sleep had done her a world of good. She took the few steps needed to get to the desk and looked out at the ocean. She'd already checked the forecast and it was going to be another beautiful day. Clear skies, a nice breeze, and mideighties for temperature was about as close to perfect as the weather could be.

But as much as she loved staring at the ocean, and could do it endlessly, the bathroom was calling. And it was at the opposite end of a long set of stairs. The night before, she'd had a lengthy shower and changed into her shorts and tank that she slept in, so there was nothing to haul downstairs except her phone. As she headed for the kitchen, she gave herself props for the decision to leave her clothes in the laundry room. Now she didn't have to run back upstairs to dress. Not that she needed to, but her bathing suit was certain to come up on her roster today.

She took care of her morning ritual of face washing, hair brushing, and everything else, then headed to the kitchen to put coffee on. After she poured the first cup, she stepped out the back door onto the small deck and sat in a patio chair. The cool morning breeze blew across her arms and legs, and she felt the weathered wood of the deck on her bare feet. She took a sip of her coffee and smiled. Perfection.

Her smile faltered for a second when all the reasons for her sitting there raced through her mind like cars in an F1 race. She shook her head and forced the smile back into place. Her reasons for being here might not be optimum, but that didn't mean she couldn't enjoy what was right in front of her. There was no point in sitting here miserable every day.

First up on her agenda was breakfast, then she was going to take a walk around the island. That wouldn't take long because the entire thing wasn't more than three acres, but she needed to start exercising more. Any movement, even slow walking, was better than sitting at the keyboard all day. At home, she hiked the wooded areas surrounding her house when she needed to work out plot issues, but her recent release and then all the stalker drama had interfered with her norm, and she hadn't exercised in weeks. If she had been, that four days of driving might not have hurt as much.

After the walk, she'd grab her laptop and head upstairs to get some work done in her beautiful room with her cute desk and that incredible view. Then after a light lunch, she'd put on her bathing suit and work on her tan. She might even follow it up with reading on the deck. The huge plus was that at least all of this disruption wouldn't cause financial hardship, because she certainly didn't need more to worry about. Since Jill wasn't enamored with world traveling, exotic cars, or designer handbags, her biggest expense had been her home. The rest of her earnings had been squirreled away for what Jill liked to refer to as 'in case shit.' Meaning 'in case shit' happened, she had cash to cover it.

And since her next book wasn't due to her editor for six months and she was well ahead of schedule on that front, she didn't have to worry about production either. Yet. So she intended to use some of her time on Tempest Island as that vacation she always swore she would take and never did.

Assuming she could find a way to relax.

She tipped her coffee mug up to her lips and was surprised to find it was empty. Time to get the day started. Giving the ocean one last smile, she headed inside. Breakfast was easy and quick—two scrambled eggs, toast, and a banana seemed healthy enough without going overboard, and enough that Bea wouldn't nag her. When she finished eating, she changed into her 'outside of the house' shorts and tank, slipped on sandals, and went out for her walk.

The lighthouse island was a small jut of earth that had risen in a spike from the ocean floor. It had a steep drop all around except for one tiny section at the opposite end from the lighthouse. That had a piece of beach entry, of sorts, that was maybe twenty feet wide. It narrowed quickly and dropped even quicker, completely unlike the gradual entry on Tempest Island, but it still allowed a swimmer to walk in.

Jill's one time on that tiny ramp of sand had been part of a school tour to learn the history of this lighthouse and lighthouses in general. Even though practically every inch of Tempest Island allowed easy entry into the water, teens always talked about sneaking onto the lighthouse island to swim. But back when Jill was a teen, there was a full-time lighthouse keeper who lived there and called the authorities on anyone who dared set foot on his spot in the ocean without permission from the Island Authority.

When she'd asked about it, Bea had assured her that the Gulf entry, while smaller, was still there. The lighthouse island had been included in all sand reclamation projects, so it had gotten a fresh batch of sand pumped onto its tiny beach area when Tempest Island was last done. Fortunately, there had been only one hurricane since then, and it hadn't swept away much of the precious sand.

The other sides of the lighthouse island were made up of giant boulders that protected the bank from erosion, and Jill headed for the one closest to the back deck. Sea oats mingled with native plants and shrubs covered most of the ground, but a well-worn path led right to the water. Jill was careful to avoid the edges of the thick undergrowth because she knew all too well that burrs lurked in that grass. And burrs had a way of finding bare skin, even when wearing sandals.

When she reached the edge of the island, the path turned and she walked the length of it to the far end, where the beach entry remained, as promised. It was definitely smaller, but she only needed room for a towel and a water bottle. She kicked off her sandals and her feet sank in the cool, powdery sand. She waded down the entry a couple steps and was already in up to her knees and was sliding downward. Before she took an unplanned dunking, she stepped out of the water, put her sandy feet back in the sandals, and headed to the path where it continued on the other side of the beach area.

When she came around the path to the dock, she paused. A boat bobbed up and down in the surf about fifty yards from the lighthouse. That wasn't unusual, she reminded herself. Fishing had always been good around the lighthouse when she'd lived here, and she couldn't imagine that had changed. Except she didn't see any fishing poles.

She continued to walk, scrutinizing the boat as she headed around to the back side of the island, and suddenly, she wished she would have unlocked the front door before she left. Then she could have been inside in a handful of steps instead of having to walk around to the back deck. The feeling of exposure was so overwhelming that her back tensed and all the progress that great night of sleep had given her was undone in a matter of seconds.

Picking up her pace, she continued around to the back of the island, drawing her closer to the boat. She kept her gaze fixed on it as she walked, knowing her sunglasses prevented anyone aboard from knowing she was staring. She saw movement in the cabin and then a man stepped out onto the deck. He glanced over and caught sight of her and lifted one hand.

She managed to get her hand up before rushing up the path toward the back door, but when she went to step onto the deck, she miscalculated and her ankle twisted. Then she went down hard. She leaped up and hurried inside, not even bothering to rinse the sand off her feet. Leaning against the back door, she tried to calm her racing pulse.

What the hell had just happened?

She limped over to the kitchen and grabbed a bottle of water from the refrigerator, then rubbed it across her forehead as she sank onto one of the barstools.

He's not here.

But could she be certain?

Jill knew if she could talk to her therapist the woman would tell her that her reaction was a form of PTSD. That the current threat had sent her emotionally back to college and her abusive ex. The tense muscles, pain in her chest, and overwhelming desire to run were entirely too familiar and completely unwelcome.

I thought I was better. I thought I was done.

She opened the water and took a long drink as her therapist's words ran through her head.

You're never completely done.

Her cell phone rang, startling her, and she squeezed the water bottle so tightly, water squirted out the top and over the counter and her phone. She saw Bea's number on the display and hit the button to answer, then put it on speaker. Bea had said she'd call this morning to check in on her, and the last thing she wanted to do was worry the other woman, especially after everything she had done for Jill.

"Good morning, Bea," Jill answered, trying to force her voice to sound normal.

"Good morning. How did your first night go?"

"Great, actually. I didn't expect to sleep much at all but I slept really well."

"I'm glad to hear it. Have you thought of anything you need and don't have?"

The water on the counter started dripping over the side onto her legs and Jill jumped up to grab a dish towel from the sink. But as soon as she took a step on the twisted ankle, she let out a gasp.

"Jill? Are you all right?"

She hopped back to the stool and sat, grinding her teeth as lightning bolts of pain shot up her leg. "I'm fine. And I can't think of anything."

"You don't sound fine. What's wrong?"

Jill held in a sigh. She should have known she couldn't fool Bea. Alayna used to swear her aunt had a sixth sense, even on the phone. Now Jill understood what her friend had meant.

"I twisted my ankle a little when I went for a walk earlier," Jill said.

"Is it swelling? Did you cut your skin?"

"I didn't cut myself and yes, I guess it's starting to swell. It's turning red."

"Can you put weight on it?"

"Well, just now was the first time I tried since I did it a few minutes ago, and you heard how it went. But I'm sure it will be fine. I'm going to set up office in the recliner, prop it up, and put some ice on it."

"I think I should head out there."

"You have your store to run, and I'll be fine in the living room. I hadn't even taken my laptop upstairs yet, so I have nothing up there at all. I can camp out in the living room until the swelling goes down."

"Okay...if you're sure." But Bea didn't sound remotely convinced.

"I promise to call if it gets worse."

"I'm going to hold you to that. Is everything else going okay?"

"It's going great."

No way Jill was telling Bea about her panic attack over a guy in a boat waving at her. She'd think she'd lent her property to a crazy person.

"Then I'm going to head to the store. You call if you need anything and definitely if that ankle gives you more trouble."

"I will. Thanks, Bea."

The water was still dripping over the counter, and now it was running down her thigh. She girded herself and rose from the stool again, this time careful to put the majority of her weight on her good foot. She held onto the counter and stepped with the bad one and felt the searing pain shoot up her leg again, but she still managed to get the rag and wipe up the water. With the water situation handled, she inched over to the refrigerator and opened the freezer to get some ice.

She smiled when she saw the bags of frozen fruit. Jill was that kid—the one who actually preferred fruit to cookies—so Bea had kept frozen fruit at her house for when Jill spent the night. And there was nothing better than a cold fruit smoothie on a hot summer day. Jill's addiction had eventually spilled over onto Bea and Alayna. It made her happy that Bea remembered this small thing. It had taken the edge off the disaster her morning had turned into. And a bag of frozen peaches was perfect to ice her ankle. Then she'd make a smoothie for lunch.

She'd left her laptop plugged in on the end table next to

the recliner, so she grabbed her bottled water and stuck it in her shorts pocket, then carefully took the couple of free steps she had to manage to the back of the couch. Once there, she clutched the couch with one hand to steady herself and slowly worked her way around to the recliner. She deposited her water and fruit on the table before removing the throw pillow and lowering herself onto the chair. Then she grabbed the remote and got the leg rest going. As it inched up, she placed the throw pillow underneath her bad ankle, then placed the bag of peaches across it.

The cold stung a bit at first but the ankle had swollen quickly. It was already bigger now than it had been when she'd talked to Bea. She bit her lower lip as she studied it. Was it broken? Surely she wouldn't be able to walk on it at all if it was. Maybe it was sprained, although she hoped not. She hoped it was just angry—assuming ankles could *be* angry—and would settle down if bribed by a bag of frozen fruit.

With a sigh, she grabbed her laptop from the table and queued up information on ankle injuries.

CHAPTER SIX

Bea entered the bookstore from the rear door, then stared at her friend Nelly as if she'd lost her mind. Not that she'd had far to go, mind you, but still. Nelly stood behind the counter, counting the cash for the register. She looked over at Bea and beamed.

"What do you think?"

"It looks like you stuck your head in Kool-Aid."

Nelly's formerly light brown hair fell to her mid-back in soft waves. She refused to get it cut but also found it hot, so it spent most of its time piled on top of her head in a giant clip. Now, the clip held a mass of hair that looked as if a Skittles bag had exploded on it.

Nelly laughed. "I don't go for the cheap stuff. I leave that to teens with a small allowance and their parents to have to fix the mess. I got this done at the salon yesterday."

"And she charged you for that?"

Bea and Nelly went to the same hairdresser, something Bea might have to reconsider.

"Of course she charged me. It was a lot of work putting in all those colors." Nelly grabbed the clip and pulled it out, letting her hair tumble down her back. "It's pretty, right?"

Bea had to admit that the colors were vibrant and blended beautifully. If the hair had been on a Vegas showgirl, she would have thought it spectacular. But on Nelly and on Tempest Island, she wasn't sure what to think.

"You know you've got sixty in your rearview mirror, right?" Bea asked.

Nelly waved a hand in dismissal. "Says the woman who jumped out of a perfectly good airplane last month."

"It's called skydiving. It's not like I was flying American and got mad and decided to leave because they ran out of Coke Zero." Bea stuck her purse under the counter, then lifted one of Nelly's colored locks. "At least it's not dry. Some of those kids who come in here with colored hair look like they stuck a haystack on their head and spray-painted it."

Nelly nodded. "This will wash out eventually, and Jewel says the product is the only one she'll use because the other stuff does exactly what you said. Although my guess is most of the teens we've seen wearing the haystack *are* using Kool-Aid."

"Well, if you're happy with it, I guess I can get used to it."

"Your enthusiasm is overwhelming."

"You don't love me for my enthusiasm."

Nelly grinned. "Harold said he saw you taking the big boat out yesterday. I thought you didn't fish in that thing."

"I don't. But it had been a while since I'd fired it up, so I figured I'd take a bit of a ride. Get some sunlight on my skin and wind in my face. Figured I should get my calm on before that interview this morning."

Nelly nodded. "How'd that go?"

Bea shrugged. "It's a reporter. She'll either write me up as the second coming of Christ or the Antichrist. Depends on how she's voting and who holds her mortgage."

"Isn't that the truth. Well, in better news, Harold caught a mess of speckled trout yesterday and we spent over an hour cleaning it all. Boy it was good fried, though. I put a freezer bag of fillets in the fridge for you."

"I appreciate it."

"You'll probably appreciate it even more if you could convince Alayna to cook them for you."

"Are you using my name in vain, Nelly?" Alayna's voice called out, and Bea looked over at the staircase to see her niece descending.

"How's the work going?" Bea asked, but she was afraid she already knew the answer based on Alayna's expression.

"You're not going to believe this," Alayna said. "The plumber's in jail and his wife refuses to bail him out. And apparently, there's not another plumber available in Florida, and since he has to be licensed here, we can't go out of state."

"Who's the plumber?" Bea asked.

"Billy Barnes."

Bea and Nelly gave each knowing looks.

"What?" Alayna asked. "What is that look?"

"Nothing," Bea said. "Just that Billy's sort of known for that kind of thing. I didn't realize that's who was doing the job. Mind you, I don't have a problem with his work. That man has enough talent to plumb for Jesus. He just needs to stay out of bars."

Tears welled up in Alayna's eyes, and Bea's heart clenched.

"I'm afraid this isn't going to happen," Alayna cried. "You've put so much money into this, Aunt Bea. What if I can't get it open in time?"

"Don't you worry about the money. There's more where that came from, and besides, this whole aggravation with the Whitmores isn't your doing. It all started with me, so if things end up going south then it's mine to worry about."

"It's a lot of money," Alayna argued.

"I'll be fine," Bea insisted. "Might have to fire Nelly to save on overhead, though, especially if her new hairdo scares off the customers."

"It's only likely to scare off Veronica Whitmore," Nelly said.

"That's an angle I hadn't considered," Bea said. "Maybe you should keep it then."

Nelly grinned. "Did I tell you that the book on flowers Veronica special-ordered came in, and when I went to send her an email, I typed in her name as 'Ms. Shitmore.' I swear I stared at it for at least ten minutes before deciding to fix it before I hit Send."

Alayna managed a smile. "The Shitmores is perfect."

Bea put her arm around Alayna's shoulder and gave her a squeeze. "I don't need you worrying. I mean that. You just keep working on the menu and the other things you can do right now—"

"Like testing," Nelly interrupted. "I really like the testing part."

Alayna laughed a little, and Bea gave Nelly an appreciative nod. Her friend had gotten Alayna out of her downward spiral.

"I guess I better run then," Alayna said. "My new idea for key lime cheesecake isn't going to make itself."

"You're making a whole pie, right?" Nelly asked.

"I'll bring some by this afternoon," Alayna promised before heading out of the store.

"How bad has Billy messed things up?" Nelly asked as soon as the front door closed.

Bea frowned. "Pretty bad. We need that plumbing done to get the inspection. Without the plumbing inspection, other things are on hold. Every day we lose is harder and harder to make up now that we're down to the wire."

"I don't suppose you have a plumber in your pocket."

"Not one who can handle a commercial install. But I've got some friends over in Tallahassee. I'm going to give them a call."

"Is anything else wrong? You've seemed more preoccupied than usual lately."

"I'm good. Same thing as always—everything hits at once."

Nelly nodded. "It sure seems to."

"Can you handle the store by yourself for a couple hours? I know it's busy season…"

"It's not a problem. Most people don't want help finding a book these days and the beach isn't going anywhere. If it takes a couple minutes longer to check them out, no one's vacation is ruined."

"Okay. But leave that new shipment alone. I'll handle it this afternoon. You just work the front end and no worrying about the back end."

Nelly shrugged. "I'm always worried about my back end, but the problem's the same—they're both getting bigger and harder to control."

Bea laughed as she hurried out of the store, then sobered as she jumped in her car. It was probably a waste of time, but she couldn't stop thinking about Jill's ankle. What if she'd broken it? If she tried to get around on a broken ankle, she could make things worse, and Bea knew Jill well enough to know that she wouldn't ask for help unless things were dire. And since Bea was already helping her, it would be a cold day in hell before Jill asked for any more favors.

Not that Bea minded. Jill had always had a special place in her heart. First, for going out of her way to befriend Alayna, and then for being such a strong young woman despite her disapproving and antagonistic parents. So if there was something Bea could do to help Jill, then by God, she was going to do it.

Especially now, when Jill was alone and really needed support.

JILL CLOSED her laptop and leaned her head back. She'd been attempting to write the same scene for over an hour and was no closer to finishing it now than she had been when she'd first started. All she'd managed to do was write and delete the same paragraph four times. Despite her best efforts to pave the way for a productive morning, the wheels had fallen off the bus.

Or in her case, one of the wheels had exploded.

Although she wouldn't dare admit it to Bea, her ankle was throbbing so hard it was preventing her from slipping into that creative zone. And every so often, the nerves decided to send her a reminder that they were trapped in inflamed tissue and not happy about it. Despite the frozen peaches, the swelling had gotten worse, and now she couldn't tell where her leg ended and her ankle began.

Even worse...she had to pee.

And even though nothing could be very far in such a small place, at the moment, the bathroom seemed at least a mile away. And the gap between the kitchen counter and the back wall was at least five steps with nothing to hold on to. Maybe she could lean against the wall. Regardless of method, she needed to get started soon because it was going to take some time and the clock was ticking on her bladder.

She lowered the recliner and placed her foot on the ground, wincing a bit as it came into contact with the floor. Taking in a deep breath, she braced herself and pushed herself up from the chair. Pain shot up her ankle and the breath came out in a whoosh, then she bent over to clutch the table and take some weight off her foot.

That's when she heard a boat outside.

It's going to go by. Boats are as common as cars here.

She'd told herself those two things over and over again after her earlier encounter, but the sound of the approaching engine still made her tense, especially when it dwindled down to an idle.

Too close!

If she could get to a window, she could see. But at the moment, letting go of the table seemed like a really bad idea. She heard noise outside coming from the direction of the dock. Then footsteps.

Someone was coming!

She balanced her weight on one arm and checked her phone with her free hand. No calls. So who was outside? Her pulse ticked up a notch when she heard the footsteps stop right outside the door. Then someone knocked softly.

"Jill? I'm coming in."

Relief coursed through her when she heard Bea's voice. Of course it was Bea. Who else would it have been? She should have known the older woman wouldn't let the ankle thing go. Bea had never been the overbearing type and definitely wasn't full of rules and standards like Jill's parents, but she took care of her own. And right now, her own included Jill.

The door cracked open and Bea looked inside. She caught sight of Jill, and her eyes widened.

"Are you all right?" she asked as she hurried over, toting a set of crutches with her.

"I guess there's no point in lying since you're here to see it. It's getting worse. I stood up, thinking I was going to go to the bathroom, but this is as far as I got. I was trying to plot a way to get from the kitchen counter to the bathroom door without anything to hold on to, but then I heard the boat and had a bit of a panic."

"I should have called, but I figured you'd just try to talk me out of it. I didn't think about causing you to panic, though. I won't do it again." Bea handed her the crutches. "I brought these just in case. Go take care of your business and then we'll see about your ankle."

Jill eyed the crutches as though someone had just given her a completed manuscript and free spa day. "I've never been so happy to see crutches in my life."

"Put them under your arms and I'll adjust them," Bea said.

Once adjusted, Jill took a step, then a crutch walk forward, and nodded. "This is so much better."

Bea nodded. "You go handle things, and I'll fix you some lunch."

She started to protest, but Bea's expression told her that arguing would be a complete and utter waste of time.

By the time she'd managed her bathroom run, Bea had a turkey sandwich, salad, iced tea, and a shot of whiskey sitting on the table next to the recliner. Jill sank down onto the chair and placed the crutches on the floor on the side where she could easily reach them. Then she took a drink of the tea.

"You brought whiskey?" Jill asked.

"Didn't have any painkiller, so it seemed like a good idea. Brought some aspirin, too, but the alcohol might take the edge off quicker."

Jill knocked back the shot, grimacing a bit at the strength.

"You didn't have to do this, but thank you. You saved my life with the crutches. Please let me reimburse you for them."

Bea waved a hand in dismissal. "Didn't cost anything. I did a number on my ankle last year on a paddleboard. Idiot vacationer came by on a Jet Ski and thought he'd be cute and send a wake my way. Couldn't control the thing and ran right into me. I almost held, but my board's not really made for surf. I use a different one in the Gulf."

Jill frowned. "I hope you caught the guy."

Bea nodded. "Easy enough to do. I knew the rental and the owner. He had the right paperwork, and the cops had a nice chat with him about how lucky he was that I wouldn't press charges as long as he sprang for the doctor's bill and a new board. He's lucky it was only a sprain. Now, put your legs up and let's see what you've got going on."

Jill pushed the button to lift the leg rest, and Bea squatted down to get a closer look at her ankle. She shook her head and put light pressure on the side with her finger.

"Does that hurt?" Bea asked.

"Not really. I think it's so swollen it's numb, at least when it comes to touching it. But the nerve pain is something out of a horror movie."

Bea nodded as she rose. "I think you should get an X-ray to make sure it's not broken."

"No. Too many people. Paperwork. The whole point in coming here was to disappear. I can't do that in a hospital."

Bea ran one hand over her hair and blew out a breath. "Okay, how about a compromise. I know a guy—a doctor—who'd look at it as a favor to me. He wouldn't have an X-ray machine on him, of course, but he'd know better than either of us if the situation warrants a harder look."

"A doctor who makes lighthouse calls?"

"He's a Naval doctor and a good friend of Alayna's man. Pete is used to handling battlefield triage, so his opinion is likely to be as good as an X-ray. And he gives us the added advantage of knowing how to keep quiet."

Jill considered Bea's suggestion and couldn't find much wrong with it. It did introduce another person into the mix, but Bea was vouching for him, and it did sound as if he had the credentials to give a good opinion. And if she was being honest, the pain had her more than a little concerned. She'd given her ankle a good twist before, but it hadn't swollen up like this and it certainly hadn't hurt this much.

"Okay. Pete sounds like a good compromise."

"I'm going to wrap it, then I've got to head back to the store. I'll give Pete a call on the way. In the meantime, you eat that sandwich. You're going to want to follow up that shot of whiskey with some food. It's the stoutest I could find."

Jill took a bite of the sandwich and stared out the window at the Gulf, wondering how her carefully structured life had suddenly gotten so complicated.

Gale Warning

"You don't drown by falling in the water; you drown by staying there."
— Edwin Louis Cole

CHAPTER SEVEN

PETE MCCORD STRAPPED HIS SURFBOARD ON TOP OF HIS JEEP and hopped in, ready to head for the island for a round of surfing. After he'd exhausted the rest of his energy in the surf, he'd grab a burger on the way home and then sit on the porch of his apartment on the Naval base with a beer and watch the sunset. If Pete had been able to script a perfect life, this was it—well, except for housing. Since he had no intention of leaving this post until he left the Navy, he needed to find a real house, and he wanted one on Tempest Island.

The drive from the Naval base on the mainland to the island wasn't bad, although summer tourists and vacationers clogged things up in the summer, but the base didn't have the same feel that the island did. Or the same sunsets. There was something about the island that improved on everything. Unfortunately, long-term rentals were nonexistent, and if people were planning on listing for six months or better, they usually did it after they'd collected all the short-term rental income from the summer season.

As he drove off the base, he considered his savings, salary, and expenses but no matter how many times he ran the numbers, he still couldn't figure out a way to afford beach property. But still, a bungalow in the neighborhood behind Main Street would be awesome too. Restaurants, groceries, and the beach were all a short walk. There would be nothing stopping him from sitting on the beach and watching the sunset every day if he wanted to. Hopefully, when the season was over, some properties would come on the market, and he'd be able to score a home.

When he stopped for gas, his cell phone rang, and he saw Bea Shaw's name in the display. He frowned as he pressed the button to answer. Bea was the aunt of the girlfriend of his good friend Luke. He knew her well enough to have her number, but they weren't exactly drinking buddies. He hoped nothing was wrong with Luke or Alayna.

"Pete, I have a big favor to ask."

"Is something wrong? Are you all right? Luke and Alayna?"

"We're all fine, but I have a friend who banged up her foot and I'd like for you to take a look."

Pete frowned. "Why don't you take her to the hospital where they can do an X-ray?"

"She's in the sort of situation where she can't risk exposure. She came here to lie low. In fact, I'm the only person on the island who knows she's here. I tried to get her to go to the hospital but she's refusing, and I get it because I know her reasons and they're good ones. But I figured if you take a look and decide it's going to require an X-ray, then she'll be more inclined to take the risk."

"Okay. I can do that. I'm on my way to the island now— probably twenty minutes out. Is she at your house?"

"Well, she's at a house I own. Sort of a house, anyway. She's staying at the lighthouse."

Pete blinked. "You own the lighthouse."

"Yeah. Very few people know that either, so I'd appreciate

you keeping that quiet as well. If people find out they'll all be hitting me up to let them picnic and have weddings there, and I'm not interested in all that nonsense."

"I get it. So do you want me to meet you at the dock?"

"Actually, I have something that I can't get out of—another interview about that damned mayoral race. I'll leave my keys in the boat. It's slip 21."

"You said she was lying low. Is she going to be okay being alone with me?"

"Her name is Jill, and she'll be fine. I vouched for you and gave her your credentials. Her father is military, so she'll be more comfortable with you than a hospital doctor. And I'll let her know the situation as soon as I get off the phone with you. In the storage compartment under the steering wheel of the boat is a key to the lighthouse. Knock first, but if she doesn't answer, then let yourself in."

"Is she armed?"

"You know, I didn't ask. Guess I just assume everyone is."

"Okay, then text me her phone number. That way, I can phone or text in case she's fallen asleep. I don't want to startle someone who's injured and in hiding and who might have a weapon."

"Good call. I owe you one."

"It's no problem," he said, and really meant it.

If he was being honest, Bea's request had intrigued him. Who was this Jill? What kind of situation had her hiding out in a lighthouse? And how did Bea know her and come to help her? He'd never heard Bea or Alayna mention a Jill, so it wasn't someone who lived here. But she'd definitely come to the right place. Bea was a good woman and one you wanted in your corner when the chips were down, and the lighthouse was the last place anyone would go looking for someone.

Twenty-five minutes later, he pulled away from the dock,

smiling as Bea's truly excellent boat glided across the water. A boat was another thing he intended to purchase...just as soon as he had a house. First things first. Then he'd see about running up some more debt, because boats like this weren't cheap. But it didn't matter. He had a long, stable career ahead of him, and what's the worst that could happen? The country stopped getting into wars and he left the Navy and went private making double what he made now?

Ultimately, the money didn't matter because he'd found his place and had no intention of leaving it. Not many people could say that at his age, so he considered himself fortunate. By the time he was ready to retire, the house and boat would be paid for, and he'd be faced with long days of nothing to do but surf and fish. Oh the horror.

He couldn't help grinning as he exited the Sound into the Gulf, where the sun reflected off the water like tiny spotlights. The wind whipped through his hair and the spray of seawater kissed his bare arms as the boat sliced through the waves. There were fewer things more perfect than a day on the ocean.

The lighthouse had always stood just offshore, visible from the beach but not within swimming distance, especially since you'd have to swim through the Pass, the name given to the channel between two islands where the Sound merged with the Gulf. The waves were always large here and often at cross purposes coming from two different, but connected, bodies of water.

He'd seen pictures of the lighthouse when he'd booked fishing charters, but everyone knew it was private property and there was no mooring on the tiny patch of land that it stood on. Although it had been decommissioned, Pete had assumed it was still owned by the Island Authority. The fact that Bea not only owned it but had apparently set it up for visitors had surprised and intrigued him.

As he drew closer, he considered for a moment what it would be like to live there, surrounded by the ocean. It wouldn't be feasible for him, of course. Sometimes he was on call, and even the Navy would frown on their doctor requiring seaworthy weather to show up for work. But it was a nice dream. Maybe when Bea's friend was done using the lighthouse, he'd ask if he could stay there for a week, use up some of his leave. She *did* say she owed him.

He eased the boat up to the dock and tied it off, then headed up the path to the lighthouse, hoping that Jill was as comfortable with all of this as Bea thought she'd be. He knocked lightly on the door and called out, "Jill, it's Pete McCord. Bea's friend."

He listened for movement inside but didn't hear anything, so he knocked again. Another twenty seconds passed, and he followed it up with a phone call that went to voice mail. When the lighthouse remained quiet, he considered the key in his pocket. Bea had said to use it if Jill didn't answer, and so far, he'd heard no signs of life. The blinds were closed, so he couldn't get a look inside. She might have fallen asleep, or she might have fallen and be unable to answer. And there was the really dark thought at the back of his mind that if whatever she was running from was a *whoever*, they might have caught up with her.

All three required him to unlock the door and go inside, but only the third required his weapon. He hesitated for a moment, then his military training kicked in and he pulled out his pistol. You could always reholster a gun. You couldn't always stop a bleed-out from a gunshot wound, especially if he was the one bleeding.

He knocked one last time before unlocking the door then inching it open. He looked through the crack but didn't see anything, so he pushed the door open wider. The living room appeared to be unoccupied, so he swung the door all the way open and stepped inside.

"Stop right there!" A woman peered around a doorway at the back of the kitchen, her hands clutching a pistol that was trained on him.

His first thought was that the young woman who had him sighted in was no 'old' friend of Bea's. His second was that her hands were shaking.

This was starting off well.

———

JILL'S HANDS trembled as she clutched the pistol. He didn't look like a stalker, but then, they weren't limited to hulking men in hoodies. Even her own books had bad guys who were the most unassuming people. That's how they got their victims. But this guy wasn't unassuming either. He was tall—at least six foot two—and built for action. His bare legs and arms gave a clear view to muscles rippling under tanned skin. His short dark hair was windblown but his stance was all military.

Jill prayed this was Bea's friend because she didn't give herself good odds if he wasn't.

"Are you Jill?" the man asked, his amber eyes flickering from her face to the pistol she held. "I'm Pete McCord—the doctor Bea sent? I knocked a couple times and called, but you didn't answer. Bea gave me the key in case you couldn't."

"How do I know you're Pete?"

"Look, I don't know your exact situation because Bea would never betray a confidence, but she said you're lying low, and if Bea is helping you then I figure you've got excellent reasons. But if people don't know you're here, and they don't know Bea, then they couldn't possibly know she asked me to come."

"Why are you armed?"

"Because you didn't answer, and I needed to make sure that was due to a nonlethal reason. That whole lying low thing..."

Jill stared at him a couple seconds, then dropped her arm and came around the door on crutches and slowly made her way forward.

"I'm so sorry. Of course you're Bea's friend. Apparently, the pain has upped my paranoia."

He shook his head. "No. Your injury has heightened your survival instincts. You're more vulnerable now. If you were already at risk before, your ankle just made things worse. The pain can cause you to be reactionary, so thank you for verifying rather than just pulling the trigger."

She smiled. "I'd never live it down if I shot the doctor who was here to save me."

"It might go on your permanent record. Do you need help, or can you make it over to the chair okay?"

"I'm good. First time on crutches but I'm getting the hang of it. Bea is a lifesaver and thought to bring them out here when she heard I twisted my ankle."

She made it to the chair, and Pete held her arm to steady her with one hand and took the crutches with the other, then helped her lower. She had to admit, it was a lot less jarring with help easing her down. Her previous sitting round had been the aim and drop, which her ankle hadn't appreciated much. When her leg was raised, Pete pulled over a footstool and removed the bandage.

He didn't so much as lift an eyebrow when he saw the swollen mass, then she remembered, military doctor. He'd seen the worst of the worst. Her ankle was practically boring compared to the things he would have experienced on a battle-field. He placed his fingers gently on the skin and gave it a tiny push.

80

"Does that hurt?"

"A little."

He nodded. "It's too swollen for you to feel light contact, but if you banged it into something—especially without a bandage—you'd be saying words you swore you'd never say. Might even pass out."

"So don't bang into anything. Is that your diagnosis?"

He grinned. "It's a start. I want to move it around and press harder. Are you okay with that?"

"Not much choice."

He lifted her foot up and held it under her calf with one hand. He had a firm but gentle grip and she was surprised that his hands were soft against her skin. Doctor, she reminded herself. He looked like he could kill people with a Q-tip, but that wasn't his day-to-day. He pressed up her ankle and around the sides, then used his hand to slowly move her foot from side to side as he felt around the ankle.

Frowning, he lowered her foot back onto the rest. "I don't think it's broken, but I can't be positive. I can't tell if there's a hairline fracture with only a physical review. Are you sure you can't go to the hospital and get an X-ray?"

Just the suggestion of the hospital had her immediately clenching her fists and shaking her head. "Not an option. If it's not broken, it will start to get better, right?"

"In theory, yes. But you have soft tissue damage. And even if there's not a fracture, you could have ligament or tendon damage."

"What's the treatment for all of that?"

He sighed. "Rest, most of the time. In severe cases, surgery."

"Well, I've got all the time in the world to rest, so that's not a problem."

"But the pain is, and I can't prescribe you anything for that or the inflammation. Over the counter will work but not nearly as quickly."

"Oh, I don't expect you to prescribe anything. I would never ask you to do something that could risk your rank or retirement. You earn every dime you get and ten times more."

"I appreciate that. Too many people don't get it, but Bea said you came from a military family."

She nodded. "My dad."

"Okay, how about this? I have your number, so I'll check in tomorrow morning. If this does not begin to improve in forty-eight hours, you have to go to the hospital."

She stared at her swollen ankle and felt the throbbing all the way into her hip. He wasn't being an alarmist and she knew that. Even she could tell her ankle was seriously damaged, and with the proper treatment and medication, it would heal faster and better, and they could be sure she wasn't causing further damage by delaying.

Finally, she nodded. "Forty-eight hours."

That would give her time to contact Detective Ward and come up with a plan.

Pete looked relieved. "Great. Okay, so while I'm here, let's get you set up the best way possible to handle all of this. Where is the bedroom?"

She pointed at the spiral staircase then straight up.

He gave her a pained look. "Does this couch fold out?"

"Thankfully, yes. And I haven't hauled any of my belongings up there because the only bathroom is down here, so there's that. But I can manage all of this. I'll just sleep in the recliner."

"So you can have a sore back as well as a bum ankle? Let me rearrange this furniture and get you set up so you have a place to sleep as well as easier passage with the crutches. I have access to a knee scooter. I'll bring that with me next time.

It will be easier than the crutches and has the advantage of a little basket on the front. That way you can carry food and drink."

She hated that a perfect stranger was doing so much for her but at this point, she also saw logic staring her in the face. Pete was a godsend and she needed to get over her own issues and be grateful that he was there and wanted to help.

"That sounds great," she said. "Bea said there are linens for the couch in the laundry room, but you don't have to do that. I can manage."

"Really? You can manage to unfold a couch bed standing on one leg?"

She sighed. "You've made your point."

He smiled. "Then I'll make the bed. But first, I'm going to grab some ice for that ankle."

He returned a minute later with a freezer bag full of ice and a dish towel. He laid the towel across her ankle, then gently placed the ice on top of it. Then he headed off for the laundry room and she watched as he walked. He was the quintessential alpha male in every way, but his gentle touch and handling of her ankle was a surprise. She'd had civilian doctors who could learn a thing or two from him. It didn't hurt that he was one of the best-looking men she'd seen in forever. She leaned back a little in the recliner.

Yep. Nice butt too.

She sighed again. Why did a good-looking man turn up in her path now? When she was literally hiding from the world and definitely didn't look her best, even if you excluded the ankle. Not that it mattered. With any luck, she'd be gone from Tempest Island before Pete even knew who she was. And even if she wasn't injured, a fling hardly fit into her plans. And that's all it could be. Her home was across the country.

"Here we go," he said as he walked back into the living room.

He moved the coffee table against the front wall, then made quick work of the couch bed. After he positioned the end tables for better passage, he checked her ankle again. "How does it feel? Too cold?"

"The cold helps, even though it's already pretty numb."

"Do you want anything to eat?"

"No. Bea set me up right before she left, so I'm not hungry yet, but I wouldn't mind another bottle of water."

He retrieved the water, then grabbed the wrap. "I'm going to rebandage the ankle. It limits what ice can do, but you need the compression and the support. Can you get in and out of the chair without putting weight on it?"

She nodded. "I'm not going to win any awards for the performance, but I can manage."

"I brought a bottle of Aleve with me. That's all I had on me. Can you take it?"

"Yes."

He pulled the bottle out of his pocket and set it on the table next to her. "Great. That should help with the inflammation. Is there anything else I can get you?"

"No. I think I'm as good as it gets for now."

"You have my number from the incoming call. If you run into any problems, call. Doesn't matter what time. I'll get the scooter and some better bandages and will be back tomorrow afternoon. Is Bea coming back today?"

"That's not necessary. I don't want to inconvenience anyone, and Bea has her store to run."

He frowned. "I really don't like you being alone all day and night."

"I learned my lesson earlier on that one, so I'll take my phone everywhere I go. If I run into trouble, I'll call."

He still didn't look convinced. "What about coming with me to the island? I'm sure Bea wouldn't mind if you stayed with her."

"No!" Her voice was a bit more forceful than she'd intended. "Sorry, but I can't do that. Bea is already more involved with my situation than I like just by letting me use the lighthouse. I won't stay in her home."

He studied her for a while, then finally nodded. She knew he wanted to ask what was going on, but he wouldn't do it.

"If anything happens, call."

She nodded. "I will. And thanks again. I really appreciate this."

"Don't thank me yet. You're not out of the woods."

"Positive thoughts."

He nodded, then let himself out. The lock clicked into place behind him, then a minute later, the boat fired up and she heard it motoring away. She stared at the closed blinds and blew out a breath. What a mess. She'd sought isolation, but sitting inside a locked room with the blinds closed was a little more isolation than she'd bargained for.

She knew there was no point in trying to write. Her mind was far too distracted to form decent sentences, so she reached for the remote and clicked on the television. Nothing caught her eye, but then she didn't figure it would. Finally, she just turned on a Hallmark movie set on a beach, figuring if she couldn't get out in the sun herself, at least she could see it on the television. She popped some Aleve and leaned the recliner back a bit.

As she started to doze off, she pictured herself in that lagoon on TV with the dolphins swimming around her. But the leading man wasn't the actor from the movie.

It was Pete.

HE SMASHED his hand onto the counter and slammed the laptop shut. Where was she? She thought she could hide, but she couldn't. She belonged to him, and as soon as he found her, he would explain all of that and then they could start their lives.

Together.

The way they were always supposed to be.

He'd spotted the cops watching her friend's building and knew she was out of the hospital, but he wasn't foolish enough to be caught that way. And since the police had issued a statement that Kate Coleson had been taken into protective custody, it was unlikely her friend knew where she was. The reward offer had been an angle he hadn't seen coming, even though he knew she was clever based on the books she wrote.

But she was no match for him.

Sooner or later, she would know that. Understand that.

She was his. She always had been. She always would be.

CHAPTER EIGHT

PETE INCREASED SPEED ON THE BOAT AS HE PULLED AWAY from the lighthouse. He was more than a little troubled with the situation he'd just left. Jill had a nasty injury and was clearly afraid of something. Whatever was going on with her was big. He was a little consoled by the gun she had, and she certainly hadn't been hesitant to pull it out. Hopefully, if it came down to it, she wouldn't be afraid to pull the trigger. That's where most things went south for good people. That hesitation.

Although he couldn't exactly complain about it because she could have shot him.

Every protective bone in his body and all of his medical training yelled at him to turn around and insist on remaining with her, but that was ludicrous. She obviously didn't want him there. Even though she wasn't afraid of him any longer, that didn't mean she'd be comfortable with him essentially moving into her space. But the stark fear on her face when he'd walked in was cemented in his mind and made his chest clench.

And that wasn't all that was clenching.

Jill wasn't at all what he'd been expecting. When Bea said

she had an old friend who needed help, he'd thought maybe she meant a childhood friend of her own, but Jill was young enough to be her daughter. Where had they met and what was their relationship? Bea had specifically said 'friend' not family, but he'd never heard anyone mention her before. Which made Jill almost as interesting as she was beautiful. And that was saying a lot given that she was one of the most incredible-looking women he'd ever seen.

Even scared, she'd been gorgeous but when she'd finally smiled, it was as if the entire room had brightened. And those green eyes... When they'd pinned him, it felt as though she were looking into his soul. Her brown hair tumbled down her back in loose waves as if she'd been in the surf and it had dried that way. Then there was her body—tall and slim with a naturally athletic build.

And there is zero point in you rehashing any of that.

He sighed. It figured. The first time in a long time that a woman had caught his eye and she was clearly running from something. And when her crisis was over, she would leave and go back where she came from. He pulled the boat into the dock and then drove to the bookstore. He hadn't known Bea for long, but there was zero doubt in his mind that she would be on pins and needles until he reported in and he figured he could allay her fears best if he did it in person. Nelly gave him a wave and a huge smile when he walked in.

"What can I do for our handsome doctor today?" she asked.

Pete glanced behind him and Nelly laughed.

"Please. No use being humble around me," she said. "If you got it, flaunt it."

"I see you've gone that route with your hair. I like it."

Her hair looked like it had been painted by kindergartners, but on Nelly, it worked.

"I'm looking for Bea. Is she here?"

Nelly hiked her thumb over her shoulder. "Checking in a shipment."

"Thanks."

He headed into the storeroom and located Bea in the back near the loading door. When she spotted him, she immediately stopped working.

"Well?"

"I can't say for certain. She could have a hairline fracture or ligament or tendon issues, but without an X-ray or MRI, I can't know for certain. I tried to persuade her to go to the hospital, but she wasn't having it."

Bea looked disappointed but also resigned. "I didn't figure she would."

"But I got her to agree to a forty-eight-hour trial. If the swelling doesn't go down by then, she said she'd come in for tests."

"Really? That's better than I thought you'd get."

Pete shifted from one foot to the other, thinking about how to approach his next question. But he couldn't figure out the magical way to do it that would guarantee answers, so he just went for it.

"I know you don't want to betray a confidence, but is she all right out there alone?" He told Bea what happened when he arrived.

"So she *is* armed," Bea said. "Good."

"Good unless she shoots a friendly. Would it help her to have someone with her?"

"In my opinion, yes, but it's not my call. I'll check in with her and offer, of course, but I won't insist. I'd rather have her here where I can keep a partial eye on her than gone somewhere else where I don't know anything at all."

He frowned. "Is someone after her?"

"Yes. And that's all I can say. The police are working on it, but until they figure things out, she's better off with no one knowing where she is."

His gut clenched. After meeting Jill and seeing her reactions to him, he'd figured it was something like that, but if the cops had told her to hide, then it went well beyond a simple case of harassment. Jill was in real danger, which explained the gun and her reaction to him.

"Don't worry, Pete. I'm not going to let anything happen to her. And since I own that lighthouse, it's my prerogative to pop in whenever I want to, but I have to balance things out. I don't want to spook her into leaving."

He shook his head. "She's afraid it would put someone else at risk, right? Well, that's crap."

Bea nodded. "My thoughts exactly, but I can't blame the girl for doing the same thing I would in that situation. I'm a lot of things, but a hypocrite isn't one of them."

"Well, she has my number, and I made her promise to call if anything changes. Otherwise, I'll check on her again tomorrow, assuming you're headed out there or I can borrow your boat. I have a knee scooter I'm going to take her and some thicker bandages for the ankle."

"What time do you get off tomorrow?"

"I'm early shift this week, so I'm off by noon."

"Good, then we can ride out there tomorrow afternoon. Meet me at the dock at one."

"I can do that."

"And Pete, thanks again. I owe you. Seriously owe you."

Pete gave her a nod and turned to leave when Shakespeare, the bookstore's resident cat, came tearing by and clipped his leg, knocking him into a stack of books that scattered as he clutched the table to keep from falling.

Bea was already yelling and he looked up to see Nelly hurrying into the room.

"Does that cat have lettuce?" Bea asked. "Why in the world does he have lettuce?"

"Because my salmon was sitting on top of it," Nelly said. She put her hands on her hips and glared up as the furry thief —who was well out of reach on the top of a bookcase— happily chewed on a lettuce leaf.

Nelly shook her hand at him. "That's the second time this week that rascal has stolen my lunch."

"Why are you leaving it out?" Bea asked. "You know better."

Nelly snorted. "I'm not. That salad was in the refrigerator in a sealed plastic container."

Bea stared. "He opened the refrigerator."

Nelly held up two fingers. "Twice this week."

"Good. God. We're going to have to put a padlock on the refrigerator because of a cat. You know if someone put this in a book, no one would believe it."

Pete grinned. "I would."

———

BEA DUG into the cases of books with gusto, marking items off the list as quickly as she could. She had always been a person who had good control of her emotions. She was the calm and rational one. The one everyone else came to when they needed someone to talk them off the ledge. But ever since she'd almost lost Alayna, her anxiety got the best of her more often. Then that nice Emma had turned up on Tempest Island and trouble had been close behind. Now it was Jill, who was like another daughter to her.

Alayna and Emma had barely come through their situations with their lives. Could luck strike Tempest Island a third time? She really hoped so. If only Jill wasn't so stubborn about staying alone. It would make her feel much better if there was another person with her. Another person operating at 100 percent.

And every time she thought about Jill being out there alone and scared and now injured, a wave of guilt rushed through her for keeping all of this from Alayna. Her niece wouldn't hesitate to go to the lighthouse and support her old friend.

But Bea had promised.

And promises for Bea were religion.

Her cell phone rang and Bea checked the display, then answered.

It was Marty, an old real estate buddy of hers from Tallahassee.

"Hey, Bea. I've called every plumber I can think of in the state, but no one has availability for a rush job. Their leads didn't turn up anything, either. I'll keep calling, but at this point, I'm out of names."

"I was afraid that might be the case, but I appreciate you doing the legwork for me."

"Of course. I'm really sorry you're in this position. Been in a similar situation myself once before and it's not a good time. I've got some more calls out...old clients, friends of friends, other real estate agents. If I turn up anything, I'll let you know."

Bea disconnected and flopped down on the stack of boxes. There was a solution. It just wasn't a great one. It involved pissing people off and the potential for losing a hunk of cash. But then, if this restaurant didn't open, the cash loss would be much larger and *she* would be the one pissed off, so when she looked at it that way, the decision was simple.

She headed to the front of the store and grabbed her purse from under the counter. Nelly took one look at her face and raised her eyebrows.

"I'm going out again," Bea said. "I'm going to solve this plumber situation."

Nelly grinned and held up her fist. Bea smiled and bumped it.

There was nothing like friends who could read your mind.

———

JILL BALANCED on one leg and crutch as she opened the refrigerator. She'd surprised herself by managing a nap, but now she was ready to eat and easy was the name of the game. When she spotted the protein shakes, she pulled one out, figuring that and some fruit would be enough to get her by. Her ankle was still aching, nerves still firing randomly up her leg and down into her foot. The swelling looked a bit better though, or maybe that was just wishful thinking. Either way, she needed to finish up this bathroom and food run and get back in the chair.

She shook her head in frustration as she inched across the living area. The lighthouse cottage that had seem so charming yesterday now felt like a prison. Before she could change her mind, she dumped her snack on the end table and hobbled over to the windows on both sides of the living area to pull up the blinds. No one was out here looking for her, and random passersby couldn't see her inside unless they were using binoculars. It was still a few hours before dark, and she could close them when she got up for her next bathroom break.

The sunlight streaming in instantly elevated her mood. Maybe if the ankle was better by the next morning, she could still manage to sit on the back porch with her coffee. She was going to think positive. This was only a bad sprain and by tomorrow, the worst would be over, and she'd start healing. She wasn't planning on Olympic-level activity anyway, so a little hindrance shouldn't affect her overall stay.

The recliner faced the big windows on the rear wall, which meant her back was to the other windows. That thought left her feeling a bit exposed, but the front windows also had plants that were a good five feet high. So unless someone was standing at the window, behind the plants, they couldn't see her either. And if they were, she had much bigger problems than open blinds.

Finally, she dropped into the recliner, wincing a little as she went, then got her foot situated just right with the leg rest and a pillow. The throbbing, which started up every time she had to walk, began to slowly subside as she drank the shake and watched rays of sunlight reflect over the water. There were two sailboats in the distance, their sails bright against the blue sky, and she smiled. She'd only been sailing a few times, but it had been wonderful. Maybe, once this was all over and her ankle was better, she could do it again.

When she downed the remainder of her protein shake, she reached for her phone and called Detective Ward. He'd responded to her text about arriving with only a thumbs-up, which was adequate but frustrating. Logically, she knew that it might take a while to resolve this situation, but there was that glimmer of hope in the back of her mind that the bad guy would foolishly show up at her house or Wanda's, they'd cuff him, and he'd be thrown into prison where he could never bother her again.

Of course, she knew better.

That didn't even happen in her books, and they were fiction. In real life, cases like this took time and many were never resolved. Well, unless you considered a dead victim a resolution, and this was one of those times where she had no desire to be part of the solution. But even if they could just figure out who he was, it would be something. At least then she'd know who to look for. Now she saw a potential killer in every male she came into contact with, hence her response to Pete earlier.

Ward answered on the first ring and sounded a little breathless. "You all right?"

"I'm fine. Just checking in."

"I'm afraid I don't have anything to report. He hasn't shown at either location and the DNA we pulled from the bookstore has all matched Wanda, her employees, suppliers, or other people who should have access, like maintenance people and the cleaning crew."

"How is Wanda?"

"She's planning on reopening the store tomorrow. I don't think her doctor is happy about it, but he can't make her stay closed. I tried to talk to her, but she shut me down."

"Wanda is a force. She refuses to let other people dictate her life."

"Well, maybe in this case, she should give a little. How are you doing?"

"Fine. Restless. Wanting this to be over. And I had a bit of a situation."

"What kind of situation?" His voice immediately went tense.

"Nothing to do with the stalker. I just had a tumble and twisted my ankle."

"Did you go to the hospital?"

"No, and I'm trying to avoid that. My friend has a friend who is a military doctor and he took a look. But if the swelling doesn't go down in two days, they're both going to insist on an X-ray."

He was silent for a couple seconds, then he took a deep breath. "I wish I could tell you this would be wrapped up by then and you could come home and prop your foot up, but you know I can't. I'm sorry, Jill, but there's just no way to know how this will go. I really hoped he'd overplay his hand and show at your house or even in town again."

"Did you find anyone else in town who saw him? Maybe so we could get a better description?"

"My guys have been working that side of things. A couple people remember someone who fit your handyman's description, but it was on that same day. No one has reported seeing him since."

"Of course they haven't," Jill said, frustrated.

"Are you sure Jacob is okay?"

"Why are you asking?"

"Because he has a record."

"For what?"

"He was kind of stalking a woman."

"What is 'kind of' stalking?"

"After talking with the officer who made the arrest, the story goes that he was working for this single woman and formed an attachment. Started hanging around even when he wasn't scheduled to work, brought her gifts, that sort of thing. She started getting weirded out by it—you know that sixth sense women have about those things—and stopped hiring him to do things. But he kept coming. So she told him she didn't need any more help, but he didn't listen. Anyway, she talked to the cops who talked to him and they thought he got it, but the next day, he was back in her yard, so they arrested him and she got a restraining order."

Jill remembered coming home to Jacob cutting down the old tree after the book signing.

"But there's no way he could have been the person who

attacked Wanda," she said, as much for her own benefit as Ward's. "He was at my house working when I got home that day and had been for a while. The work was right there to see."

"I'm not saying he's the card writer, because you're right, the timing of things doesn't fit. And honestly, I don't attribute the brain power for this to him as he seemed a rather simple sort. But when this is over and you're back home, I want you to be very careful where he's concerned. If he's not completely stable and forms an attachment to you like he did the woman before, we don't know what he's capable of."

Jill shook her head. "Maybe I should just change my identity again, sell my house, and move out of the country."

"That would definitely be a solution. Not that I'm suggesting it, but for a woman who is clearly trying to keep a low profile, you're on a lot of radars. And I hate to add another blip, but I've run into a problem with your old college boyfriend, Trevor Jones."

"What kind of problem?"

"The disappearing kind. You made a good call getting clear of him back then. He's been in and out of jail for domestic abuse and harassing women he's been in relationships with for years. Unfortunately, no one's thrown the book at him. He got out from a stint a little over three months ago, got evicted while he was inside, violated parole and went back for another six weeks, and when they released him two weeks ago, he bounced. No one has seen him since."

Jill's back tightened. The timing wasn't lost on her. He'd gotten out of jail about the time she'd received the prior card, then back in and out again right before she'd received the latest one.

"We have all the particulars on him," Ward continued. "And I know it's a wide range, but he fits the description Jacob gave us, at least in regard to size and age."

"But the notes are coming to Kate, not me."

"If the guy is obsessed with you—the one who got away and all—then he might have made the connection. It was always a possibility. How much does this guy know about your childhood?"

"We dated for two years, so a lot, I suppose, assuming he was paying attention. But I was a military brat. We lived a lot of places."

"So you don't think he could zero in on where you are by those stories? Anything you said that indicated you had attachment to that area in particular?"

Jill pursed her lips, trying to stretch her mind back to college and everything she'd said to the person she'd dated for half her time at the university, but there was no way she could recall every sentence spoken.

"I'm sure I told him how much I loved it here, but we lived a lot of places that I loved."

"But when you had to go somewhere to hide, that was the place that immediately came to mind."

"Because it was the only one that ever felt like home. And I knew Bea would help because that's just who she is. She was more of a mother to me than my own."

"And did Jones know that?"

"I don't think I ever went into that much depth with him. I know we dated for a long time, but I never took it to the next level. I think I knew it wasn't going anywhere even though I wasn't aware yet of his abusive side. But the entire relationship lacked depth, not just our conversations. I'd be surprised if he zeroed in on one place, but there would be nothing stopping him from checking everywhere he could think of, I guess. Well, except money and the fact that there's probably a warrant out for his arrest."

"A warrant has been issued, but money is never a problem

for criminals. They always manage to find enough to get by. Your case is my top priority. I'm going to keep working everything until we settle this. You have my word. And if you have to get an X-ray, then let me know. If you need to move again, I can arrange something and help with transport, because it doesn't sound like you'll be doing much long-distance driving anytime soon."

"Probably not."

"I'm sorry I don't have better news. When I get something, you'll be the first to know."

"Thanks. Please let Wanda know I'm all right."

"Will do."

Jill dropped her phone back on the end table and stared out the window. She'd told herself before she made the call not to get her hopes up, knowing full well that if anything had happened to move the case forward, she would have already heard about it. But the disappointment was still very real. And even though it made her entire body clench to think that Trevor might be the stalker, she was also happy that the cops had zeroed in on him—sort of—as far as suspects went.

Now, if they could just find him.

She would never admit it to Bea, but despite her secluded location, she now felt exposed because of her ankle. Or what was it that Pete had said—that being injured had heightened her survival instincts? That made sense, except that she'd already assumed they were high enough after what happened to Wanda, which meant now they must have gone right past overdrive and be in explosion territory.

You should leave.

She blew out a breath. And go where? This was the only place she could go where she felt somewhat safe and had the advantage of a friend who could help. If she went somewhere else, she'd be totally on her own. On the plus side, that meant no one else was at risk, but surely, her stalker couldn't connect the famous author with a bookstore owner who lived across the country.

Unless her stalker was Trevor and he'd listened more than she'd given him credit for.

She shook her head. No, staying put was the right call, especially given the situation with her ankle. And staying put literally meant sitting in this chair until she moved to the couch bed. She hadn't come to Tempest Island for a vacation, but she had pictured it being a little more enjoyable than this.

She grabbed her laptop and opened it up. All this dwelling on things wasn't going to get her anywhere, and it certainly wasn't going to get any work done. Crappy work was better than none at all. Nora Roberts always said you couldn't edit a blank page. Getting some words down—even if they were crappy—would help take her mind off things.

Sort of.

Except that her stories were about killers.

———

BEA KNOCKED on the front door of Billy Barnes's house. She could hear kids yelling inside and Billy's wife, Minnie, yelling on top of their yelling. Apparently, Billy's actions were spreading good cheer everywhere. Or maybe that's how the house always sounded. It wouldn't surprise her. She'd known them both the forty-plus years they'd been on this earth and neither had portrayed calm and tranquil as personality traits.

Bea knocked again, louder this time, and finally the door flew open, and an aggravated Minnie stared out at her.

"What do you want, Bea? I'm already voting for you and don't have time to hear no political nonsense. If these kids don't shut the hell up, I'm going to kill them and bury them in the backyard. Since it's getting toward sundown, I got to make a call on that one soon. Back porch light's busted."

"Now, Minnie. We can't have both their parents in jail."

"Don't need parents if they ain't breathing, do they? Now, what's this about?"

"It's about your husband. He's supposed to be doing the plumbing at my niece's restaurant, and we're at a critical point. If he doesn't do that work, we might not get to open before the city council can block us."

"I don't know nothing about that mess and don't want to. What I know is that man put himself there and I'll be damned if I'm getting him out. I'm tired of it. He needs to learn a lesson."

"I don't disagree, but I'd prefer if his lesson doesn't come at my expense, and it will. If I can't open that restaurant, I lose everything I've invested and it's substantial."

Minnie put her hands on her hips and pursed her lips. "I'm sorry, Bea. I really am, but I'm not spending the last of our tiny savings to bail him out. Got two kids with teeth coming out their ears and braces don't come cheap. Besides, I don't know that I would bail him out even if I had a million dollars. He never has done right by me."

The last thread of patience that Bea was grasping slipped away.

"Oh bullshit! That man was beating up boys in high school if they looked twice at you, and back then you thought it was romantic. When he stole a keg two counties over for your sweet sixteen, you thought it was proof of his ultimate love. He punched a man at your wedding for standing too close to you, and you laughed and fed him cake. That man acquired the nickname 'Fracture' when he was in eighth grade because of his propensity for fighting, and he still goes by it today. Don't you give me any lip over 'right by you' or any other nonsense.

You got exactly what you wanted, and you went into it with both eyes open."

Minnie's jaw dropped. "I can't believe you're talking to me that way."

Bea threw her hands up in frustration.

"And I can't believe you're letting whatever petty argument you had—that likely sent him to the bar in the first place— cost me a bunch of money and my niece her restaurant. I get that you're mad. So pack up your kids and leave. Or change the locks and tell him to get right or don't come home. But you've been whining about him as long as you've known him, and one thing is for certain—you never did anything about him then and you won't now. In a week, you'll bail him out and go right back to your regular programming. But in that time, I will have lost my butt."

Bea wagged her finger at the obstinate woman. "This is how it's going to be. I'm going to bail him out myself, and he's going to finish that job."

"You can't do that."

"I certainly can, and I'm going to. I'm not letting your ridiculous choices ruin this opportunity for me and Alayna."

"He's not coming back into this house unless he gets in a program."

"I don't care if he's living under a bridge. As long as he finishes my plumbing job."

Minnie crossed her arms across her chest and huffed. "Well, I guess I can't tell you different, but I have to say, I'm not happy with you, Bea."

"Get over it. Or not. I don't really care. I'll check in with you again in a few years when you're still married to him and still complaining about the same things, and I'll say, 'I told you so.' In the meantime, head back inside and explain to the *five* kids you had with him why you're leaving their father in jail until rent's coming due."

Minnie glared at her, then stepped back and slammed the door in her face. Bea jumped into her car and pulled out her phone and dialed.

"Yeah, I need to post bail for William Barnes. Can you help me with that?"

CHAPTER NINE

JILL CLOSED HER LAPTOP AND SLID IT ONTO THE END TABLE. She'd managed an entire chapter. It wasn't any good, but it could probably be salvaged for the final draft, and at least writing it had worked out another plot point that needed finessing. On her earlier bathroom run, she'd fixed a sandwich and grabbed an apple and had polished those off with some Aleve before starting to work. Her ankle hadn't throbbed as much during that round of walking, so maybe it was already getting better. More likely, it was the perfect wrapping job that Dr. Dreamy had done.

Good. God.

Now that she thought about it, she was the heroine in a romantic comedy and had cast Pete as the hero. Except that nothing about her situation was funny.

She lowered the leg rest on the chair and reached for the crutches with one hand. Then she pushed herself up with her arms and one good leg, taking the crutches with her as she went. She balanced carefully on one leg in the couple seconds it took to get the crutches under her arms, then lowered her weight onto them and headed for the windows to draw the blinds. The sun had set at least an hour ago, but she hadn't wanted to make the effort of getting up just to close them, figuring when she did her final bathroom run—so to speak—she'd handle them then.

Once the blinds were closed and she was ready for bed, she flipped the covers back on the couch and grabbed the television remote, handgun, water, and her cell phone and put them on the table next to the couch. Pete had brought an extra pillow down from the upstairs room so that she had something to prop her foot on in bed. She climbed in, one pillow behind her back and another under her foot, so that she was inclined enough to see the TV.

She flipped it on and found an old movie she'd already seen a million times and let it run. She'd never been able to sleep in absolute silence, maybe because there was no such thing. Her father had played the television all day and night long and that was what she was used to. When she'd gone off to college, her dormmate had been the same way with music. After graduation, when she got her first apartment alone, she'd turned off everything and climbed into bed, relishing the thought of finally getting a night of silent sleep for literally the first time in her life. But it didn't go at all as she'd thought it would.

Buildings, bugs, wildlife, neighbors, and a host of other things made noises all night long. Noises that had been drowned out by the television or radio all those years. And since she wasn't used to the noise, every little sound jolted her awake, and then that overactive imagination that made her such a great thriller writer kicked in and made her an even better insomniac. After three nights of terror-inducing attempts to sleep and a threat from her new boss when she'd fallen asleep in a team meeting, she'd bought a small television for her dresser and went back to old habits.

She watched as the heroine traveled across the rocky

shores of Ireland and smiled at the beauty of the coast. The ocean had always been her happy place. Thank God her father had chosen the Navy and not another branch that might have left them living in landlocked places. Lakes and swimming pools were okay but simply weren't the same as looking over a vastness of water that didn't appear to end. Like the view outside the lighthouse. It was perfection.

And she drifted off, remembering exactly that.

She bolted upright in the dark room, her heart pounding in her chest, and panicked when she couldn't discern where she was. Then her ankle sent a jolt of pain up her leg, and everything came back to her in a flash. The television was off now—probably on a timer—which meant an unknown noise had probably awakened her.

It's nothing. You're scaring yourself. Just turn the TV back on and go back to sleep.

But as she reached for the table, she heard a bang outside. Like someone had dropped something heavy on the back deck. She pulled her legs over the side of the bed and turned toward the back door. In the dim light, she could barely see the outline of it, but she could hear someone jiggling the doorknob.

Fighting the urge to turn on the lamp next to the couch, she grabbed her cell phone and dialed Bea, who had clearly been asleep.

"Bea, there's someone trying to get in the back door."

"Huh, what?" The older woman went from half asleep to wide awake in a second. "Call the police. I'm on my way."

Shit!

This was exactly the kind of situation she'd needed to avoid. Calling the police would mean more eyes on her and official statements and records and the local gossip would run wild with it. But then, if she shot someone and hadn't called the cops, how would that stand up? Silently cursing, she dialed 911 and told them she was renting the lighthouse and there was someone trying to break in. They said they'd send someone immediately, but it would take at least twenty minutes for them to get there. She couldn't imagine it would take Bea any less time, which was beyond frightening. Twenty minutes might as well be a lifetime if you were under attack.

"Ma'am," the 911 operator was still talking. "Ma'am, I want you to stay on the line with me."

A huge bang on the back door made her gasp and she clenched the phone. "They're trying to break in the door," she whispered. "I have to set the phone down so I can hold my gun."

"Ma'am, that's not a good—"

Jill dropped the phone onto the couch and clenched her pistol, crouching so that she was mostly concealed by the back of the couch and could use the top of it to steady her aim at the back door. She hoped there weren't more than fifteen of them, because that's how many rounds she had. And that was assuming she made every shot count, which was an iffy proposition.

She heard the clink of metal against metal and figured they were trying to jimmy the lock. Not that it would help as Bea had installed dead bolts on both doors that could only be drawn from the inside. And Jill had made certain they were both completely closed. Even if they could get the lock undone, they'd still have to break down the door to get inside. She said a silent prayer that picking the lock would take long enough for the cops to get there.

The minutes ticked by, slow and agonizing, and after ten had passed, the noise stopped. Jill suddenly realized her phone was silent as well and wondered if she'd accidentally discon-nected when she'd dropped the phone. Maybe they'd given up and were leaving. Then she heard footsteps outside the living room window.

They were walking around the structure!

She knew the windows were all locked—she'd watched Bea check them and then she'd double-checked them herself when she'd opened the blinds. And they were hurricane windows, so thicker than a normal window and wouldn't be nearly as simple to break as standard fare. The front door was part of the original lighthouse and was a solid chunk of heavy wood, so it didn't offer easy access either.

The footsteps paused at the window, and she heard the sounds of hands touching it, then voices. Two at least, and male. Her chest constricted even more as she shifted into a better position to aim at the windows.

"They're locked," one man said. "Probably all the same way."

"So break it."

"With what? I'm not hitting hurricane glass with my hand. I'd just break my hand, and even if I managed to break the glass, have you ever seen a hand sliced from breaking a window? I gotta work tomorrow."

"Well, we're not getting through that front door. It might as well be a tree planted there."

"Then let's try the back door again. I felt it give a little."

Jill listened in disbelief. Maybe they thought the place was empty. Why else would they be talking so loudly?

Because they figured no one could get to her in time, so there was no point in being quiet.

"Breaking a window would be easier," one of them said. "You don't have a board or something?"

"I don't make a habit of carrying lumber around in my boat, and I lost my anchor fishing last week. Let's just try the back door again. We're running out of time. This has to happen tonight, or we can kiss that pile of money goodbye."

She sucked in a breath, their words sending her shifting once more on the couch to fix herself up for the perfect shot at the back door. Despite everything she'd gone through to hide, he'd found her. And he'd sent someone—*two* someones—to finish the job, or worse, kidnap her. She clutched her gun tighter. She had her plan. If they got the door open, she'd fire one warning shot, and if they didn't bolt, she'd unload.

Each second felt like an hour as time crept forward. The outside had gone silent again, except for the sounds of waves crashing against the rocky barrier behind the house and the wind blowing through the palm trees. Long, silent seconds turned into minutes, and she felt a bead of sweat trickle down her face. Her palms grew sweaty despite the cold metal of the gun, and her eyes were dry from not blinking often enough. Her heart pulsed in her throat and her temples.

Then there was a huge crash at the back door, and she saw it shake and heard wood crack. One of them let out a cry of pain and frustration and a couple seconds later, they slammed into the door again. This time the frame splintered, and two young men came crashing inside, the porch light illuminating the kitchen. They fell over each other and onto the floor, giving Jill a great opportunity for a warning shot. She squeezed off a round above their heads and into the palm tree out back, and they jumped up from the floor, eyes wide as they spotted her on the couch with her gun leveled at them. They practically fell over each other as they scrambled back out the door.

Jill heard a second cry and then a gunshot and the sound of a round hitting the side of the house. She involuntarily ducked but kept her hands up and her pistol ready. Then she heard a familiar voice.

"You two fools damned near got yourself shot!" Bea yelled.

"Don't you even think about running, either. The cops are on their way, and they're gonna want to talk to you two."

"We're not going in there," one of them said. "Some crazy lady shot at us."

"So let me see—you were breaking into her home in the middle of the night, but she's the crazy one for shooting at you? I don't think the law is going to be on your side on this one. Nor is the court of public opinion. And since I own this lighthouse and that woman is my guest, I'm absolutely certain you don't have permission to be here. Now get in there before my next shot goes through your dad's boat."

A couple seconds later, the two young men walked inside, giving Jill nervous looks as they stepped through the splintered doorway, darting glances behind them as if trying to decide if they could make a run for it. The calculations must have determined that even if they could outrun Bea, they couldn't outrun her gun, because they finally shuffled all the way in and stood with their backs against the refrigerator and hands in the air.

Bea stepped in after them, turning on the kitchen light as she came inside, and Jill was relieved to see that her gun was lowered. The older woman appeared irritated but not remotely frightened. A boat engine sounded nearby, and Bea looked outside, then back at the boys, shaking her head.

"You really outdid yourselves this time," she said, then looked over at Jill. "It's all right. These two idiots are locals, known for their stellar decisions. But this one is going to land them in it big time. Criminal trespass, breaking and entering, threatening the life of my tenant..."

"Ah, come on, Bea. We were just trying to make some money."

"So you were going to steal from me?"

"Heck no. Rowdy Miller said he'd pay us a hundred bucks

if we set off some fireworks from the top of the lighthouse. It's his girlfriend's birthday, and he was trying to do it up special."

"And you thought breaking into private property and terrorizing the person living there was worth a hundred dollars?"

They both slumped. "Didn't know anyone was staying here and didn't know you owned it either. But if we get arrested, we're in big trouble."

"You can say that again." A cop stepped in through the open door and glared at the two boys. "You're not minors anymore. We've had to put up with your nonsense for years now, but things are about to change."

Their eyes widened. "You're not arresting us, are you?"

"Got no choice. We got a 911 call saying someone's breaking into a private residence and I see a door torn off the hinges here. Got damage to personal property, trespassing, and breaking and entering at a minimum. Those call logs don't just disappear because people are stupid and didn't mean no harm, and this door isn't going to fix itself. Now turn around and I'll get the cuffs on you. Then you can park it in my boat while I help Bea get this door covered."

He looked over at Jill. "Are you all right, ma'am? Dispatch lost signal and couldn't get an answer on callback. I apologize for that. Cell service is sometimes spotty, especially when there's a storm moving in."

She nodded. Her heart still raced, and her mind was whirling with too much information. Even though she was safe and the break-in hadn't been about her at all, she couldn't force herself to calm down. Bea made her way over to Jill as the officer cuffed the boys and headed out with them.

"Are you all right? Seriously? You're pale as a ghost."

"I thought I was going to be one. I'm having a little trouble calming down."

"I don't blame you. If I could have bashed those two fools, I would have. I'm so sorry. This was a bunch of trouble and stress you didn't need. All these years with no trouble out here and then this."

"I heard them talking about having to get it done fast or they wouldn't be able to collect a lot of money. I was certain they were hired to kill me, even though that doesn't make sense, really. Stalkers are stalkers because they like to star in the finale. Then I thought maybe they were here to kidnap me so he could finish me off somewhere else, which isn't the way they operate either."

"We're not always rational when we think our lives are threatened. I'm afraid that door isn't going to be fixed tonight though, and I don't have any plywood out here to cover it. I think you best come back with me tonight until I can get it covered, because you're not going to feel safe with just a tarp up there."

Jill bit her lip. She certainly didn't want to stay in the light-house without a back door, but she also didn't want to put Bea at risk. And the risk of other people seeing her was far higher on the island than here.

"You can hide out at my house," Bea said. "I'll pull into the garage, and no one will see you going in, assuming anyone is even up at this hour. I can bring you back at night so no one sees you leaving either. But I can't let you stay here tonight. You're shaking."

Jill looked down and realized she was still clutching her pistol, and Bea was right. Her hands were trembling. She put the gun on the end table and covered her face with both hands.

"I'm so sorry, Bea. I didn't mean to bring trouble here."

"This has nothing to do with you. Those boys have been trouble since the crib. I'm just angry they picked tonight, of all times, to take their tomfoolery up a notch. I'll gather up some of your things. Is there anything in particular you want as far as clothes go?"

She shook her head. Given her solitary profession and personal life, she pretty much existed in T-shirts and yoga pants, sweats, or shorts. She had her public-facing wardrobe, of course, but she didn't have to dip into them often. She switched to jeans when running errands in town and that was the extent of her fashion life.

"Just my bathroom things and any change of clothes. And I'll take my laptop."

"And your gun." Bea smiled. "I'm glad to know you have no problem defending yourself. I saw that round in my palm tree. You could have taken them out, but you didn't, and I don't think for a moment that you just missed. I know you think you're not firing on all cylinders, but you seem pretty darn aware."

Jill nodded but she didn't feel as if she'd done a good job of handling things, especially since she couldn't lessen the tension in her body.

It wasn't about you. You're safe.

For now.

CHAPTER TEN

Bea stepped into the jail with the bail bondsman and took a seat while he went about the business of getting her plumber set loose. She'd taken care of the paperwork and the payment at the bondsman's office that morning, and she didn't have to be here for this part, but she intended to have some words with Billy, and if he didn't show the right amount of respect and contrition, she was going to pull her bond money and send him right back inside.

The last thing she was looking to do was bail the guy out and then still not have the plumbing done. Bea had the advantage of not being in love with the man or having five of his kids to raise, so she could be as hard on him as needed. And after the nonsense she'd dealt with last night, her tolerance for stupidity was at an all-time low.

It took a good thirty minutes for the jailer to go through the process of filing everything and releasing Billy, but finally, he walked into the lobby behind the bondsman, looking sheepish.

Good.

He glanced around and when his eyes locked on Bea, his expression changed to one of surprise.

"Bea? What are you doing here?"

"I'm here doing what your wife won't do. You've really stepped in it this time, Billy, and your timing couldn't be worse. If you don't finish that plumbing job at my restaurant, I'll be out of business before I open."

He shook his head, looking contrite. "I'm really sorry, Bea. But that guy started it."

"It's always someone else who started it, but you finish it and therein lies the problem. So here's how this is going to go. I've posted your bail, which means I'm on the hook for ten grand if you don't toe the line. And trust me when I say, short of the Whitmores, I'm the last person in this town you want to screw over."

"I would never—"

Bea held up a hand to stop him. "I'm taking the bond fees off your bill, and you're going to stick to drinking water until that job is finished and approved by the inspector."

"No problem. Whatever you want. Can you give me a ride home?"

"No point. Your wife has her own stipulations, and in my mind, they're long overdue. You're not welcome back home until you're in a program. Since you are officially sober until you finish my job, I figure you can start working on that right away. When was the last time you got into a fight sober?"

His brow scrunched in concentration.

"You've made my point," Bea said.

"If I can't go home, where am I supposed to stay?"

"I've got a sleeping bag. You can bunk in the restaurant. Assuming you do your job as well as you're supposed to, you'll have a working toilet for tonight."

He stared at her in dismay. "You want me to sleep on the floor?"

"It's that or you pay for a hotel, but I wouldn't want to run that expense by your wife, especially during tourist season."

"Ah, come on, Bea."

"There's a cot back inside that cell with your name on it. I can pull my funding and you can opt for that if you'd prefer."

His eyes widened. "No! The floor's fine. Shouldn't take me more than a day or two to get it all done anyway."

"Good. Because that's all you've got."

"What happens when I finish? Where am I staying then?"

"That's something you'll have to work out with your wife." She handed him some flyers. "Here's some pamphlets on local programs. I suggest you get signed up for at least one before you go talk to her."

He took the brochures and sighed. "Yes, ma'am."

"So we've got a deal, then. You'll finish my work, stay out of trouble, and meet all the conditions required by the courts so that I get my bail money back?"

"Don't see as I have a choice."

"Not if you want to continue to do business here."

"Then we best get going. I need to get those toilets working before my breakfast kicks in."

———

JILL SHUFFLED into the kitchen balanced on the crutches but managing them a bit better than she had the day before. There was something to be said for practice, she supposed. After all the stress of the previous night plus getting in and out of the boat and all the additional walking, she'd been afraid her ankle was going to let her have it. And it had ramped up on the throbbing by the time Bea had gotten her secured in her guest bedroom, feeling just as it had right after she'd injured it. But some ice and Aleve had helped.

It was better now, but if she was being honest, it was still a little stiffer than it had been before all the evening drama took place. All the movement hadn't done her any favors. As she walked, the bandage sagged a bit, so she clung to the hope that the swelling had gone down, even though she knew it was more likely the fabric had stretched. Regardless, she wasn't even going to look until she'd downed at least two cups of coffee.

She'd had a fitful night of sleep, awakening with every sound and startling herself by being in yet another unfamiliar place, but had finally drifted off around 6:00 a.m. and managed to sleep solidly until a few minutes ago, which had given her a surprising three hours of rest. Bea wasn't in the kitchen but there was a note on the counter.

Had to take care of something first thing. Coffee is ready to go. Breakfast stuff in the fridge. I'll check in later this morning. Call if you need anything.

She pressed the button on the coffeemaker and pulled a container of grapes out of the refrigerator. Then she slid onto a stool at the counter and gave the house a look as she munched on the fruit and waited for the coffee to brew. The room had a new coat of paint since the last time she'd been here—both the walls and the cabinets. The walls had been yellow but now were a soft blue. The cabinets, previously a light maple, were now painted white with glass-paneled doors. The old white Formica countertops had been replaced with white quartz with the tiniest gray vein running through it, and tile in various shades of blue sea glass made up the backsplash.

Even with the blinds on the front windows closed, the ocean color created a cheery glow to the room. Canisters, dishrags, dishes, glasses, and other decor and utensils splashed spots of blue and coral everywhere. The kitchen, living room, and dining area were all one large room as was common for the older beach houses, and as she glanced around, she felt a wave of familiarity and contentment wash through her as she spotted art, pillows, and objects on tables and bookshelves that she remembered from when she was a teen.

She'd spent a lot of hours sitting at this counter with Alayna. Had probably eaten her weight in testing Alayna's recipes. Even then, she'd known her friend was destined to be a great chef. There was plenty of trial and error, but Lord, when she hit on the right combination, the results were incredible.

A pang of regret hit her when she thought about how she and Alayna had lost touch over the years, but that seemed to be the norm. Even with the internet and smartphones making it easy to stay in touch, people moved on from high school and lost track of the past while they struggled to create their future. Jill had stayed in touch with Bea though. Not often, but at least a couple emails a year.

Bea had always encouraged Jill to write and had given her book after book on the craft. Even after college, every time Jill had felt like giving up, Bea's words had filtered through her mind, telling her that she had natural storytelling ability, and that her characters were well developed, and her plots interesting and complex. So when she'd signed that first contract, Bea had been the first person she'd told. Her sincere and overwhelming happiness for Jill had helped balance out the complete and utter lack of enthusiasm her parents had displayed for her choice of professions.

Both of Bea's 'girls' had become successful. Jill hadn't kept in touch with Alayna, but she'd followed her online when she'd started making a splash in New York. And she had followed, along with the entire country, when everything went down with her ex-boyfriend and the subsequent fallout that happened on Tempest Island, almost costing Alayna her life. Jill had picked up the phone a million times in the past few weeks to call Bea and ask for Alayna's phone number, but she'd always hesitated and ultimately done nothing, afraid it would appear that she was only interested in the sensationalism.

Deep down, she knew Alayna would never think that, but somehow, it felt intrusive and rude to contact her old friend after everything that had happened. Now she was literally hiding in Bea's kitchen, just a couple miles away from her, and still couldn't work up the courage to make that call.

She sighed. More than anything, she wished Alayna were sitting right here, gossiping with her and telling her all about her adventures since high school and all about the new man in her life, who, according to Bea, was magical. But Alayna was barely past her own brush with death. The last thing Jill wanted to do was bring that back front and center with her own screwed-up situation.

If something happened to Alayna because of Jill, she'd never forgive herself. She already had overwhelming guilt for involving Bea. And now, instead of being isolated in the lighthouse, she was sitting in the kitchen of the very woman she hadn't wanted to expose. She hoped the back door could be easily secured and she could get back to her hiding place. Even if they had to board it up until it could be properly repaired, that would work.

Hopefully, long enough for Detective Ward to do his job.

———

ALAYNA STEPPED out of her car and headed into the hair salon on the mainland. She'd stopped several local women who had good hair and asked where they got it done. Two had named this shop, so when she'd come over that morning to run some errands for the restaurant, she'd decided to step in and if things felt right, make an appointment. She didn't have to do a lot with her hair, but she liked to keep the ends trimmed, and all the time in the sun and water were rough on them, so she probably needed to see to that more often now than she had when she lived in New York.

The inside of the salon was pretty—all white marble and gold finishes—with that glitz and glamour look. A young girl with beautiful long black hair at the reception desk smiled at her as she walked in.

"Do you have an appointment?" she asked.

"No. I've just moved back to the area and am looking for a new stylist. People have recommended this salon, so I thought I'd check it out while I was over on the mainland."

"You live on Tempest Island? Isn't it great? I wish I could afford it, but life goals, right? We're booked about two weeks out but I'm sure one of the stylists will do an excellent job for you. You don't color, do you? If you do, someone did a fantastic job."

The girl finally paused long enough for Alayna to reply, but before she could get a word out, she heard a woman's voice behind her.

"Alayna. What a surprise."

Alayna's back clenched because she knew that voice, and it was one she'd hoped to never hear again. She turned around and got her first look at Poppy Bettencourt since she'd graduated from high school.

Head cheerleader, homecoming queen, and best friend to Melody Whitmore, Poppy came from one of the well-to-do families on the mainland. Her sweet sixteen presents had included veneers, extensions, and a Mercedes convertible. Her eighteenth was breast implants. And from the looks of her poreless, unlined skin, puffed lips, and a butt that belonged in a rap video, the cosmetic enhancements hadn't stopped there.

Obviously, her disdain for Alayna hadn't, either.

Poppy stared down at her from her perch on six-inch Louboutins, wearing an expression as if she'd smelled something foul.

"Poppy," Alayna said finally. "I didn't know you still lived here. I thought you'd gotten married and moved away."

Poppy lifted her nose a bit higher and sniffed. "He wasn't good enough. I came home and took one look at the horrific way these people wore their hair and decided to open my own salon. My divorce settlement covered the costs—naturally—so here I am."

"So this is your place. It's really nice."

"Of course it is, but I don't think you're the kind of clientele we're looking for."

The receptionist's eyes widened, and she leaned back in her seat as if trying to remove herself from what was obviously an old grudge match.

Alayna gave Poppy an insincere smile. "I would think the clientele you're looking for are the ones willing to pay enough to keep you in Botox and butt injections, but that's okay. This isn't the kind of place I want touching my hair. I'm used to New York salons. I'll probably just drive to Atlanta."

The receptionist let out a strangled cry and fled the front of the shop. A flush crept up Poppy's face, and Alayna could tell she was attempting to come up with some biting retort. Unfortunately for Poppy, brains had never been her superpower, so she was still standing there, mouth half open, when Alayna turned around and left.

She forced herself into a careful stroll on the sidewalk, refusing to let Poppy see how angry she was. Good God, what was it with some women? High school was a million years ago, and Poppy and Melody acted as if it were yesterday. She'd just bet Poppy had gotten a divorce settlement large enough to pay for that high-end salon. He'd probably been happy to give her everything just to get rid of her.

She climbed into her car and pulled away, still shaking her head. One more thing she couldn't check off her list. With everything in the restaurant being a disaster, she'd thought making a hair appointment was the one thing she could be sure to manage, and therefore, feel like she'd accomplished something. But even that simple task had been complicated by old grudges.

And Alayna had never even done anything to Poppy. Hell, she'd never done anything to Melody. But whatever. If they wanted to dwell in their pitiful little existences, there was nothing Alayna could do about it. Except find another place to cut her hair of course.

I can't believe I called her out on her butt implants.

She started laughing. The longer she was back home, the more she understood Aunt Bea's direct manner and lack of filter. Some people just brought it out in you.

And since Aunt Bea was on her mind, she headed for the bookstore. At least the linens she'd scored on clearance had come in and she was going to need to squeeze a corner out of her aunt's already very full stockroom to store them until the restaurant was open. Assuming it opened, of course. If not, then she saw a long summer of eBay sales ahead for her to get the storeroom back to normal. With construction going on everywhere upstairs, the only place she could safely store things was the walk-in refrigerator, but she'd maxed it out quickly.

She said a quick prayer that things were going better with the construction than they had with her failed hair appointment attempt and headed back to the island.

BEA GAVE Alayna a nod when she walked into the bookstore, then turned her attention back to the women she was ringing up. They thanked her as they signed the credit card slip, then headed off with a bag of books, ready for a week at the beach.

"What's wrong?" Bea asked as Alayna stepped up to the counter. "The linens?"

She knew that look, and something had her niece riled.

"No. The linens are perfect. The only thing to navigate there is storage."

"We're putting out some new releases today, so there's room for more. I can squeeze them in."

"Great. Then I'll schedule the delivery."

"So the linens are good, and your plumber is literally living on the job, so what's that frustrated look about? I know it's not Luke, because although no man is perfect, he comes dangerously close."

Alayna smiled when Bea said Luke's name, and Bea couldn't blame her. If she'd been able to build the perfect man for her niece, she was pretty sure Luke was better than anything she could have come up with. Something Bea said prayers of thanks for every day. After everything that had happened with her ex, Bea had worried that Alayna would close herself off from relationships altogether, so Luke was an answer to a prayer.

"You know that salon on First Street?"

"Oh no." Bea started shaking her head.

"How come you didn't tell me that Poppy Bettencourt was back here and owned a hair salon?"

Bea shrugged. "We don't exactly run in the same circles. I'm sure as heck not paying someone hundreds of dollars for a trim, and Poppy probably hasn't read a book since high school, so I'm not going to run into her here. I had forgotten about it until you mentioned it, which I'm assuming means you had a chance to get reacquainted."

"No reacquaintance time was necessary. Poppy just picked right up where we left off in high school. If anything, she's more antagonistic."

She told Bea about their exchange, and Bea started laughing at the butt comment so hard she had to reach for a tissue.

"I have to admit," Bea said when she'd caught her breath, "I didn't think you had it in you. People are going to start accusing you of becoming more like me if you keep telling the truth."

"There's far worse things, and you know what? It felt good. I think I finally get it. I'm not saying I'm ready to go full-on Bea, but I'm ready to borrow the hat now and then."

"You might need that hat if you can't find a place to cut your hair."

"Thank God my hair doesn't have a lot of maintenance. I can give myself a trim in a pinch, but why in the world is she still so nasty?"

"Rumor has it that her husband did her dirty. Of course, given that he wasn't from here, the source of the rumors would be what Poppy is saying, so you have to take it all with a grain of salt. My guess is he chewed his leg off and ran but since he was the golden goose and she only got a portion of his net worth in settlement, he's the villain in the story. I don't even recall you talking about her much in high school, which is probably why it never occurred to me to pass along that gossip."

"Poppy never had problems with me exactly. It was Jill she directed all her hating energy on."

"Why Jill?"

"Because Poppy was dating Drew Alderman in high school, but it was clear he had a thing for Jill."

"Yuck. Please don't tell me Jill had a thing for him? I can't stand the guy."

"God no! Drew was a total creep then and now."

"A good-looking *rich* creep, which explains why Poppy wanted him."

"Probably. Or maybe she cared about him. I don't know—can demons have feelings? But I'm surprised you know him so well. Not that it takes much knowing to dislike him."

"It's from the local business functions, like that meeting I dragged you and Luke to a couple weeks ago. He likes to make sure everyone knows he has money and status. And hit on anyone he deems available."

"Yeah, nothing has changed since high school."

Bea nodded. "Even less than you think. Poppy turned up at two recent events, and every time I spot her, she's trailing after him. I figured she was trying to reel in her next big payout, but I had no idea about the high school stuff. He's not biting, though, but then, he spends most of his time chasing tourists who are a good ten years younger. You'll probably run into him on the island this summer, with some completely inappropriate young woman in tow."

"Gross."

The door to the bookstore opened and Alayna looked over and saw Pete come in. She gave him a smile.

"Hey, stranger," she said. "I was just telling Luke last night that we needed to have you over for dinner. It's been a minute."

"At least a week, but I didn't want to admit I'm counting the days 'til I get more of your cooking."

"Luke's got night training the next few days, but maybe after that?"

"I would love to."

She glanced at her watch. "You must be on the early shift. Going to get in some surfing?"

"Actually, I was considering a book and maybe just a long sit on the beach."

"Sounds wonderful. Bea, I'm going to run. I'll let you know about the delivery."

Bea gave her niece a wave as she hurried out of the store, then leaned across the counter. "You're early."

"I am, but there's a couple books I wanted to see if you could find for me. Figured I might as well take advantage while I was here."

"Well, why didn't you say so? What are the titles?"

He pulled a list out of his pocket and passed it over to Bea, who scanned it and raised one eyebrow.

"These are all rare editions. There's not a book on here less than twenty years old. You're making me work."

"There's no urgency. I'm just hoping to fill out my own collection. I do the usual internet searches, but I figured you probably have connections I don't have access to."

She nodded and tucked the list under the counter. "I'll make some calls. Before Nelly wanders up here and catches us, there was a situation last night."

She gave him a brief rundown of what had happened at the lighthouse.

"Jesus. Their timing couldn't have been worse."

"I know. I've got her holed up at my house, but she's not going to want to stay put. I've got to get that door fixed up so that she can head back to the lighthouse or I'm afraid she'll bolt. Fixing it properly is going to require a carpenter, but I have to get it covered at least, and I can't get away from here for at least another hour or so."

"I can handle it if I can borrow your boat."

"Of course. I've got some plywood in my garage and screws and a drill in the blue cabinet. Take whatever you need. You might as well check on Jill's foot when you get the boat keys. They're hanging on a hook in the laundry room. Now, duck on out of here before Nelly finishes up in the back. The less she sees us together, the better."

"Please give Jill a call and let her know I'm on my way."

"On it."

CHAPTER ELEVEN

Pete hopped in his Jeep and headed for Bea's house. The first thing he noticed when he backed into the driveway was that the blinds on the front windows were closed. But that made sense. He made his way onto the porch and rapped lightly on the door, hoping that Bea had been able to get hold of Jill. She must have because the door opened seconds later, and Jill gave him a brief smile as she darted a glance out the door. He slipped quickly inside and shut the door behind him before anyone could get a look at Bea's other guest.

She looked surprisingly good given the night she'd had. He'd expected her to look exhausted and stressed, but apparently, she'd managed to bring some calm back in. In fact, she looked better than good. Even the circles under her eyes couldn't detract from her overall beauty. She had one of those faces that would look good at any age. Great genetics, his mother had always groused, especially when she was complaining about her lack of them. She'd left her long hair loose and it hung down her back in waves that looked so soft, he had the overwhelming desire to touch them.

Shaking himself out of his stupor, he followed her to the

kitchen, noticing that while she was maneuvering better with the crutches, her limping was a bit more pronounced than it had been the day before.

"I heard about the excitement last night," he said.

She sat in one of the chairs at the dining table and shook her head. "I almost shot them. I mean, I could have. I fired a warning shot over their heads, hoping it would scare them away."

"They're lucky you were so levelheaded. It would be a shame for someone to take a bullet over youthful stupidity, but no one could have blamed you for it."

"Except me. So I'm glad I didn't panic. Or I should say, I'm glad I didn't panic more, because I was pretty sure I was going to have a heart attack."

"You're in the worst possible scenario for that to have happened—hiding from a threat, isolated, injured—so it's no wonder you hit peak stress level. How's your ankle doing?"

"I was hoping it was better today, but that's probably wishful thinking."

"Let's take a look."

He turned a chair to face her and sat then gently lifted her leg up and placed it on his. Since he was here in a medical capacity, her bare skin pressed against his shouldn't have felt so good, but it did. Pushing that thought away before it could head down an avenue he had no business going, he carefully unwrapped her ankle and studied it. He pressed gently on the swollen areas and then moved the foot slowly around in a circular motion while continuing to feel the injured area.

Frowning, he reached for the bandage and began wrapping it again. "It seems a bit worse today than yesterday. I know you had to do a lot of walking, and getting in and out of the boat probably didn't help matters, and just the stress alone can contribute to inflammation, but I was hoping to see more progress."

She bit her lower lip. "I still don't want to go to the hospital. Not yet. I swear, it was getting better before all that stuff happened. Can we still wait until tomorrow? I promise if it's not improved enough, I'll go."

"Improved enough by my standards or yours?"

She sighed. "You got me. Yours, okay?"

He'd hoped since she was already on the island that she would agree to an X-ray, but he hadn't expected her to. Especially not after being scared half to death the night before. And like Bea, he didn't want to put pressure on her so that she felt she had to leave in order to make her own decisions. Clearly she was in danger, and at least she had people looking out for her here.

"How's the pain?" he asked.

"It throbbed some last night, especially when I first went to bed. And it sent me some warning signals when I first started moving this morning. But all that had calmed down last night before everything went crazy."

He nodded. "I'm hoping it's still a sprain, but you have to promise me you'll be very careful. The additional aggravation last night was enough to set you back, so you need to keep weight off it as much as possible. Even if it improves by tomorrow, that doesn't mean you can run out and start hiking or anything."

"I'm not going to 'run' out and do anything, but if I could slow walk out and swim in a couple days, I'd be happy."

He frowned, pushing thoughts of Jill in a bathing suit out of his mind and forcing himself to focus on her injury. "There's no graduated entry at the lighthouse, is there? Because it's best to stay off ladders for the time being. The weighted compression would set you back."

"There's a tiny beach area. It's graduated, but it is a little steep. Kinda goes down quickly, then disappears."

"It's probably not a good idea yet. Honestly, it's not a good idea to do it alone, even if you were in tip-top shape."

She raised one eyebrow. "Bea said you're a surfer. Do you always go out with a buddy?"

"Touché. But I'm in the Navy. We're half sea creature."

"Nice try, but I get your point. How about I promise not to go swimming until I can walk without the crutches, and I'll take them anyway and bring a float, which I'd already intended to do. Worse case, I can crawl up that incline and then get back up onto the crutches."

He was a smart enough man to know that was as good as he was going to get, so he nodded.

"Okay. Well, I told Bea I'd give her a hand with the door situation, so I need to get Bea's boat key and some plywood out of her garage. I'm going to board it up until she can get a carpenter out to repair it properly. I hope that's okay for you."

"That's fine. I didn't expect she could get it repaired quickly. Those boys really did a number on the frame. The whole thing is probably going to have to be replaced. I hate that they damaged her property. I almost wish I would have confronted them before they kicked the door in."

"You had no way of knowing who was on the other side or what their intent was. It could have been more than two people and all of them armed. It sounds like your response was the best one possible under the circumstances."

"I suppose in the big scheme of things that's true. But still." She sighed and waved a hand around. "You'll see that Bea's made the lighthouse an extension of her home. I hate that it's been damaged. And while I know it can be fixed, that's not the point. A lot of thought and care goes into making a place so welcoming."

Pete looked around the room and nodded. "I've always loved the cottages on the island. I'm hoping to buy one someday. And Bea's definitely got a knack for design and decor. I might have to tap her if I ever find the right place."

"It's more than that. Yes, the colors and materials and items are all beautifully blended, but it doesn't feel like a sterile magazine ad. Even though she's changed the colors on the walls and cabinets in this main area, it's always had that warm and inviting feel...like it's just waiting to welcome you home."

He studied her for a moment. "You've been here before...I didn't realize."

Her eyes widened slightly as it dawned on her that she'd told more than she'd been intending, then she slowly nodded. "At this point, I don't suppose it matters if you know some of my history. My father was stationed here when I was in high school. Alayna and I were best friends."

"Really?" Pete didn't bother to hold back his surprise. He'd assumed, given Jill's age, that she was the daughter of a friend, but he'd never gone as far as thinking she'd lived on the island and had, at one point, been an integral part of Bea and Alayna's lives. Now that he knew, her desire to remain hidden from the islanders made even more sense. If her stalker came around asking questions, people probably wouldn't remember a random woman, especially with tourist season under way. But they *would* remember someone they knew previously and had recently seen again.

"Seems like a lifetime ago. Alayna and I lost touch after high school. School, work, trying to have a life... You know how that goes. They say absence makes the heart grow fonder, but in my experience, it just makes the heart forget. Not that I forgot Alayna or Bea, and they didn't forget me, but when you're a young adult, you think you're supposed to conquer the world alone."

"Truer words. An old friend of my family is a very well-known cardiac surgeon and wanted to give me a recommendation to a top-tier medical school where he was on the board. I hesitated for way too long before finally accepting. Youth, arrogance, limitless energy...whatever. At least I came to my senses. Anyway, you don't have to explain to me how people lose touch. I've lived in six countries in the last five years alone."

"I think I was used to losing people because of all the moving around with the military. But I always kept in touch with Bea. Not often. Maybe once or twice a year and just an email, but I never could completely let go of that connection. Bea was more of a mother to me than my own was. She's an incredible woman."

He nodded. "I haven't known her for very long, but what I do know makes her an admirable person. Alayna too. Have you contacted her?"

"No. I don't want her involved. I only involved Bea because I knew she was dialed into the real estate market and would know of a good place to lie low. My connection with this place as an adult is nonexistent, so my stalker is unlikely to track me here, and even if he goes back to my school years, this was just another stop on my father's itinerary."

"So as long as the locals don't see and recognize you, then you're good. It makes a lot more sense why you don't want to risk going to the hospital now."

"And why I don't want to expose Alayna to my problems, especially after everything she just went through. I don't want her reliving her own worst nightmare again."

Pete frowned. "I know you didn't ask for my opinion, but I'm going to give it anyway. I think you're making a mistake.

Alayna is one of the strongest people I've ever met, and more importantly, she has a heart bigger than the Gulf. She would want to help, and if she ever finds out that you were here and purposely avoided her, she'll be hurt. She doesn't need protecting, and even if she did, she's got my buddy Luke for that."

Jill shook her head. "I have a friend back home...a very strong, capable woman. A woman I deeply admire. She was attacked by the man looking for me. He put her in the hospital. She'll be fine, but if she hadn't been on the phone at the time, and the person on the other end hadn't dispatched the police when she screamed, he might have killed her."

Pete felt his heart clench. No wonder Jill was so frightened and so adamant about not involving others. "Who is he?"

"I don't know. That's the worst part. He could be the guy who sold me firewood, or the man who delivered my washer and dryer, or Tom Cruise. Well, maybe not Tom Cruise. He probably has an alibi."

Pete forced a smile because he knew she wanted him to, but he was certain it didn't mask the dread he'd felt at her words. "So your suspect list is the entire male population, sans Tom Cruise."

"Well, and you."

She managed a small smile, and he had the overwhelming desire to draw her into his arms and promise her that he'd never let anyone harm her. That she was safe with him. Now and for as long as it took. But her vulnerability was as acute as her fear, and the last thing she needed was a man making any kind of physical move on her, even in friendship.

Especially since what he felt wasn't *only* friendly.

Any move like that on his part would probably only scare her more. Even now, her expression had shifted from somewhat relaxed to tense, and he could see the walls going up around her. Because he didn't want to cause her any more stress, he changed the subject.

"I've got that knee scooter with me," he said. "Do you want me to bring it in or take it to the lighthouse?"

"I think I'm okay with the crutches for now, but if you're going to the lighthouse to secure the door, there's no reason for me to sit here waiting so that Bea has to take me later. I could go back with you."

"You're not worried someone will see you?"

"Technically, those two boys and the cop have already, but I didn't know any of them from before, so I'm probably good. Regardless, I don't want Bea heading out there at night again just because I'm worried about someone getting a peek. If you back into the garage, I can climb in and duck down until we get to the dock. I have a ball cap and sunglasses. If anyone sees me at the dock, you can always claim Bea let you borrow her boat for a hot date."

He stared at her for a bit, wanting to refuse, but he was also afraid of what other plans she might come up with if he did. "Let me give Bea a call and make sure she's all right with that. But if for any odd reason I can't secure that door, you'll have to come back."

"Deal. I'll go throw my things back into my overnight bag. It's really getting a workout."

———

JILL SAT on the bench in the cabin of Bea's boat as Pete guided it across the Sound. She had the strange feeling of déjà vu but then she'd just made this ride a couple days before. Same boat. Different captain. But her role was the same—hide until they reached the Gulf. That way, no one would spot her on the boat and Pete wouldn't have to make up lies on her behalf. The man

135

had already gone above and beyond. She didn't want to drain any more of his time and energy away from his own life, which she assumed was full.

"The coast is clear," Pete said, and grinned.

She laughed at his use of the rather applicable cliché and headed onto the deck to sit in the passenger chair across from him. It was another beautiful day on the Gulf, and she leaned toward the side of the boat, allowing the spray of salt water to mist her face. She closed her eyes as the sun warmed her skin and let out a sigh of contentment.

"It's pretty incredible, isn't it?" Pete said when she leaned back in her chair.

She nodded. "The best place in the world. I don't suppose you could slow down a little? I mean, unless you have to hurry. I know I'm already cutting into your day."

He smiled and cut speed to a slow cruise. "I'm good. And there's few places better than being on or in the water."

"I totally agree. My home has a water view but it's from a distance. And the water's not the same. It's so clear here and the sand is like powder."

"I can't think of a prettier place in the continental US. Can I ask a personal question—not about your situation?"

"Okay."

"It's clear you love this place, and you have good history with Bea and Alayna, so why don't you live here? Or at least, visit more often?"

"You're a surfer. Why don't you live in Hawaii?"

"My job, for starters. I guess I should have figured. That's why most people are where they are."

"Yes, but there's more to it than that for me. Where I live now is across the country from some bad history. After college, I just started driving until I ran out of road, found a nice place, a good job, and eventually a good friend, and decided to stay. But technically, I'm remote now, so staying is a choice."

"So it's home?"

"It is. I guess." She frowned. "Apparently, I haven't given it a lot of thought."

"Seems like a lot of change is going on now. It might be a good time to rethink everything."

She blew out a breath. "I suppose so."

"So are you planning on staying gone until the cops catch this guy?"

"That was the initial plan, but the reality is I can't hide forever. At some point, I'll have to make a choice."

"How long have they been looking for him?"

"Seriously looking—since he attacked my friend. Claiming they were looking—five years."

His eyes widened. "Five—holy crap! This guy has been threatening you for that long and the cops still don't know anything about him?"

"Until last week, he'd only sent cards. Creepy, unsettling cards. But there are no fingerprints, the cards are produced by the millions, and he always prints the words."

"Man, that's...just wow. I can't imagine."

She nodded. "Of course, my initial reaction was fear, as any woman with a lick of sense would feel. Then after a couple years, I got to the point that I felt more annoyed than afraid. When they started coming more often and the messages increased in intensity—like he was on the cusp of acting out on his feelings—I got scared all over again."

"And you have no idea where this guy attached to you? Social media, work?"

"I'm not on social media." Which was true. Kate Coleson was, but Jill Smith/Morgan was not. "Work is the most likely place for us to have crossed paths, I suppose, but so far, we haven't come up with anything."

"No coworkers who you turned down for a date? A boss that wanted you to earn a promotion the old-fashioned way?"

"I've never had anything like that happen, and even before I starting working remotely, I didn't really interact with coworkers much. Now most everything is by phone or email. My friend who was attacked—I was at her place last week. She has an apartment above her business in one of those historic buildings. He was inside the building while we were in her apartment and attacked her after I left."

He frowned. "But if he's after you, why did he let you go?"

"Because he wants me alone. And he's obsessed, so I doubt killing me is his only objective. But once he does, the game is over. He didn't spend years on buildup to simply put a bullet through me from across the street."

"Jesus. I hadn't thought of that. I'm so sorry. But then why did he break into your friend's place if he wasn't there for you?"

"We're pretty sure he was in her building looking for my home address."

"But if you've been receiving cards for five years...?"

Crap. Jill's mind rushed to cover her faux pas.

"He sends them to my corporate office."

Bookstores were sort of an office, right?

"This last one he sent to my friend," she continued. "I've been careful about keeping my home a secret, but apparently, he's reached the point of action beyond the cards."

"He's escalating—looking for a face-to-face."

"Yes. He printed a long address list from her computer. He would have had to work through them all to find me, because my friend didn't use my real name on it, but a few days later a card showed up at my house, slipped through the mail slot."

"And you contacted Bea and came here."

"Where I promptly injured myself because I panicked when a guy in a boat waved at me."

"That's how you twisted your ankle?"

She nodded. "It was stupid. Boats pass there all the time and it would be stranger if someone *didn't* stare and wave when they saw someone at the lighthouse. It hasn't been occupied since I was a kid and was always restricted. But instead of thinking of all of that, I rushed to get inside and twisted my ankle. And here I am—injured and hunted."

"You need to stop beating yourself up over your reactions. There's nothing you've done since you've been here that doesn't make perfect sense given the situation. But are you sure you want to stay at the lighthouse after all of that? I know your stalker can't get to you easily, but neither can the good guys."

"I know. But the isolation is what I hoped would protect me...and everyone else."

She held in a sigh. Unfortunately, that might not make a difference unless her stalker was a stranger. But what if Trevor was the stalker? He knew she loved the ocean. What if he remembered all the places she'd lived? He was already a criminal on the run. What would stop him from checking out every town he could recall, seeing if he could locate her? And since she'd spent the majority of her life on Atlantic and Gulf Coast bases, that would be the logical place to start.

"I get why you think the location is more secure," Pete said, "but I still think you'd be better off staying with Bea, at least until your ankle heals."

"But then every day would be staring at four walls with the blinds closed. I couldn't even step into the backyard without her neighbors starting a chat. And some of them might recognize me. Besides, I need sun and wind on my face.

I can't sit in the dark all day, and ambient lighting isn't the same."

"I get it," he said finally.

"I figured with that tan you have this early in the season, you might."

He smiled. "I did one very limited tour on a sub. Let's just say I wasn't a fan. I'm not claustrophobic, but I definitely prefer being *on* the water, not below."

"I don't think I'd like that either. Don't get me wrong, I prefer a good deal of alone time, but when I want, I can get in my car and be with people or at a business in a matter of minutes. I know there are sailors on the sub, but you can't exactly duck out at midnight for a Taco Bell run."

He laughed. "Taco Bell? That's what you come up with as the shortage in your life if you were trapped under water in a giant metal container?"

"Not the *only* thing. There's also midnight pancakes."

"Okay, I can see that." He pointed to the lighthouse as they approached. "Almost there. Do you want to take a spin around a bit before we dock?"

She stared at the lighthouse and the ocean, trying to make up her mind. Finally, she looked back at him. "I don't want to tie up your whole day or even half. I'm sure you have things to do...work, a girlfriend, laundry, hobbies..."

"So that's a yes to the spin," he said and guided the boat toward one side of the island to make a big circle.

"And for the record," he continued, "I'm done with work for the day—early shift. My hobby is being anywhere near the ocean, so that box is checked, and my laundry is caught up. The girlfriend box is glaringly blank."

"Then you must not be trying."

Too late, she realized she'd blurted out her thoughts before she could check herself.

"Oh my God, I'm sorry," she said. "It's none of my business. I just... Well, you're young, successful, horribly nice, have the patience of a saint, and you're hot."

Good. God. You just told him he was hot!

She felt the blush rush up her neck and onto her face as he stared at her, looking a bit stunned.

"Wow," he finally said. "Thanks. I've never had that kind of glowing review before."

"I can't believe I just said that."

"Were you lying?"

"No! But I'm usually far better at keeping my thoughts to myself."

"Sometimes abnormal circumstances contribute to abnormal behavior. But for the record, you're right."

"You *are* hot?"

Now it was his turn to blush.

"How the heck do I answer that without sounding like an ass? I meant you're right that I haven't been trying to find a girlfriend."

"Can I ask why not?"

He shrugged. "I got stationed here recently, so that's some of it. My first objective was to get comfortable with my job and staff and determine where support for the sailors under my care can be improved and then wage a budget war to get the funds for those improvements."

"So all work and no play."

"No, I've played, but it's mostly been surfing or just relaxing at the beach. I've spent a good bit of time with Luke and Alayna, and honestly, that might be part of my hesitation to jump in the dating pool again."

"I don't understand. Why would they hold you back?"

"Oh, Lord, they aren't actively preventing me. In fact, they've pointed out every good-looking woman on the beach, without fail, trying to spur me on. But it's seeing them together that's made me reevaluate that part of my life. What they have is special. I want something like that, and I refuse to settle."

"But how do you know you can't have it with any of those good-looking women on the beach if you never even talk to them?"

"They're mostly tourists. I'm not looking for something temporary."

"I get it. And I suppose it's always been hard before to find the right person with all the moving. It takes a special kind of partner to be willing to uproot themselves on the whim of the military."

"Very true, and that's always been on my mind up until now. But unless things go seriously wrong, this is my final assignment. I'll be here to retirement. If they attempt to change that, I might bow out early and head for the private sector. But this is where I want to be. I found my place."

She smiled. "Now you just need to find your person."

"I have a dog, if that counts," he said.

"Oh, I love dogs. I keep telling myself I should get one, then I end up not doing it. I don't even know why. What kind of dog?"

"A Lab named Gus. He's an older guy who belonged to a soldier who passed. I took him in so now he gets to keep living here, which is the only place he's ever known."

"That's awesome. How come you don't have him with you?"

"I only take him out for leisurely beach strolls. Otherwise, he spends most of his day couch surfing, which is his favorite thing. A military wife who lives in the apartment next door walks him for me when I'm working or away. She has a couple of young kids and they really enjoy him but aren't in a position to get a dog of their own. Her husband will probably post overseas soon."

"Couches and beach walks sound like an excellent life."

"What about you?" he asked, trying for a casual tone. "Do you have someone you're making those emergency Taco Bell runs with?"

"No. I had a relationship in college that went south. Criminally south. I got away, concentrated on building my career, then the creepy cards started...I guess it's just never felt like the right time to take that next step."

"The college relationship... Was that the reason for your cross-country drive?"

She nodded.

"That sucks, and now this. I guess the cops have run down that guy as part of their investigation, right?"

"They tried to, but he's apparently made a career out of poor decisions and has now disappeared. There's a warrant out for his arrest for violating parole, but so far, they haven't come up with anything."

"It sounds like he's the guy. Why aren't they trying harder to find him?"

Jill could hear the frustration in his voice.

"They're doing everything they can, but he doesn't have a bank account or credit card, not even a valid driver's license. There's APBs out to all police departments in the country for him and his car, but he's a thief. He probably steals different license plates every week along with money, pays cash for the kind of motels that don't see or hear anything, and bounces too fast for anyone to catch up."

"Does he know you lived here?"

"Probably. I mean, I told him about the places I lived, but that was a lot of places, and I don't know that I focused on

Tempest Island any more than the others even though it was my favorite."

"But he could be checking them all."

She nodded. "Yeah. That's what I'm afraid of. Assuming he even remembers."

"If he's fixated on you, he remembers. Who is this guy? Does Bea know? If we had a recent picture, that could be useful."

Jill frowned and he could tell she was conflicted.

"Bea runs a bookstore," he said. "I'm on the island all the time. If either of us spots this guy, we'd know to call the police."

She blew out a breath. "You're right. I just... Man, I was hoping that I could be here and not get anyone else involved. I don't want that weight on my shoulders."

"We're better off knowing than not."

"Okay. The detective handling my case sent me a recent photo. I'll tell Bea he's a suspect and send her the information, but if you don't mind, I'd like to keep the rest of the story between us. Bea will get all parental, which on the one hand is nice since my own mother is lacking that gene, but I don't want her so close that she gets hit by the fallout like my friend did."

"I won't say a word."

"Thanks. For everything you're doing. I feel better telling someone about him, even though I didn't want to put my crap off on someone else. Bea's already in deeper than I'd like."

"You're not putting anything off on me. I asked. And I want to help."

She nodded and looked out toward the lighthouse island. "Look, there's the beach."

He turned a bit more toward the island to get a better look at the patch of sand she'd indicated. "Boy, you weren't kidding.

It's small and given the change in water color, it does drop off pretty fast."

"It does, but how cool is it that they built that little beach there? The whole property is special. I swear, if I didn't already have a home, and all of this wasn't going on, I would try to talk Bea into selling it to me."

"I can definitely see the draw, especially if you can work from anywhere and don't like people all that much. But that midnight Taco Bell thing would be a lot of work."

She laughed. "I guess I'd just have to keep ground beef and taco shells in stock. But since I go days or even weeks sometimes without leaving the house, it wouldn't be all that difficult. The worst part would be having to evacuate for hurricanes, although Tempest Island evacuates as well."

"They're supposed to, you mean."

"That's true. Some of the old-timers aren't packing their bags for anything less than a Cat 4."

He guided the boat around the island and the dock came into view. "Are you ready to get off the boat?"

"I guess I should. I've taken up enough of your day and you still have that plywood to hang. I can help you."

"No way. You're not doing anything to aggravate that ankle any more than last night did. Getting in and out of the boat is the extent of the exertion you're allowed for today."

She frowned. "I hate that they ruined the back door. I was really looking forward to sitting on that deck."

"Is there a walkway from the front to the back?"

"Of sorts. It's more of a path though."

"Well, you can go out the back door and take a seat before I start work, then when I'm done, I'll help you walk around. If you can find a spot out front to put the chairs, I'm happy to move them."

She smiled. "That sounds about as perfect as it can get."

CHAPTER TWELVE

AT THE FIRST BREAK IN CUSTOMERS, BEA HEADED UPSTAIRS to check on the plumbing progress. It was a good thing Pete had offered to handle the door situation because with the perfect weather, the store had been swamped with beachgoers. It had taken both her and Nelly to handle them all. Under different circumstances, she would have tapped Alayna to help, but she was already working the afternoon shift at the ice cream shop, filling in for Birdie, whose husband, Tom, had just had surgery for prostate cancer. Birdie and Tom had worried about closing their business during the busiest part of the year, but all their friends had offered to fill in and had created a schedule so that the business was always covered.

Bea and Nelly had their hands full at the bookstore during business hours, but after hours, Bea was helping Emma, a new islander and an accountant, make sure the books and inventory for the ice cream shop were running on all cylinders. Nelly was doing her part by keeping the couple in casseroles and desserts. Bea was really pleased with how everyone had jumped in to contribute help where they could.

As she tromped up the stairs, she said a prayer that Billy

had been as diligent about the plumbing as everyone else had been about helping Birdie and Tom. When she walked into the restaurant, she heard a toilet flush and crossed her fingers that was a good sign. Billy walked out of the bathroom, set eyes on her, and smiled.

"Got half the toilets in and working. I'm going to handle the rest of the bathroom plumbing, then I'll tackle the kitchen water and gas hookups. Are the appliances ready to go?"

Bea felt some of the tension leave her shoulders. "Yes, and a lot of them are downstairs in my storeroom. When do you think you'll be ready for them?"

"Tomorrow afternoon probably. Plan on burning the midnight oil. Going to be better on my back than sleeping on that floor."

"Good, then I'll tap a couple of strong backs for first thing in the morning to help you get them all in place."

Billy looked down at the floor and shuffled a bit, and Bea started to worry that there was something wrong that he wasn't telling her.

"Have you run into any problems?" she asked.

"No, ma'am. Least not on the plumbing, but that's never been a problem for me. I guess I was wondering if when I'm done here you'd talk to Minnie for me."

"And tell her what? That I'm holding you hostage with bail money until you finish the job? Hell, she's mad at me for bailing you out."

"You're the one out the bail money. Why's she mad?"

"Like you said, your professional ability isn't the problem. Minnie already knows you're great at what you do, and me telling her what she already knows isn't going to get you anywhere. But you're a disaster when it comes to being a husband and father. Now, I know Minnie thought all that male posturing was sexy when you two were younger, but it's a bad look for a grown man with a passel of kids to set an example for."

Billy frowned. "I don't know about no male posturing. How am I supposed to stand?"

Bea silently counted to five before replying. "It means you have to stop beating up everyone who challenges you. Stop acting like a caveman and act like a man who has something to lose if he keeps using his fists to solve his problems. The judge threw the book at you this time because he's tired of seeing you in his court. What happens next time when bail is double or triple? Who's going to spring you then, because it's not going to be Minnie, that much I know."

Billy gave her a crestfallen look. "I thought Minnie liked being married to a strong man."

"She does, which is why she's just as guilty as you for continuing this childish way of life, but she's ahead of you on realizing it's not going to work anymore. You can be a strong man without beating another guy's face in. Give it a try. And get into one of those groups. The only way you're going to change Minnie's mind is by changing yourself. There's nothing I can say to fix that for you."

He sighed. "I guess not. Thanks for getting me out, Bea. At least I can make the rent money, and that's something. I'm going to look into those classes just as soon as I'm done with your job. Maybe signing up will be enough for her to let me move back in at least."

"Maybe so. I'll go arrange that help. Let me know if you need anything else."

He gave her a nod and headed back to the bathroom, a resigned look on his face. Bea shook her head. Marriage had never been on her bucket list, and relationships like Billy and Minnie's only confirmed her choice. She had no doubt they loved each other, but what worked at sixteen was completely different from what one needed at forty. Making something work for a long time was a constant requirement of compromise.

And Bea had never been very good at it.

———

JILL SAT in the patio chair on the back deck, attempting to enjoy the view. The problem was, instead of staring past the palm trees and tropical bushes and out over the clear turquoise water, the most enticing view was the shirtless man ten feet from her, hanging plywood over the back doorway.

His body glistened with a sheen of sweat, which only accentuated the ripple of muscles on his back, shoulders, chest, arms, legs, abs... Good Lord, she needed to stop with the inventory. The man was perfect. So perfect that he almost made her want to hit the gym on a regular basis. Almost. Jill was in reasonably good shape, and her diet was usually decent except for her pizza-when-stressed habit, but she wasn't even in the same fitness realm as him. Pete had the kind of body that graced magazine ads and romance book covers. And it hadn't even been touched up with Photoshop.

Which almost seemed unfair to every other man in the world.

It was definitely unfair to her, because this level of attraction to someone had been absent from her life for years. There had been the occasional man she'd dated, but none had stuck or made her tingly in all the right places the way Pete did. And he wasn't even trying to romance her. The whole thing didn't bode well, especially given her current situation.

She wasn't in a place where she could allow herself to get drawn in, regardless of her attraction. For one, someone was trying to kill her, and that pretty much put a crimp into any kind of normal life. And introducing a man into her life when another had mentally claimed her for himself would probably be viewed as throwing down a gauntlet. Then there was the fact that she lived on the opposite side of the country. Yes, that could be changed, but was that what she wanted?

She'd made the comment earlier about buying the lighthouse from Bea if it was possible, but would she really want to move back here? She had a great life where she was and an awesome friend in Wanda. Assuming her stalker was caught and she could go back to normal, would she really want to leave her beautiful home and great friend to move back to Tempest Island?

But the island is even more beautiful and Alayna is here. And Bea. Wanda could visit and there's always video chatting.

She shook her head. This whole line of thought was a waste of time. Until the cops caught her stalker, nothing in her life could be normal, so there was no use making plans based on something that might not happen anytime soon. Every day her stalker was loose was another opportunity for him to find her. And anyone in the way would be collateral damage. Which meant any thoughts of moving here needed to be off the table, even in her imagination. Why work herself up just to be disappointed?

Bea had already stuck her neck out more than Jill was comfortable with, but her ankle injury had complicated things. And she'd already shared too much with Pete, but she'd been so comfortable with him because she knew she could trust him. And she had to admit that she'd felt better after she'd told him the basics of her situation.

"Are you sure I can't help you?" she asked as he set the plywood in place.

"Positive. I don't want you standing unless absolutely necessary."

He pressed one knee into the huge sheet of lumber, then reached up with the drill and deftly sank a screw into the top. That one screw was all he needed to keep it in place while he made quick work of securing the rest of them. Then he followed that up with a tarp that he stapled around the frame.

Clearly, he had everything under control, but Jill couldn't help feeling guilty about it all. He'd helped her out of the boat and down the dock. Then he'd gotten her situated in a chair on the deck with her foot propped up and a bottled water before going back to lug everything out of the boat. Jill wasn't the kind of woman who felt comfortable sitting around while other people did all the work, even though she acknowledged that his job was easier with her out of the way.

"This will hold well enough, unless we have one of those huge storms," he said when he finished. "There's some cracks around the frame that water could still find a way into, though."

"Hopefully Bea can get someone out here to make the repair soon. She said she's got someone good working on Alayna's restaurant. Maybe she can convince him to fit in a side job."

Pete frowned.

"What? Is something wrong with the restaurant?"

"Not exactly. There's some asshat on the city council trying to block it from opening, and Bea and Alayna are pushing to get it going before the next meeting when they'll hold the vote. A business has never been shut down after opening, and they think that will hold true for them. But they've run into a lot of issues with the construction."

"Oh no! And here I am causing Bea to step away from her responsibilities even more."

"Bea's not the one doing the build-out, so you're not interfering with that at all."

"But I'm adding more stress and it sounds like she's already dealing with enough. And that's even more reason to leave Alayna out of this. Who is this person? And what is their problem with Bea?"

"His name's Carlson Whitmore, and—"

Jill held up her hand. "No need to explain any further. The Whitmores have been a thorn in the side of decent people since the dawn of time."

"That's right. Since you lived here, you probably know them."

"Unfortunately, Alayna and I attended high school with his daughter, Melody. She was a real treat. She hated Alayna and went out of her way to make her life miserable."

Pete nodded. "Alayna's told some stories. I'm afraid she didn't improve things by settling in with Luke. Melody was making a hard play for him before he locked in on Alayna."

"Oh boy. That explains even more clearly why Carlson is pushing so hard to prevent Alayna from opening her restaurant."

"I don't get it. What's wrong with those people?"

"Jealousy, for sure. Alayna was everything Melody wasn't—smart, beautiful, and someone everyone liked to be around. Melody isn't all that bright, and she's pretty, but in a very plastic sort of way. Her personality, though, is nasty."

He nodded. "Luke told me he was afraid of her. Coming from a SEAL, that statement is a lot to unpack."

She laughed. "I don't blame him. You must not have run into her yet because otherwise, you'd understand what he's talking about. You're just her type."

"Which is?"

"Good-looking, built, good career. You'd fall down on the religion part of things, though."

"How do you know I'm not religious?"

"Melody requires that you worship *her*."

"Ha. You're right. I have not had the displeasure of meeting her and God willing, I never will."

"You keep surfing and hanging out at the beach, you're bound to eventually. Even in high school she trolled the vacationers because she'd exhausted the local population."

His look of dismay made her smile, and even though she'd been teasing him, everything she'd said was true. Pete was 100 percent Melody's type, but then Pete was every woman with a pulse's type.

"When is the next city council meeting?" she asked.

"Two weeks."

"Crap. That's not a lot of time. How close are they?"

"I think it's almost done. There was an issue yesterday with the plumber getting arrested. His wife was done with his bad behavior and refused to bail him out, so Bea went and posted this morning."

"Good Lord! No wonder she was out of the house so early. That woman has done more in a single morning than I will all week."

"She does seem to pack a lot into her days."

"I hope they finish it on time. I can't stomach the thought of the Whitmores standing in the way of Alayna's restaurant, especially after everything she went through."

"Me either. She's a good woman. Bea and Luke were afraid that after the situation in New York she wouldn't take the chance of opening a restaurant again, and that would have been a shame. I've had the good fortune to eat her cooking on several occasions, and I will pay anything she's charging to be a regular."

She smiled. "She was always so talented. Even in high school, she could cook circles around all the other kids' moms. And Bea, well, let's just say she's not domestic, so Alayna had all the opportunity in the world to hone her craft. But Bea has other talents."

"Real estate appears to be one of them. That woman has a nose for an investment. Like this one. No one even knew the county would sell this property and she goes and makes a deal before anyone realized it was there to be made. She could probably make a small fortune renting this place out during the season."

"I know. I told her I'd pay market rate, but she refused to take anything."

"Didn't figure she would." He looked out at the ocean. "Does that seawall have any rocks in front of it?"

"No. I looked when I did my walk the other day. It's a straight drop down. Maybe about five feet deep right in front of the wall when the tide was out, but with the tide in like it is now, it will be a lot deeper. Why? You thinking about fishing?"

He grinned. "Not exactly."

With that said, he jumped off the porch and sprinted to the seawall, then bailed off into the ocean. She was still laughing when he came up for air.

"How's the water?" she asked, feeling more than a little jealous.

"Refreshing," he said. "It will get to bathwater state before long, but right now, it's the perfect cooldown."

She gazed wistfully at him as he treaded. "I wish I could get in."

"Hopefully soon. But your job is to baby that ankle until we know for sure it's on the road to mending. I'm sorry to tease you like this, but it was just too good to pass up."

"Oh, I don't blame you. If I'd just spent time carting plywood and fixing the door in the hot sun, I would have done the same. Heck, if I wasn't relegated to this chair, I'd be in there with you, and I wasn't even part of the manual labor."

He smiled at her, and she felt it all the way down to her toes. Then she remembered why she was sitting here, on this secluded patch of land, and she forced herself to ban all thoughts in that direction.

But good God, he made it hard.

He swam to the seawall and pulled himself up and over the wall in one fluid motion and headed her way. His ripped, tanned body glistened with salt water and all thoughts of a ban instantly fled her mind. Why was she denying her attraction to him? She was a writer, for Christ's sake. An intimate understanding of emotion was necessary to be a good one. Accepting that she was attracted to him did *not* mean she had to act on it.

So there was the line.

As long as she didn't act on her attraction, silently lusting was perfectly fine.

He plopped in the chair next to her and waved a hand at the ocean. "This is incredible, right? I still can't believe Bea owns this—that it's even a house. I mean, it's perfection. Nothing but ocean disappearing into the horizon. If only I were rich. I'd sit here forever."

"You'd probably get hungry."

He laughed. "Yeah, but a grill right there on the corner of the deck would solve all of that. The only real problem is being lonely. Don't get me wrong, I like my solitary time like the next guy, but every day all day would be hard."

"You wouldn't be a very good doctor if you didn't like contact with people."

"That's true. Unfortunately, my work is often centered around young men injured or disabled by war. It's a tough thing to see every day. So a break from it is necessary in order for me to provide high-level care."

Her heart clenched at the thought of caring for men, some

who hadn't even hit drinking age, who would live with permanent health issues because of their service. She knew she wouldn't be able to handle it without breaking down. It took a strong person to dedicate their life to the care of others.

"That must be hard," she said. "I couldn't do it, but I'm glad there are people like you who can."

He gave her a curious look. "What do you do for a living exactly? You don't have to say if you don't want to, but you mentioned you worked remote and mostly only talked to clients..."

"I'm a claims adjuster for an insurance company," she replied, trotting out her standard lie. "And yes, it's as boring as it sounds, but it pays well and has excellent benefits. And working from home there's less expense than being in an office and commuting."

"Obviously it pays well enough to afford a house with an ocean view—even from a distance. Can't argue over that."

"Oh, well, I had an uncle with money and no kids. He left it to me and that helped me get ahead on adulting."

"That's a great deal if you can get it. My mom's brother— my only uncle—has zero money, is an addict, and is currently not speaking to me because I refuse to write him prescriptions for painkillers."

"Oh man, that sucks. What does your mom think about it?"

"She hasn't spoken to him in twenty years and thinks I should do the same. But when he heard I'd moved here and called to ask for medical advice, I couldn't just say no without going to see the man. Unfortunately, my mom is annoyingly right most of the time."

"Better she thinks she's right and actually is than glaringly wrong and refuses to acknowledge it."

"I take it you and your mother don't see eye to eye?"

"I don't even see kneecaps with either of my parents. They have different world views, professional views, personal life views. I feel like every conversation with them is another opportunity to increase their disappointment in me. Do you know what my father said when I called to tell them about the stalker and that I was going off-radar for a while?"

"I'm afraid to ask."

"He said that it was unbecoming of a lady to have such things in her life. Like it's somehow my fault that a psycho has fixated on me."

His face flashed with anger. "Your mother is either a saint or a doormat to tolerate that kind of mentality. It's victim blaming at its finest."

"My mother essentially married her father, who was a sexist, hateful know-it-all. I don't like to say those things about my father, but he's not a nice man. Oh, but he's an excellent soldier. The military sings his praises all the time."

"And you didn't fall in line. I'm sorry. I'll take my mildly annoying parents over disinterest and disapproval any day."

She nodded. "That's why I've stayed in touch with Bea all these years, even though it wasn't nearly the effort I should have put in. Those handful of years here on the island were the only time I felt I had a real mother. Bea isn't the stereotypical mother type, but she always gave me advice based on who *I* was, not who she envisioned me to be. She cared about me as an individual, and to a teen with no visibility or guidance, that was worth everything. Alayna was really lucky to have Bea after her parents were killed."

"Bea is an awesome person, and she and Alayna are really close. It's no surprise to me that she's looking out for you now. But I still think you should reconsider letting Alayna know you're here."

Jill sighed. "I want to...you don't know how badly. It's

killing me to be just across the water from her and not see her, hug her, sit up all night talking. I want that more than you can know, but I want to keep her safe even more. And she's got enough on her plate right now without adding my worry to her own."

"I understand. Your face is starting to redden. Do you want me to grab some sunscreen?"

"No. I probably ought to head inside and prop this ankle up."

"Good answer."

She'd gotten out onto the back deck through the house, but now that the door was boarded up, it was going to be a slow and careful walk around the lighthouse to the front door. The crutches were leaning against the wall of the house next to her chair, and she gathered herself, ready to push up, when Pete extended his arm.

Grateful, she clutched his arm and rose, leaving the majority of her weight on one leg, but even with his help, she was still off-balance and had to shift some of the weight to her injured foot. A jolt of pain shot up her leg and she must have flinched because in a flash, he scooped her up off the deck and she automatically circled her arms around his neck.

"You can't carry me," she protested as he started off the deck.

"This is the option with the least amount of risk and pain. Or do you want to go to the hospital?"

His skin was already dry, and pressed against the hot, firm mass, she could feel the flush creeping up her face and prayed that he dismissed it as being caused by the sun. She couldn't even look him in the eye, afraid her face would give away her intense attraction. When she finally managed a glance, she realized his gaze was ahead and down, concentrating on the terrain to ensure her safety.

Which just sent another wave of heat running through her.

Pete McCord was the kind of man women wrote romance novels about. He was handsome, caring, and strong, and he actually listened. She'd never met anyone like him and was fairly certain she probably never would again.

At the front door, he leaned in a bit to twist the doorknob, then carried her inside and leaned over, gently placing her in the recliner. His face was almost touching hers as she sank into the seat. She looked up and locked eyes with him, and every reason she'd given herself for why getting involved with Pete was a horrible idea fled completely as she was overwhelmed with the urge to kiss him.

Pete's eyes widened just a tiny bit as it must have dawned on him exactly how she felt, and he only hesitated a split second before lowering his lips to hers.

His lips were hot and rough from the sun and salt water, but nothing had ever felt as good on her mouth as them. The kiss was as tender as his care of her had been and despite all the good reasons to stop, she wasn't about to take her own advice.

She reached up and placed one hand on his chest and he answered her by deepening the kiss. When she was ready to offer him the sun, the moon, and the stars, he broke the kiss and rose up.

"I'm sorry," he said, instantly contrite.

"You better not be. I know I'm not."

His eyes widened, and he stared at her for a second before the smile crept onto his face. "Thank God. The last thing I wanted to do was make things uncomfortable, especially when you need my help."

And then that tiny bit of doubt crept back in. Was her overwhelming attraction to him spurred on by her situation—life threatened, injured, and surrounded by the only place she ever felt at home? Was she trying to find comfort in creating that perfect life she'd envisioned when she was a girl? Nothing wrong with that, except... And it was the except that had her rethinking things. Was this really the right move—getting involved with someone who had become a caretaker during a highly charged emotional situation? Would both of them regret it when her life was no longer in danger?

He must have noticed her shift to indecision because the smile faded. "This isn't the right time. You've got too much going on, and I refuse to add any stress to your life. I won't lie and say that I'm not interested because there would be no point. But I won't go there again. Not until things are resolved and you've said it's okay."

She nodded, unable to speak, afraid her mouth would spill out what her heart and body were screaming rather than listen to her mind, which was backing up everything he'd said.

"I'll go grab those chairs and your crutches."

He was gone before she could even reply, and she tried to force her racing heart to calm. Holy crap, on top of every other stellar trait, the man could kiss. Never before had she felt so much in such a small amount of time. But was it real or was it her situation driving all of it?

She was still rolling it all around in her mind when he walked back inside with the crutches.

"How would you like the blinds?" he asked. "Opened or closed?"

"Go ahead and open them. I like the sunlight."

He opened all the blinds and hauled the knee scooter and her bag with her laptop over to her chair.

"I'm going to grab you something to drink," he said finally. "Are you hungry?"

"No. I had plenty at Bea's. And besides, I don't want to

keep you any longer than I already have. You still have some daylight left to get in some surfing."

A flash of sadness passed across his face, and she knew he'd taken her statement as dismissal rather than the free pass to go that she'd intended. But that couldn't be helped. And even though she wanted nothing more than to grab his hand and ask him to stay, she knew it would be the wrong thing to do.

For both of them.

He headed to the kitchen and grabbed her a bottled water and then placed the ice pack on her ankle. "I'll be back tomorrow afternoon. I'm hoping the swelling goes down by then but if it doesn't, I'm going to insist you get an X-ray. The risk of additional damage you could do if it's more serious than what we hope would be too high."

"Okay," she agreed. He'd been more than fair about the entire thing, and she didn't want to cause him more worry by being too obstinate to admit that she needed access to medical tests that he couldn't deliver by boat.

He placed one hand on her shoulder and squeezed. "If you need anything, call. I can't be here in a minute, but I'll be here. And remember to send that picture to me and Bea."

"Thanks, Pete. For everything."

He gave her a single nod and was gone.

And the feeling that she'd just let something important slip through her hands overwhelmed her.

CHAPTER THIRTEEN

PETE KNEW A DISMISSAL WHEN HE HEARD IT. HE DIDN'T think for a moment that he'd misread her, but as soon as she'd had time to think about the kiss, it was clear that she'd not only moved into Park but into Reverse. She'd said she didn't regret it, and he was fairly certain she was telling the truth, but clearly, she wasn't on board with repeating the performance.

And that was fine.

He should have known better. Hell, he *did* know better. And yet he'd gone and done it anyway. Just sign him up for the world's biggest fool award. He'd spent years avoiding romantic entanglements because of the requirements of his job, and now, when he had an opportunity to finally pursue that avenue of his life, he'd fallen for a woman literally running for her life and who lived across the country. He couldn't have made a worse choice if he'd tried.

But what if it's not a choice?

He blew out a breath as he guided the boat from the Gulf and into the Sound. Did he really think that? He didn't want to believe that life was one of those Hallmark movies his mother was so infatuated with, but how else could he explain feeling no desire whatsoever to go out with any of the attractive, available women that he'd been exposed to when he'd taken a post here? And several had put out the right signals. He just hadn't taken them up on the offer.

Why?

It wasn't fear. He didn't have some tragic love story in his past that had caused him to erect barriers and cast a side-eye at women as a species. He wasn't a child of divorce—in fact, his parents were still very in love after thirty-eight years of marriage and very clearly enjoyed each other's company. So what explanation was left besides the attraction one?

The one with zero science behind it.

Not that any of that mattered. Why he was so attracted to Jill wasn't at issue, but what he did about it was. And right now, he had to curb all feelings until she was healed and safe. Given administration of the correct medical testing, he could assign a timeline to her ankle healing, but the stalker was a huge unknown. He'd already been at it for five years. What if it continued another five years? What if Jill decided that the only way to completely rid herself of him was to change her identity and leave the country?

He couldn't exactly blame her if she decided to go that route, but he felt his chest constrict at the thought of never seeing her again. Because of the things she'd said—the island was the only place she'd ever felt at home, Bea was the only mother she'd ever had, she could work from anywhere—he'd started to build an image in his mind of a potential future. But that opportunity all rested on one glaring issue that controlled everything.

And he knew that unless Jill's stalker was caught, she'd never stop running.

He secured Bea's boat and jumped in his Jeep, trying to decide what to do with the rest of the day. He kept his surfboard at Luke's cottage, so he didn't have to lug it back and forth. The surf was still decent and he had plenty of daylight left, but for the first time that he could remember, he wasn't dying to get into the water. He started the Jeep and sat there, waiting for the universe to hit him with the desire to do something. Unfortunately, the universe must have been on coffee break. He pulled out his phone and sent Luke a text.

You sleeping?

Already done. Sitting on deck drinking a beer.

Is Alayna around?

No. Working at ice cream shop.

Mind if I drop by?

Do I even want to know what this is about? You sound very deep state.

Just on the island and thought I'd check in. You had me at beer.

I'll grab another.

He slipped his phone back into his pocket and drove the short distance from the marina to the beach cottage that Luke rented from Bea. She also owned the cottage next door and technically, Alayna occupied that one, although Pete guessed they spent most of their time together in one or the other. But both were cautious and not yet ready to officially label themselves as living together. Pete couldn't blame them. It had only been a little over a month, but he also had no doubt that his friends were destined for permanent.

Luke hadn't specified which deck he was sitting on, so Pete opted for Luke's cottage and headed around back. His buddy was seated in a lawn chair under a canopy, feet propped on a table and holding a beer. A second bottle sat on the table near Luke's feet. Pete sank onto the chair next to him, lifted the beer bottle, and clanked it against Luke's.

Luke waved his free hand at the Gulf. "Look at that. It's

absolute perfection. Some days I marvel at just how good we've got it."

"Well, you have a front-row view and a gorgeous, talented chef serving up awesome food to go with that beer, so I'm thinking you've got it a tiny bit better than me. But yeah, it's definitely the best place I've lived."

Luke studied him for a moment. "I have to say, I was a little surprised that you chose here for your permanent station. You're a top-rate surfer. I figured you'd pick the big surf—California, Hawaii, maybe even Okinawa. You've been stationed in all of them, right?"

Pete nodded. "Don't think it didn't cross my mind, but Hawaii and Okinawa are too far from my folks. They're in great shape now, but they won't be forever. And even though they would have visited, my dad will probably work until he dies, so it would have been minimal. At least here, they're only a couple hours away. And cost of living factors in as well. Tempest Island is as beautiful as those other locations but not nearly as expensive."

"Not yet. But the more people that find out about it, that's definitely subject to change, especially with every available piece of land already developed. Prices got nowhere to go but up."

"Don't remind me. I'm still hoping to get a house here, but the prices are going up faster than my savings."

"Bea says they always go up in the summer. The time to buy is during the winter."

"She would know."

Luke nodded. "She's definitely been ahead of the real estate game here. I can only imagine what these two cottages would go for. And the bookstore building as well. Talk about prime real estate."

"Millions, I'm sure," Pete said.

They were silent for several seconds and finally, Luke said, "So why aren't you surfing today? The waves are definitely right for it."

Pete shrugged. "I wasn't feeling it."

"Uh-oh."

"What?"

Luke shook his head. "Man, you've seen some of the worst stuff humanity has to offer, but I've never seen you turn down spending time in the water. There's only one thing that could be worse than a military battlefield. You've got woman trouble."

Pete stared at his friend with what he hoped was an appropriate amount of confusion and outrage, because he was already regretting coming over here.

"What?" Pete asked. "How can that be? I'm not even dating anyone."

"And yet Lieutenant Fuller saw you carrying a woman into the lighthouse today, which I find fascinating for a lot of reasons."

"Fuller needs to have his eyesight checked."

Luke laughed. "He's the base optometrist. And the fact that you didn't even look me in the eye when you threw out that weak denial tells me Fuller's eyesight is just fine. So did you have a quickie marriage and didn't tell your best buddy? Carrying her over the threshold is old-fashioned, but you're a traditional sort of guy."

Pete sighed. "It wasn't what it looked like. I was doing a favor for a friend."

Luke stared. "Your other friends are asking a heck of a lot more from you than I do."

"It wasn't *that* kind of favor—look, the woman twisted her ankle and didn't want to go to the hospital. I was just checking it out."

"Not checking *her* out?"

"Only her ankle."

"Hmmm. And you took her to the lighthouse to perform the examination? That's an interesting medical approach."

"She's staying at the lighthouse."

"Really? I thought the county owned it. So what is it, like a VRBO or something now?"

"Something like that."

"You're being horribly evasive, but since I know you'd never lie about medical things, I'm going to assume part of this favor means keeping your mouth shut."

"That's correct."

"Okay, then what *can* you tell me that will explain why you're sitting here with me when you could be spending your afternoon off in the water?"

"Can I ask you something? Something personal?"

Luke shrugged. "Ask anything you want, but I don't promise I'll answer."

"Fair enough. How did you know when Alayna was the one for you?"

Luke studied him for a moment, then shook his head. "I'm not certain, really. I told you the story about how we met that same day when I talked to you on the beach."

Pete grinned. "I remember."

"I guess I'd have to say that she captured my attention from the start, and obviously I was attracted to her."

"Who wouldn't be?"

"Hey, watch it," Luke joked. "But I can't give you a specific moment in time. There was so much going on—I was trying to figure out the rest of my career, she was running from trouble —and emotions were heightened due to all of that. I'm sure plenty of people thought we'd be done in a flash once it finally sank in that all that mess was behind us."

"But that didn't happen."

"Not even close. In fact, it's the opposite. Every day, I discover something new about her and it's like taking that dive all over again. And before you say it, I know we're still in the honeymoon period, but she's it for me. I'm certain."

Pete frowned and stared out at the ocean.

Luke leaned forward and locked his gaze on Pete's. "Look, I can't tell you when attraction turned to love and love became forever, but what I *can* tell you is that from the moment I met Alayna, I couldn't stop thinking about her. Even though I didn't want to."

Pete sighed. "Yeah."

"You got some of that going on with this 'favor'?"

"No. Maybe. Hell, I guess I do, but it can't go anywhere."

"Why not? Is she married? Gay? A relative?"

"No to the first two and gross on the last one."

"Then what's stopping you? The worst that can happen is she's not into you and you can stop wasting brain time on her."

"I think she *is* into me. But she's not in a position to get involved."

Luke narrowed his eyes. "Why didn't she want to go to the hospital?"

"I can't say."

"She's got trouble." Luke sat back in his chair and blew out a breath. "God knows, Alayna had trouble when we first met. Is she expecting a solution anytime soon?"

"No way to know. Might be tomorrow, might be never."

"That's a pretty big window."

"Trust me, I'm no happier about it than she is. And I mean that for her, not me. I mean, me as well, but you get what I'm saying."

Luke nodded. "You want her trouble to end for her sake,

but if it opens a door for the two of you, then you're going to carry her through it."

"You've really developed a romantic streak since you settled down."

Luke grinned. "Wouldn't you?"

"Yeah. I totally would. Hey, I appreciate the advice, man. And if you wouldn't mind, can you keep this all between us? The woman doesn't want anyone to know she's here, and I promised I wouldn't tell."

"As far as I'm concerned you were right here with me all afternoon and Fuller needs to get his eyes checked."

———

JILL HAD DOZED off in the recliner and the ringing of her phone brought her out of a somewhat frustrating dream. She'd been in a scene from *Charlie and the Chocolate Factory*. All she needed to do was cross the room and pick up the golden ticket, but she couldn't walk. Then a dark figure with a blank face appeared in the doorway of the room and she couldn't run, either. It didn't take a genius to figure out the meaning.

She lifted the phone and saw Bea's name on it, and barely answered before it went to voice mail. "Hi, Bea."

"Did I wake you?"

"Sort of, but that's a good thing. I was having the most disturbing dream."

"Given your situation, that's not surprising. Pete told me you went back to the island with him."

"Yeah, I sort of forced his hand on that one."

"You know I would have been happy to take you."

"I know, but there was no use in my hiding in your house and causing you another trip when he was coming here anyway. I can sit here like a lump just like I could at your house."

"I suppose that's true enough, but I won't deny that I liked having eyes on you."

"You've got enough to deal with. Pete told me what's going on with the Whitmores and Alayna's restaurant. And that the reason you were out the door first thing this morning was to bail out the plumber. I'm so sorry, Bea. Are you going to be able to get it open on time?"

"I'm doing everything I can to make it happen. My girl deserves a break, and more people than just her family and friends and some strangers in New York need to experience her talent."

"I agree with that. She was incredible in high school. I can't even imagine what her dishes are like now."

"You wouldn't have to imagine if you told her you were here. I'm sure she'd launch a feast fit for a queen."

"I know, and I wish I could, but it's just not the right time. I promise when this is all over that I will have a nice long visit in full view."

"I'm holding you to that. Do you need anything? I can make a trip over and bring supplies if there's something you don't have."

"I'm good, really. You stocked the kitchen well, and Pete brought that knee scooter for me. It's a lot more convenient than the crutches. Even has a little basket on the front so getting food is a lot easier as well."

"Sure, as long as it's in a bottle or surrounded with a rind. Don't you go living on protein shakes and fruit. If you don't cook up some meat, I'll hike back out there and do it myself, and neither of us wants that for a lot of reasons."

Jill laughed. "I promise I'll throw a chicken breast in a skillet tonight."

"And a can of baked beans."

"I can do that."

"What about French bread?"

"Pushing it, but I might toast a slice with some butter and garlic."

"Okay then," Bea said, sounding pacified. "If you're sure you don't need anything, but you call if you do. Doesn't matter what time. I don't anticipate any more problems out there, especially as the gossip's already circulating that those idiots frightened someone staying there."

Jill sighed. "I figured that would happen."

"I wish I could have kept it from getting around, but you know how it is here. Probably going to have some boats cruising by slower than usual, too, trying to get a look. But at least that gossip has included the fact that it's private property that has been rented, and the sheriff is aware and ready to arrest people for trespassing. That should keep anyone from coming ashore."

"Well, the farthest I'm going is out the front door where Pete moved the patio chairs to, so they'd need binoculars to see anything worthwhile. And I have sunglasses and a big floppy hat."

"And if they cruise close enough to try to talk?"

"I look confused and reply in French. That's what I do when I'm on vacation and men hit on me because I'm alone."

Bea laughed. "That'll do. You have a good night, Jill."

Jill sat down her phone and stared at the kitchen. Even though Bea wasn't there to see if she cooked that chicken or not, Jill wouldn't feel right unless she did. And Bea was correct—she needed something more substantial than shakes and fruit because being healthy was more important than ever.

In case you have to run again or defend yourself.

She rose from the recliner, pushing that thought from her mind. It didn't do any good to think about what might be. Her best bet was to focus on the right now and make the most of it, because it could change in the next five minutes.

So if things go way negative, you want cooking chicken to be the last thing you did?

She sighed and propped her knee on the scooter. Why did her inner voice have to be not only right but sarcastic? Still, there were worse last things to do before death—getting a tooth filled, having a colonoscopy. Cooking chicken was practically a trip to Disney in comparison.

Thirty minutes later, she sat at the counter with her plate of chicken, baked beans, and a slice of garlic toast. Everything looked delicious, and when she took the first bite, she smiled. She'd used Alayna's instructions for seasoning the chicken and it came out perfect every time. She really should make an effort to cook more, but it always seemed like such a lot of preparation and time for just one person.

Pete would have joined you for dinner...and much more.

She stabbed the chicken with her fork and cut off a piece. Thinking of Pete was definitely stepping outside of the moment, but it was hard not to. She'd never felt this strongly about someone, especially someone she barely knew. And yeah, maybe some of it was her heightened emotional state, but not all of it. The reality was, she was horribly attracted to the good doctor—physically, mentally, and emotionally.

So what are you going to do about it?

She shook her head. Nothing. That's what. Because nothing was her only option. Maybe if Detective Ward caught the stalker, then she could venture off into that line of thinking, but not until. Because she wasn't going to put anyone in the same position as Wanda had been.

Thinking of Wanda made her heart clench. She wanted so badly to call her friend and see how she was doing, talk to her about everything that had happened, especially about Pete.

She didn't always share the same views on things as her friend, but Jill could always count on her to dole out her honest opinion on everything. It was the thing that had endeared her to Jill the most, because she knew Wanda would never be one to hedge. If she thought it, she said it. Which meant Jill could trust her words even if she didn't necessarily align with her judgment on matters.

Wanda would tell you to go for it with Pete.

Jill smiled. Yeah, she probably would. Wanda's primary goals in life were happiness and joy. After so many years playing an off-screen role as a Hollywood producer's wife, she sought to live life to the fullest, and that meant living every second as she saw fit.

Living every second as if it were her last.

The smile turned into a frown. But what about Pete's life?

He knows your situation and can make his own decisions.

But did he really know her situation? She was still lying about who she was. Jill Morgan didn't have a stalker. But Kate Coleson did. Heck, Jill Morgan wasn't even her real name anymore, and Pete didn't know Jill was Kate.

She sighed.

If Pete didn't have all the information, then he couldn't make an informed decision about just how deep he wanted to get into her mess. It wasn't fair. And Jill was all about fair.

So tell him.

She took another bite of the chicken. Maybe she would. Tomorrow. She'd see how things went with her ankle and then if the moment felt right, she'd confess. Then Pete could decide.

Because although she didn't want to admit it, her mind was already made up.

She wanted him.

BEA'S DOORBELL sounded and she hurried to unlock the door. The Jokers, Bea's poker group, had all arrived at the same time and came trailing into her house, laden with containers that smelled like heaven. Three different conversations were already going as they headed straight for the kitchen and started the food set up. Bea smiled as she watched the incredible group of women she called her friends.

There was Nelly, her coworker and partner in crime at the bookstore. Birdie, her friend of three decades, who owned the ice cream shop with her husband Tom. Scarlett was their drama queen, who'd made marrying well an art and divorcing well a business. And at forty-eight, Izzy was the youngest member, widowed several years back, and owned her own physical therapy practice on the mainland.

"Thank you for taking care of everything tonight," Bea said. "I wasn't sure I'd even have the bandwidth to meet, much less come up with food."

"Your work plate is overflowing," Nelly said. "The least we could do is fill up your dinner plate."

Birdie nodded as she cut Mexican casserole into squares and served them up on plates. "Absolutely. And helping Tom and me has added to everyone's plate as well."

"We've all been happy to do it," Scarlett said as she unwrapped cheese dip and a peach cobbler. "Especially me. I've got three dates lined up already. That's one date per shift. At this rate, I'll be booked for the rest of the summer."

Nelly shook her head. "Leave it to you to figure out how to turn an ice cream shop into a speed dating event."

Scarlett waved her heavily jeweled fingers at Nelly. "We all have our individual talents. And our own preferences for how we like our ice...cream."

They all grinned.

"Even when Birdie and Tom are back in full swing, I might have to keep working at the shop." Scarlett winked at Birdie. "You can pay me in customers."

"I'm pretty sure the Department of Labor would have a problem with that," Birdie said. "I don't even want to consider what our insurance man would say."

"He'd probably say you're underinsured, having an asset like me in the shop," Scarlett said.

"I don't think 'asset' is the accounting term Birdie had in mind," Bea said.

"I'm convinced Scarlett could find a man in a convent," Izzy said.

Scarlett grinned. "Challenge accepted."

"The bigger challenge will be finding a convent that would let you across the threshold," Bea said.

They all laughed.

"This food is ready to go," Nelly announced. "Bea's got the beer on the table, so let's load up and get to gossiping. I know Bea had drama this morning, but we were so slammed all day, she hasn't even had a chance to tell me about it."

"I love good drama," Scarlett said, "especially when it's not mine."

"Because it's so rare," Bea said as she stacked more food around her casserole.

"Not lately," Scarlett said. "You've totally kicked me off my drama throne this summer. Well, you and people who are you-adjacent."

If only Scarlett knew just how true that statement was. Between Alayna, Jill, the restaurant, and now her bid for mayor, Bea hadn't just kicked Scarlett off her throne, she'd had it reupholstered.

They all sat at the table and Bea pointed to Birdie. "You

first. Give us the Tom update. I'm surprised you let him out of your sight long enough to make poker night."

Birdie rolled her eyes. "He has one of his fishing buddies over. Leaving was self-defense. They have six tackle boxes spread out on the dining room table. I've already threatened lives if one of those hooks snags my chairs."

"I hope you removed your grandma's tablecloth," Nelly said.

"As soon as Tom hung up the phone. I could hear him hollering that he was coming over from another room. He refuses to wear his hearing aid."

Scarlett shook her head. "I don't blame you for leaving, honey. Two men shouting about fishing lures half the night is enough to turn me off dating. And you know how big a statement that is."

"How's Tom doing otherwise?" Bea asked.

"He's good," Birdie said. "The worst of the pain was done within a week or so, and he came off the painkillers. That helped with his muddled mind. I can't tell you how many times he was grousing about losing the TV remote only for me to find it in places it didn't belong."

"Like where?" Nelly asked.

"The pantry, which makes a little sense as he probably carried it in there while looking for a snack. But I don't even want to know why it was in the washing machine. I'm just glad I looked before I dumped a load of towels in. Twice, I found it in my pot plants on the patio, and once in the freezer. That was the worst one."

"Why?" Scarlett asked. "Sounds like he was looking for a snack again."

Birdie blushed a bit. "It's what he did with it after. His ice pack wasn't quite frozen again yet and he needed some cooling relief...in the down there."

They all howled with laughter, and Birdie gave up propriety and joined in.

"Izzy has been a real blessing," Birdie said when they'd all regained control. "Especially those first few days. He didn't want to move at all, and the doctor said walking was important. Izzy came by in the morning before she went to her clinic, at lunch, and then again in the evening and made him get up and move. He has no trouble telling me no, but he wasn't about to say it to her."

Izzy smiled. "I'm afraid that's typical, and probably the primary reason physical therapists have jobs. If everyone listened to and followed doctor's orders, half my client list wouldn't exist."

"I'm glad he's doing well," Bea said. "I know it's been hard on you too."

Birdie grimaced. "He gets his stitches out tomorrow. I might go back to work. I can't watch TV until I replace that remote."

"I can set up your phone to do everything the remote does," Nelly said.

Birdie's eyes widened. "You can? You hate technology."

"It's the only way I could get the channel on something besides fishing or golf. Harold has no idea. I just switch it over to HGTV and after a couple back-and-forths, he thinks there's something wrong with the cable and gives up. He's already called them twice this week complaining."

"That's diabolical," Scarlett said. "And impressive."

"So Bea, tell us about your drama," Birdie said. "I hope it isn't about the restaurant opening."

"Unfortunately, that's exactly what it was about, but it has a happy ending. Sort of." Bea told them about her argument with Minnie the day before and posting bail for Billy that morning.

Scarlett shook her head when Bea was done. "Minnie should have left him years ago."

"Minnie's just as bad," Bea said, "which was my point. And she doesn't need to leave him now that they have darn near a half dozen kids."

"Reason number eight hundred sixty-two for why I never had kids," Scarlett said. "The thought of having a permanent tie to any of my exes causes serious anxiety."

"You get alimony," Nelly pointed out. "How is that not a permanent tie?"

"Checks don't have graduation parties, and don't get married and have grandchildren," Scarlett said. "Checks mean never having to see someone face-to-face again. Heck, I don't even have to hear their voices."

"Valid," Bea agreed.

"So speaking of significant others," Scarlett said, "what about you, Izzy?"

"I got one big life insurance check," Izzy said, "but I would love to see and hear my husband again."

Scarlett leaned over and gave her friend a squeeze. "That's because you had one of the good ones. But I meant your new man."

Izzy blushed a bit and shook her head. "He's not my man."

The last time they'd met, Izzy had told them that she'd had coffee with a client. She'd tried to play it off as nothing big, but the Jokers knew better. Izzy deeply mourned her husband Antonio, a doctor who'd shocked everyone when he'd passed away from a heart attack five years ago. Showing even a tiny bit of romantic interest in a man was a huge deal for Izzy.

"He's a man, and you're having coffee with him," Scarlett said. "In your world, that's practically engaged."

Izzy smiled. "I have always envied your ability to have casual relationships with men."

"She's been married three times," Bea said. "How's that casual?"

"But she's dated hundreds more," Izzy said. "And no matter how many come and go, she maintains her positive outlook."

"That's because the checks keep coming but not going," Scarlett said. "Now, stop deflecting and give up the scoop. Have you had coffee again?"

"Twice," Izzy said. "And we have dinner plans this weekend."

They all cheered and clapped. Izzy looked a little embarrassed but also pleased.

"I really like him," Izzy confessed. "Sometimes I feel a little guilty about just how much I enjoy talking to him."

Bea reached over and squeezed her friend's hand. "Antonio was more full of life than anyone I've ever met. He would want you to live the rest of yours with no limitations."

Izzy's eyes filled with tears, but she smiled and nodded. "I know he would, but it still helps to hear it."

They all gave her encouraging smiles and nods and Bea felt her chest constrict. These women were worth their weight in gold, and Bea didn't know what she would do without them.

———

HE SLAMMED his hand on the motel desk in frustration, all his research spread in front of him. Pictures, news articles, and all his notes. Every fact that he had assembled about Jill. But this place was another dead end. She thought she could hide, but she was wrong. No one could remain in the shadows forever.

Everyone revealed too much about themselves over time, and he knew enough about her life to know where to start. He had a list—places she'd lived, visited, or had friends or family.

It was lengthy because she'd covered a lot of ground, but there was no ticking clock.

Jill or Kate or whatever else she chose to call herself thought she was playing things smart by hiding, but he'd find her. He'd gone years looking for her before she'd popped up on his TV screen. She believed she'd fooled everyone with the wig and the makeup, but he'd know her anywhere. That's how it was when you loved someone the way he loved her.

He needed to calm down and regroup. After all, what was the worst-case scenario—that she eventually gave up hiding and returned home? She couldn't stay on the run forever, and even if she decided to move, she'd have to pack, sell the house...any number of things forced her to return to Oregon. And then she'd check in on that friend of hers. The woman who had interrupted his address search by ordering a pizza of all things. It still galled him, but there was nothing to be done about it now. He hadn't left any evidence, and she hadn't gotten a good look at him, so nothing was really lost.

After all, he'd gotten what he came for. He'd just had to work for it a bit more than he'd liked.

He probably shouldn't have left a card at her house. He'd gone there, hoping to find her alone. But instead, that odd landscaper had accosted him, refusing to provide any information on Jill. He'd intended to leave if he found the house empty and stake it out, waiting on her to return, but he knew he'd already tipped his hand with the landscaper, so he'd left the card, unable to help himself. Jill needed to know that their time was drawing near. That soon, they would be one forever.

She'd surprised him by fleeing. He'd assumed she'd stay put and the police would put an ineffective guard outside, just as they had with her friend's building. But none of that mattered. It was just a small delay. Hollywood had delays all the time when filming. The bigger the story, the more problems might arise. But this story would have its fantastic finish.

He had no doubt that Jill had hidden somewhere among her past.

And he was going to find her because he was patient. Very, very patient.

Even if he found his patience running out, there were ways to make her surface. Her friend could have another incident, or maybe he'd make the trip to Italy and pay a visit to her parents. That would be the sure bet to draw her out, but it had other risks he wasn't prepared to handle, starting with the ease of being tracked across countries. He couldn't figure a way around it just yet, but he had a feeling he wasn't going to have to.

Sooner or later, Jill would come up for air.

And then she'd pledge her love to him, or he'd strangle it back out of her.

CHAPTER FOURTEEN

Jill awakened the next morning, somewhat surprised that she'd managed to sleep through the night. Well, maybe 'the night' was stretching it, but the last time she'd looked at her watch it was close to midnight and now it was 6:00 a.m., so a really good stretch compared to what she thought she'd have. Unfortunately, she'd started dreaming close to waking time and that last one was bad enough to prompt her eyes to open.

For a woman who wrote thrillers and had intentionally made herself familiar with self-defense and weaponry, she simply couldn't understand why every time the bad guy was after her in her dream, she was unable to fight and couldn't pull the trigger on a gun. Clearly, that character flaw had been proven incorrect because she'd had no problem firing off a round over the head of the two miscreants who'd broken into the lighthouse.

Frustrated that her otherwise decent sleep had been marred with last-minute weapons incompetence, she sat up on the couch bed and threw the covers back to get a look at her ankle. It was still bandaged, so she couldn't really tell if the swelling had gone down any, but the bandage still seemed well wrapped. Crap. She was hoping to wake up to a loose bandage and a much-improved ankle.

She swung her legs over and gently touched her foot onto the floor. Pain immediately shot through her ankle, and she sighed as she pulled the knee scooter over and used it to rise on one leg. With her bad ankle perched off the back of the scooter, she headed for the bathroom. After taking care of the basics, she peered into the walk-in shower to assess the situation and was surprised to see a small wooden stool sitting in the middle. She was certain it hadn't been there two days ago, so Pete must have brought it along with the knee scooter. She hadn't thought he could endear himself to her more than he already had, but she felt her chest constrict at his thoughtfulness.

With everything else going on, she hadn't even considered how she would shower, but it was past time. Deciding it was easiest to undress while sitting on the stool, she lifted a towel from the rack over the toilet and hung it on the hook just inside the shower entry. Then, using the shower entry to brace herself, she stepped over the lip and inside, then used the walls for bracing and made another single step to the stool. Her ankle sent up a single shriek of protest both times it connected with the tile but calmed down as soon as she was seated. She looked down and realized he'd even repositioned her hair products, liquid soap, and loofah next to the stool.

He had moved past bonus points territory and was approaching sainthood.

She bent over to address the ankle wrap and hoped for the best as she unwrapped the layers. When the last piece came off, exposing her bare ankle, she gave it a critical eye and frowned. She was no doctor, but it looked the same as the day before. Maybe a tiny bit smaller, but not significant enough to break out mimosas. Crap. When Pete saw this, he was going to insist she get an X-ray, and at this point, it was hard to argue with him.

But that was something to worry about later. First, she was going to take a shower and wash her hair so that she felt somewhat human again while she fixed breakfast. She made quick work of her T-shirt, then eased her yoga pants and panties off around the hurt ankle and flung them all out of the shower to be gathered when she was done.

She turned around on the stool, bracing herself for the shot of cold water that was coming, then turned on the faucet and let out a few choice words as the chilly stream hit her. It didn't take long for the water to warm up, and she sat for a couple minutes, just relishing the hot water on her skin. Then, afraid her ankle would stiffen up too much if she sat there very long with it unwrapped and not elevated, she took care of her shower business and then turned off the water.

She could just reach the towel on the hook inside the shower entry and remained seated to dry off. Then she did the two steps again to get out of the shower and back onto the scooter. Her ankle protested a bit, but not in an alarming way. Maybe it was improving more than she could see. Once out of the shower, she sat on the toilet and pulled on undergarments, shorts, and tee and managed to do a somewhat credible job rewrapping her ankle.

Then she scooped up the dirty clothes and tossed them in the laundry basket. Now that she was done showering—in what had to be one of the most inefficient ways possible—she scooted into the kitchen to decide on breakfast. Since she didn't want to get crap from Bea later when the older woman was certain to ask about her food intake, she decided to fix eggs with cheese and have some slices of pineapple with it. That should be enough protein to satisfy Bea.

When she was done preparing her plate, she placed it on the counter and made a quick round on the scooter opening all the blinds to let the sun stream in. She'd never been a fan of dark rooms. It was the one thing that sometimes bothered her about her home. She loved the seclusion, but that meant all those trees reducing the sunlight that entered. She'd cut back some of the foliage to allow for more passage and had installed skylights in her living room and office, which had helped tremendously, but it was still nothing compared to the light that filled every square inch of this room. And the proximity to warm, clear water wasn't anything to sniff at either.

Not that she could get in it.

So currently, that stellar view was just a tease but still so relaxing. And since Pete had relocated the deck chairs right outside the front door, at least she could venture outside for a bit and enjoy the sun and breeze on her skin and fill her lungs with salt air. The view toward the island wasn't quite as spectacular as the giant expanse of never-ending water on the back side, but it was still gorgeous and calming, and just relaxing in the sun would help lift her spirits.

Her cell phone rang just as she finished breakfast, and she saw Detective Ward's name in the display. She answered immediately, hoping the fact that he was calling so early meant he'd discovered something.

"Did you find something?" she answered.

"Yes, but I'm afraid it's not good news. I didn't wake you, did I?"

"No. I've been up for a while, but it's early for you."

"Yeah, I got a call from a cop in Norfolk. They put out an alert on the news for Trevor and someone called in a tip that turned out to be good. He was spotted at a motel near the Naval base. Unfortunately, he'd already cleared out before they got there, but they have him on video. I'd like you to verify this, but as far as I'm concerned, it's him. I'm texting it now."

Her pulse spiked up as she accessed the message and started the video. When she saw a man walking across the parking lot, she sucked in a breath. It was definitely him.

"It's him. I recognize that ridiculous swagger." Then he turned toward the camera. "Definitely him. He's older and worn as hell, but it's him."

"Okay. Well, the good news is we're closing in on him. The bad news is it looks like he's visiting your old stomping grounds, and if he's working his way south, it's going to be sooner than later when he hits the island."

She clenched the phone, not wanting to think about having to flee again, especially now.

"How is your ankle?"

"It's okay. Not doing as well as I hoped. I'm afraid the doctor will tell me I have to get an X-ray. He said he'd wait until today, but I think he's going to say it's necessary."

"I thought when I talked to you the other day, you didn't think it was going to be a big deal."

"I didn't, and it might just be because I was on it too much. There was an incident here night before last." She told him about the break-in at the lighthouse.

"Damn it!" Ward exclaimed when she was done. "Those idiots couldn't have picked a worse time."

"I know. The sheriff had to issue a statement but didn't give any information other than the boys had broken in and the property was now privately owned and rented, and trespassers would be prosecuted. That will keep people off the lighthouse island but won't stop the gossip."

"And now that people know someone is staying there, the lookie-loos will gear up. I know how small towns work. I grew up in one."

"At least they can't walk by. They can only get a glimpse of me by boat."

"Uh-huh. And how many people there *don't* own a boat?"

"Probably two at least."

"Exactly. Maybe it's time you thought of changing locations. With this crap and your ankle, you're probably better off going someplace where no one will recognize you."

Jill blew out a breath. He wasn't wrong necessarily, but another place wouldn't have Pete, and even though it defied logic and good common sense, she wasn't ready to leave him.

"Let me think on it," she said. "Did you send Trevor's information to the sheriff here?"

"Yes, but only as part of our general request. Given what's happened with those two idiots, I think it's time to fill him in on everything. You're hiding in his town, and he's already met you. Professionally, he has an obligation to protect his citizens and I have an obligation to provide him information in order to do that."

"I get it and I agree. I don't want anyone else caught in the middle of this."

"I don't have to go into detail about you being Kate as that's not relevant in the big scheme of things. But I can advise him that Trevor previously attacked you and served time for it and has skipped out on parole. That there's a warrant out, and we have reason to believe he's looking for you. That will only give the sheriff more reason to keep quiet about your presence there."

"I agree. I'm also going to tell Bea and the doctor who's taking care of my ankle as well. He knows the basics but no details, and I'm still going to leave out the Kate Coleson part. But I'll share pictures and this video."

"Good. The more people keeping watch, the better. Let me know what happens with your ankle."

She disconnected and stared out the window. On the one hand, she was glad that someone had finally laid eyes on Trevor. On the other hand, his location had given every indication that he was, indeed, trying to track her down. It concerned her that he had abandoned the West Coast and headed to the other side of the country, but then it would have made sense for her to get as far away as she could, and her father had been stationed in Norfolk for several years. She'd taken horseback riding lessons there and loved them, something she was certain she'd shared with Trevor as she'd been wanting to take lessons again after graduation.

On the plus side, Norfolk was so big, it would take a while to cover the area, but if he'd seen the alert, that might have sent him off to the next base. Maybe that's why he'd checked out of the motel. Or maybe he was still in the area but changed rooms often to keep the cops from pinpointing his location. And he could always don the fake beard, sunglasses, and a hat and most people wouldn't look twice, even if they'd seen the alert.

Frustrated, she rose from the stool and got herself positioned on the scooter. There wasn't anything she could do about it, and thinking in circles was only going to frustrate her even more. If she was going to have to leave soon, she might as well enjoy what time she had. So she was going to get a book, go outside, and sit in that chair and read until she was tired of it or until her skin told her she had to go back in.

———

ALAYNA GRABBED Bea's hand and gave it a squeeze. "Is it wrong to be so excited about toilets?"

"Not these toilets," Bea said. "These toilets deserve Dom Pérignon and a marching band."

Chance grinned. "I played the trumpet in middle school. I was horrible at it, but I'm so happy about this work being done that I'd be willing to dig it out of the attic for you."

"I'll just use my iPhone," Alayna said. "So what's the next step?"

"Inspection, and I've got him coming this afternoon."

Alayna felt some of the tension in her neck lesson. "Thank God. I was afraid the inspector would drag just to keep this from happening."

Chance nodded. "I was a little afraid of that myself, but in awesome news, as of this week, there's a new guy assigned to the island. I talked to him yesterday and poked around in a general conversation sort of way. The awesome part is he inherited his house, so he's not beholden to the Whitmores, and he made it clear that he's voting for you, Ms. Shaw."

Alayna clapped her hands and squealed. "Things are finally going our way!"

Chance grinned and gave Bea an appreciative look. "I can't tell you how much I appreciate you getting this plumbing situation handled. I guess I should have bailed him out myself."

"That's not something that should be on your tab," Bea said.

"Shouldn't be on yours either and yet…"

"Oh, I'll get my bond money back and the fees are coming off his bill, so when you get it, let me know."

"Absolutely. You know, for a man who spent last night sleeping on a floor, he didn't seem in a hurry to leave after he got those appliances hooked up."

"I'm guessing that's because he's still not welcome at home, and given that it's season, every motel room for a hundred-mile radius is going to be booked. But none of that is our problem. Maybe this one will set him straight."

"I hope so. He's a darn good plumber."

"But a lousy husband," Alayna said. "Luke manages to be an alpha male without beating up everyone."

"True," Bea agreed, "but you're also not encouraging him—something I called Minnie out on. Those two are too darn old to still be living like they're teenagers. Mind you, some of their kids are about to *be* teenagers, which makes the entire situation even more problematic."

"Well, he's officially Minnie's problem again, so what's after the inspection?" Alayna asked.

"Assuming no issues with the plumbing, the tile guys will start on the decorative finish out in the bathrooms and kitchen tomorrow. Then the wood flooring goes in the dining area. The elevator shaft off the back deck is done and the cab will go in tomorrow. That wasn't dependent on the plumbing, so it's kept moving forward."

"Oh my God!" Alayna exclaimed. "When those floors are done, it's just a matter of the light fixtures and moving everything from storage and into place."

"And cleaning, and decor, and getting those people you've hired trained," Bea said.

Alayna waved a hand in dismissal. "All of that is the easy part, and Lord, I never thought I'd hear myself say that, but construction is not for the faint of heart."

Chance sighed. "I really wish things hadn't been so stressful. The Whitmores sure did everything they could to ruin it."

Alayna squeezed his arm. "None of this is your fault. You've been great, and the next time I have something to build, you're the first person I call."

Bea nodded. "You've done a great job here. A job to be proud of."

Chance blushed and gave them a nod. "I've got to go pick up some hardware that came in. I'll give you a call once we're cleared with the inspector."

He headed out and Alayna waited until the back door had closed behind him before looking at Bea.

"This is a big 'if,' but assuming the restaurant does okay and I actually have income again, Luke and I have been talking, and we were wondering if you'd sell us one of the cottages?"

Bea blinked and stared for a moment, and Alayna wondered if her aunt had heard her correctly or if she was just in shock.

"You want to move in with Luke? Well, hallelujah!"

Alayna felt a blush creep up her neck. "You don't have to be so excited about my romantic life. It's been going fine."

"Oh honey, I was fairly certain the romantic part of your life was going gangbusters. I just didn't understand this Puritan view of waiting and all that. You almost died. What better reason to live every day at 100 percent?"

Alayna bit her lip and shuffled a bit. "You're not worried about what people will say? I mean, Luke and I haven't known each other very long. And there was so much negativity surrounding my coming here with the trouble that followed me."

Bea put her hand on her niece's arm and squeezed. "Honey, I stopped caring what other people think so long ago, I'm not even sure I ever did. It's the kindest thing you can do for yourself. The only people who will talk crap about your choices are the ones who don't matter anyway. So what are you waiting for?"

"Well, to ask you about it, for one."

Bea rolled her eyes. "Of course you can have one of the cottages. But you're not paying me for it. You'd inherit it anyway, so you might as well take it now and make it your own. Pick the one that works best for you."

Alayna felt the tears forming in her eyes and she sniffed.

"Okay, then I'd like our cottage—the family one. I know something horrible happened to me there, but so many wonderful things did as well, and that's what matters."

Bea wrapped her arms around her niece and Alayna heard her sniff as well. "I'm so happy for you. And I'm thrilled that you'll be living in the cottage. I wouldn't want it any other way."

She released Alayna and smiled. Alayna swiped at her tears and laughed. "Okay, then the next big thing I'm hitting you with is construction. Luke has money for improvements, and we'd like to make some. Is that okay?"

"It's your cottage. Why would I care?"

"It's mine as of two seconds ago. But I still wouldn't make changes if you had an objection."

"I can't think of anything I'd object to. But out of curiosity, what kind of changes are you wanting to make?"

"We'd like to add another room and bathroom and enlarge the back deck."

Bea grinned. "Thinking about using cohabitating to make buns in more than just the kitchen?"

"God, Aunt Bea! I mean, maybe. Someday. But right now, we were just thinking about closet space and not having to share a tiny bathroom. The extra bedroom will be an office with a Murphy bed so that we can have guests."

Bea threw her arm around Alayna and laughed. "It just so happens that I know this really good contractor, and I think he's going to free up soon. And there's this lady who owns the cottage next door. You're probably going to want to stay there while this construction happens."

"I love you, Aunt Bea."

"Love you too."

CHAPTER FIFTEEN

JILL HAD JUST FINISHED UP A BATHROOM AND WATER refilling break and gotten back into her chair outside when she saw Bea's boat approaching the island. She'd gotten a text from Pete thirty minutes before asking if she was ready for him to head that way. Given that her pulse had spiked as soon as she'd seen his name in the display, she was fairly certain the answer was yes.

Just maybe not about her ankle.

She'd tried putting a tiny bit of pressure on her foot a couple times that morning, and both times, pain had zinged up her leg like a lightning bolt. Not as acute as when she'd first injured it, but still clearly there. She had no doubt that Pete was going to insist on an X-ray, and at this point, she couldn't argue against it anymore. If she had a fracture, she could do more damage if it wasn't treated properly.

He spotted her as he guided the boat toward the dock and smiled and lifted his hand. She waved back, her heart already pounding at the sight of him. All the common sense her mind had thrown at her when it came to Pete McCord had been completely undone. She was in the woman-in-jeopardy version of *Jerry Maguire*—he'd had her at a smile.

He tied off the boat and headed up the dock. "I see you're getting your dose of vitamin D. Is the chair and that crate working out okay for you?"

"Working great. I've been out here for a couple hours now, reading."

"It's hard to beat a salt air breeze for relaxing. Unfortunately, it's time to make that final assessment."

She sighed. "And I'm pretty sure I already know what you're going to say. Go ahead and take a look."

He lifted her foot and sat on the crate, then propped it on his leg and carefully unwrapped the bandage. The immediate frown told her everything she'd suspected. The swelling wasn't going down quickly enough. He pressed on it a bit and asked her if it hurt, then moved it gently around before letting it rest back on his leg.

"I would love to tell you it's just a really bad sprain and that's why the swelling isn't going down as quickly as I'd like, but I can't do that with any certainty. There could be a hairline fracture, and I wouldn't be doing the responsible thing at this point if I didn't insist on an X-ray."

"I know." She stared out at the water, frustrated all over again even though she'd known this was coming.

"Is anything else wrong? You look really upset."

"The detective in charge of my case called this morning. They got a tip on Trevor and tracked him to a motel near Norfolk, but he was gone before they got there."

"He's checking towns with Naval bases where you lived."

"It looks that way. We suspected that would be the angle he'd take, but I guess I was really hoping we were wrong. Or at least that he'd stick to bases on the West Coast first."

"Do they think he's moved on to a new location?"

She shrugged. "They have no way of knowing. Obviously, he couldn't have scoured every square inch of Norfolk, but if he remembered any names from my past, he could have spied on them to see if I was lurking in the shadows."

"So he might still be in the area, just changing motel rooms."

"Yes, but the locals issued an alert, which is where they got the tip about the motel. We have to assume he knows about it as well. He wasn't in disguise in the video footage I saw taken at the motel, but if he stayed, he would be now. And he might have decided to move on altogether until things cool off. There are other places to check."

"That still doesn't mean he's headed here."

"No. But ignoring the possibility would be irresponsible."

He blew out a breath. "I get that. Look, medical records are private, so there's no worry that he can track you that way, assuming he even had hacker-level skills. The wife of one of my assistants works for an orthopedist on the mainland. I can call in a favor—doctor to doctor—and get you in for an X-ray. It's just that one office, so it's a lower chance of being seen by someone you know than at the hospital."

"At this point, I don't think I have a choice, but a smaller office does make me feel a bit better about the exposure. And if Trevor is headed this way, it's better for me to know exactly what I'm dealing with before I have to move on."

Pete nodded but she could tell her comment about moving on bothered him. It bothered her too.

"Do you want to do this today?" he asked.

"If they can get me in, might as well get it over with."

"Okay. Give me a second and I'll make the call."

"I'll go get ready to leave."

He assisted her up from the chair and handed her the crutches, which were propped against the front door, then he

195

pushed the door open so she could step inside. She'd left the knee scooter right next to the front door, so she made the transfer and headed to the bathroom to brush her teeth and hair and try to steady her warring emotions.

Pete was waiting in the living room when she exited the back room.

"They will work you in whenever we can get there," he said.

"Wow. That's nice. It took a month to get into an orthopedist last time I needed one. These doctor favors are awesome."

"I can't guarantee you won't have to wait a while."

"I'd be waiting if we went to the ER, right?"

"Given that life threatening injuries take priority, yes, and often a long time."

She grabbed her cross-body purse from the table next to the recliner and slipped it over her head. "Well, I'm as ready as I'm going to get."

They headed out, Jill using her crutches again, and Pete helped her into the boat, but when he opened the cabin door, she shook her head. "No one will recognize me from the boat. But if you don't want people asking you about who you were with, I understand."

"No worries." Pete fired up the boat and guided it away from the dock. "One of the sailors caught sight of me carrying you into the lighthouse yesterday. He asked Luke about my secret marriage."

"Oh no! What did you tell Luke?"

"That you had a medical issue and I was doing a favor for a friend who needed things to stay quiet. He agreed to say that I'd been sitting on the dock drinking beer with him all day."

"Just like that, he said he'd cover for you?"

"Sure."

"That's really cool. To have a friend who trusts you enough to lie for you even when they don't know why they're lying."

Pete nodded. "He's a good friend and a good man."

"I'm so glad Alayna found someone special."

And I wish I could too.

Except that she already had. He was sitting right next to her. But her messed-up life had ruined anything that might have been. Just the night before, she'd decided to live in the moment, but that call with Detective Ward had slammed the brakes on her plan.

Maybe Trevor hasn't left Norfolk. Maybe the local cops will get another tip and catch him.

But she couldn't make plans on 'maybe.' It wasn't fair to Pete or anyone else. Right now, she had to assume that everything in her life was temporary.

And unfortunately, that included Pete.

He was quiet most of the drive from the marina to the doctor's office, but to be fair, she wasn't exactly spurring on conversation either. He stared straight ahead with the appearance of concentrating on the road, but the occasional frown told her he was locked in thought, just as she was. She wondered, selfishly, if he was thinking about her. She was definitely thinking about him. Him and Trevor and her entire life, but at the moment, they were all connected. The question was what would be left when all of this played out.

He pulled up in front of a nice brick building with a sign that indicated it was a medical complex and stopped at the curb in front. Then he hurried around to help her out. "Go ahead inside. They're expecting you. I'll find a place to park."

She gave him a weak smile of thanks and took a deep breath before heading for the door. On the one hand, letting her off at the front door was the logical and kind thing to do, but on the other hand, she was feeling vulnerable entering on her own.

Stop being stupid. He's only seconds behind you.

A woman at reception smiled at her as she stepped up and gave her name.

"Oh, yes, Ms. Smith. I'll get you into rotation as soon as we have an opening. Your ankle, right?"

"That's correct."

"It shouldn't be too long. We had a cancellation, so we'll easily be able to fit you in. Just take a seat in the lobby and please fill this out for me. Do you have your insurance card?"

"I'm from out of state, so I'll be paying for this myself."

"Perfect, then I'll make a note to give you the patient pay discount."

"Thank you."

Jill tucked the clipboard under her arm and headed to a pair of chairs in the back corner of the room. Only two other people sat in the lobby. She could feel their gazes on her as the crossed the room and had to remind herself that was normal behavior. Pete walked in right after she got seated, and when he sank into the chair next to her, she felt some of the tension slip from her shoulders.

"Sorry it took so long. The parking lot was packed. I had to wait for someone to leave."

"It's no big deal. I have to fill out the paperwork anyway, but they had a cancellation, so hopefully, it won't be a long wait."

"That's good. Do you need any help with the paperwork? For the injury description, I mean."

"I don't think so, but you're going to talk to the doctor, right? I mean, about what you've observed."

"Absolutely. And I'll pay as well. I know you've got to put

your real name on the paperwork, but medical records aren't as easy to trace as credit card transactions."

"Trevor's not smart enough to hack the credit card company or even figure out my password."

"No. But there are people he can pay. And you're assuming Trevor is the stalker. What if it's the guy working down at the bank, who has access to your account? Or a cop?"

She sucked in a breath. "Good Lord. I hadn't even thought. I guess I locked in on Trevor as the obvious person and hadn't... Fine, you can pay, but I'm reimbursing you."

She lifted the pen and tried to concentrate on the paperwork, but Pete's words kept running through her head. What if Trevor wasn't the stalker? Sure, things seemed to fit, and God knew, he was evil enough to do something like this, but Pete was right to consider other suspects, especially people with easy access to her personal life.

The manager at the bank was, in her opinion, overly friendly. His wife had walked in one day shortly after Jill and based on her expression as she walked up behind him, she felt the same way. Could the manager be her stalker? But the notes were addressed to Kate, not Jill.

Stop it! Next, you'll be suspecting Old Jim, the retired fisherman who lives at the docks and whittles animals for the kids in town.

But Pete's admonition was still accurate. Trevor might not be the stalker, and even if he was, there were plenty of criminals he could pay to do dirty work for him. She knew from her research that incarceration more often produced better criminals than it did rehabilitate people. She finished up the paperwork, and when she signed the last page, Pete took the clipboard back to reception.

He'd barely sat back down when his phone buzzed. He frowned when he checked the display. "This is the doctor on shift today. I have to take this."

She nodded as he hopped up and stepped outside to take the call, then pulled out her phone and opened up the book she was reading. Five minutes later, she'd read the same paragraph ten times and still had no idea what it said. Frustrated, she closed the book and searched her apps for a mindless game.

The man's voice echoed down the hall and into the lobby before she saw him, but she stiffened. Trevor Jones was the last person she wanted to see, but Drew Alderman was barely above him on the list.

CHAPTER SIXTEEN

Jill started to reach for the crutches on the off chance she could make it to the ladies' room before he finished paying and exited, but the door swung open and her high school nightmare stepped into the lobby.

She ducked her head, pretending to stare at her nails while praying he'd head straight out without paying attention to the people seated there. But luck was something Jill had always been short on, especially, it seemed, when it came to men.

"Jill? Jill Morgan?" Drew's voice boomed across the lobby.

She looked up and forced a surprised look. "Drew."

He gave her a huge used car salesman grin as he swaggered over, and Jill was immediately struck by how little he'd changed since high school. Of course, he'd aged physically, but clearly, he was still the same insincere, egotistical douche.

He gave her a long look from head to toe and she struggled not to whack him with one of her crutches. "You're looking good," he said. "Even better than high school. Can't say that about most of the girls we went to school with."

Jill clenched her jaw and remained silent, mostly because

she was afraid of the words that would come out of her mouth if she opened it.

"You here visiting Alayna?"

"Yep."

"That's cool. She looks even better than high school too. 'Course she hooked up with a military guy as soon as she stepped on the island. Didn't even give the locals time for a run at her, but then, she was never my favorite anyway."

He gave her a wink, and disgust coursed through her.

"I own a couple businesses here," he continued. "Doing really well. Just bought a brand-new Mercedes convertible. I can take you to dinner...let you ride in my car?"

"No thanks. I don't have much time, and I want to spend it with Alayna."

"Ah, come on. You gonna let Alayna cockblock me again? High school's over. You don't have to let her run your life."

Jill clenched her jaw and struggled to keep her voice level. "I know you're not going to believe this, but Alayna was never the reason I didn't go out with you. And you had a girlfriend."

He shrugged. "You mean Poppy? We were never serious."

"Was Poppy aware of that?"

His face flashed with a bit of anger. "Look, Poppy and me were never going to be a thing. It's on her if she decided differently because I never told her we were exclusive. The truth is, I'm over here doing you a favor. I'm the hottest ticket in the county. So you going to take me up on that offer, or are you going to be a loser just like in high school?"

"Ms. Smith?" A man's voice sounded from the doorway, and Jill looked around Drew and spotted a man in scrubs standing at the doorway next to reception and frowning at Drew.

"I'm ready for you now, Ms. Smith," he said. "Mr. Alderman, you need to get home and ice that shoulder, or you won't be golfing next week."

Drew flushed at the obvious dismissal and Jill could tell he was mad, but he must have decided his golf game was more important than harassing Jill, so he whirled around and practically stomped out of the office. Jill pushed herself up and made her way across the waiting room on her crutches. The doctor stared at her as she approached, then his eyes widened and he checked his clipboard.

"Jill... Morgan?" he asked.

She'd thought he looked familiar, but then she hadn't seen anyone from the island in over a decade so she couldn't place him. Then she glanced at his scrubs where his name was stenciled.

Dr. Nelson.

"Isaac?" she asked.

He smiled and pushed his glasses up on his nose, and then she recognized the boy who'd once tutored her in math.

"I was afraid you didn't recognize me."

"I didn't at first. It's been so long since I've seen anyone here. A doctor, huh? I always knew you were going to do great things."

"Thank you. I'm glad to see you again, but sorry for the circumstances. Let's get you back so that I can take a look at that foot. And I apologize for Mr. Alderman. When the receptionist alerted me that he was bothering you, I came out as soon as I could."

Jill followed him down the hall and into the first examination room. "I guess all of us didn't grow up after high school, huh?"

He motioned for her to sit on the table and started unwrapping her ankle. "Those might be the truest words I've heard today. So are you moving back or just visiting?"

"Oh, visiting. It's long overdue."

"So what have you been doing since high school?"

"The usual things—college, then work, a little travel when I could fit it in."

"I hope your work doesn't require you to stand or walk for long periods of time."

"No. I do boring insurance work from home, so at least there's that in my favor as far as this injury goes."

He nodded and began to press on her ankle, then gently moved it around as Pete had.

"How are your parents?" Jill asked.

Isaac looked pleased that she'd asked. "Doing great. Dad retired a couple years ago—they were a bit older when they had me, if you recall. Dad and I thought Mom would never retire, but she surprised us and pulled the plug last year. She's still in the thick of the local theater stuff, but now that she's not teaching anymore, she has more time to devote to being on stage herself."

"Good for her. I always loved seeing her on stage." Isaac's mom had held a couple roles on Broadway back in the day. The local college had been fortunate to have someone of her caliber on staff. His father was an engineer and had worked for a defense contractor. They'd both been very welcoming to Jill when Isaac had tutored her.

He smiled. "She's rather terrific. Still disappointed that her only child didn't inherit her ability or interest, but becoming a doctor helped ease that a bit."

Jill laughed. "I would hope so."

There was a light knock on the door, then it opened and Pete walked in.

"I'm so sorry," he said. "That call got more involved than I thought it would."

"Mr. Smith?" Isaac inquired.

"Huh?" Pete looked confused and Jill realized that Isaac had assumed Pete was her husband.

"No," Jill said. "This is Pete McCord. He's a friend and a doctor with the Navy. He took a look at my ankle because I was hoping to avoid a big production, but he insisted that I come in for an X-ray."

"You're the doctor my assistant told me about." Isaac stuck his hand out. "Nice to meet you. Isaac Nelson. Is there anything I need to know about the injury?"

Pete gave him a rundown of her situation, using all the five-syllable words that doctors always seem to have on hand. When he finished, Isaac nodded.

"I concur with Dr. McCord. I suspect it's a moderate to severe sprain or you wouldn't be walking on it, even with crutches. But I'd like to get an X-ray just to be certain there's not something more serious going on. Give me a minute and I'll get the tech in to get you back for that. It shouldn't take long, then Dr. McCord and I can have a look and get you a plan."

"Thanks, Isaac."

Pete looked over at her, one eyebrow raised as Isaac left. "Isaac?"

"He was a couple years ahead of me in high school. Scary smart. He tutored me in math."

"Ah, crap, I'm sorry. Here you are trying to lie low, and I bring you to the one doctor in town who tutored you."

"It doesn't matter. I ran into another old classmate in the waiting room. One I'd rather hoped to never see again in this lifetime. He was busy trying to pressure me into going on a date with him—the same thing he did in high school—when Isaac interrupted and sent him on his way."

Pete's face flashed with anger. "The guy hasn't set eyes on you since high school and was harassing you to go on a date while you're waiting in a doctor's office? What's wrong with him?"

"There are not enough hours left in the day for me to cover that. Suffice it to say, he hasn't changed one bit. He was an asshole then, and if anything, it appears he's upped the ante."

"What is this guy's name?"

"Drew Alderman."

Pete shook his head. "Yeah, I know him a little. Owns a business or two on the mainland. Loves to sponsor events so that he can show up and talk about how great he is. Always showing pictures of his car."

"That's him. He was trying to tempt me with his Mercedes convertible."

"I take it that didn't work."

She grinned. "I'm more of a Lamborghini girl."

"That's one way to narrow your dating pool."

She laughed. "I'm also the kind of girl who can buy her own car."

"The car in Bea's garage wasn't a Lamborghini."

"Now, how could I hide out driving a Lambo?"

He laughed. "That's a good point. I imagine if you drove one onto the island, you'd be surrounded in a matter of minutes. I got stopped three times last month when I upgraded the wheels and tires on my Jeep."

The door popped open and a tech walked in. "Ms. Smith? I'm going to take you for an X-ray. Can you walk okay with the crutches? It's not far. If not, I can grab a wheelchair."

"I'm good," she said.

Pete helped her off the table and handed her the crutches. The tech gave him a nod. "You can wait here, sir. We'll be right back."

Jill hobbled through the X-rays then back to the room. Isaac walked in shortly after and stuck them up on a light board for them to see.

"Everything looks good, per se," he said. "No fracture, so

best possible outcome. An MRI is the only way to see ligament damage, but it would probably take another couple days before I could get you in for one. They stay pretty booked."

Jill bit her lower lip. "Do you think I need one?"

Isaac shook his head. "I think it's a moderate sprain and if I had to guess, you didn't stay off it as much as you should have."

"Probably not."

He nodded. "Then I'd suggest icing it for another day, then switch to heat and see if that helps. I'm going to prescribe an anti-inflammatory to help get the swelling down quicker. You can take Tylenol for pain as needed. I'm also going to give you a boot to wear when you're walking. Otherwise, I'd prefer it be open so that you can start to get some of the flexibility back as the inflammation goes down."

"Thank you so much," Jill said. "I'm glad it isn't anything serious."

"Well, you can still make matters worse if you don't give it some time to recover, so I'm afraid your visit needs to be conducted mostly in a chair. I know telling people on Tempest Island in the summer to avoid going into the water is like cutting a vein, but you can't risk walking in sand or surf. Not yet. Maybe in a week or so, you'll be better. How long are you visiting?"

"I haven't decided. I work from home, so my return is flexible."

"Well, if you have time in your schedule, give me a call. I haven't seen Alayna yet since she's returned and would love to catch up over dinner. Then the two of you can meet my wife. She's a social worker. Awesome woman."

"I'm sure she is. I'll see how it goes and let you know. It was really good seeing you again, Isaac."

JANA DELEON

He gave her a big smile. "You too. And nice meeting you, Dr. McCord."

Isaac headed out and a few minutes later, an assistant came with the boot and got it fitted. Then Pete helped her back onto the crutches and out to pay. Before she could protest, he pulled out his card and took care of the bill. Isaac, who was handing her file over to the records nurse, gave them a nod as he set off to the next patient.

When they got into Pete's Jeep, Jill slumped into the passenger's seat and blew out a breath.

"Relieved?" Pete asked.

"Yes. And no. Relieved about the ankle, but now two people I knew from high school have spotted me. It's going to get around. Not from Isaac, but Drew has probably already told everyone he came across since he left the doctor's office."

Pete nodded. "Your cover is officially blown. So what do you want to do?"

Jill stared out the windshield, considering her options. Leaving didn't seem like the best one, although at least now that she knew her ankle wasn't broken, that helped. But still, even a few days of rest were likely to improve it by 50 percent or better. Unfortunately, if Trevor was looking for her, news was going to spread that Jill Morgan was officially back on the island.

"I think the first thing I need to do is see Alayna," she said finally. "I don't want her to hear about this from anyone else."

"Good call," Pete said as he started the vehicle. "I'll give Luke a buzz and see if Alayna's at home. We can stop and pick up your prescription on the way."

Jill stared out the window as they pulled out of the parking lot, her nerves on edge. Not that she wasn't excited to see Alayna, but she wished the circumstances were different—for her sake as well as her friend's. And how did she even start a conversation about all of this with someone she'd lost touch with so long ago?

———

DREW ALDERMAN LOOKED up as the bell on the door of his printing business rang and held in a groan when Poppy Bettencourt walked in. She wore heels as high as her blouse was low and he wondered how she managed to stand all day balancing on tiny stilts and holding up all that extra chest she'd had put in. But no way he was asking. The slightest bit of interest shown to Poppy might as well be a marriage proposal, and Drew wasn't interested in settling down in any way, shape, or form. And even if that changed, Poppy would be the last person he did it with. She took high maintenance to a whole new level and wasn't nearly good-looking enough to demand it.

Now Jill, that was a whole different story. Sure, she could use a set of boobs—not as big as Poppy's, but maybe another cup size—and she really shouldn't go out without fixing her hair and putting on some makeup. But even with her hair in a ponytail and no makeup at all, she still looked better than Poppy. Something the other woman had always hated her for.

He was still a little pissed that weasel Isaac had interrupted him. If he hadn't, Drew was certain he could have convinced Jill to go out with him. Maybe he'd finally get in that tumble he'd never gotten in high school. But in the meantime, Jill was the perfect tool to use to get rid of Poppy. People often insinuated that Drew was living in the past, and he supposed some of that was true, although he had yet to figure out why that was a problem.

Until he ran into Poppy.

No one held on to old grudges like Poppy Bettencourt. For her the past was the present and the future. In high school, as soon as she'd found out Drew was attracted to Jill, she'd decided she hated her. The easiest way to get Jill riled up would be to sic Poppy on her. Then maybe Jill would rethink that dinner offer. If she was going to catch hell anyway, might as well enjoy his company.

It was about time Jill acknowledged what she was missing.

"Hi, Drew." Poppy sauntered up to the counter, batting her eyes in what he assumed she thought was a sexy look.

"How can I help you, Poppy?"

"You ask that like I'm just any ole customer. That's not the case, now, is it? Are you going to the Business Leaders' meeting tonight? I wouldn't mind a ride in that pretty new car of yours."

"I don't think I'm going to be able to make it. I'm working on dinner plans."

She frowned. "Anyone I know?"

He grinned. Lord, she was easy. He'd set her up and she'd played right into his hands. "Yeah, matter of fact, you'll never guess who I ran into today."

"Who?"

"Jill Morgan. She's in town for a visit, but I get the impression she might be looking to make it more permanent. She hasn't changed a bit. Still thin and with that mass of hair. You'd probably love to get your hands on it."

"I'll just bet I would."

Drew struggled not to laugh at her tone, and the snit she was in was written all over her face. Poppy wasn't overweight, but he knew she existed on air and diet soda to keep her figure. She always had. Women like Jill, who seemed to be naturally thin and fit, were the bane of her existence.

"Are you sure you want to miss tonight, though? I heard we're discussing the next mayoral election. You know we don't want Bea in there."

He shrugged. "Neither candidate is going to affect my business any. I don't really care about politics, and all they do at the meeting is rehash the same stuff over and over again. If I miss anything, I can hear about it next month."

"We could have lunch tomorrow. I could fill you in. I've got a two-hour gap in my schedule midday. Plenty of time for eating...and anything else we might think of."

"I'm busy this week. Maybe another time. Was there anything you needed printed?"

Poppy's face flashed with anger. "I'll just wait until you're not so busy."

She whirled around and hurried out, slamming the front door behind her.

"Did she need anything?" A young man who worked in the back office poked his head through the office door.

"Not anything we're offering."

He turned back around and smiled.

Poppy was locked and loaded. Jill was going to wish she hadn't turned him down.

CHAPTER SEVENTEEN

JILL BIT HER LOWER LIP AS PETE PULLED INTO THE DRIVEWAY of Alayna's cottage. If she was being honest, she was nervous about seeing her old friend, and no matter how hard she'd tried to 'logic' with her emotions, they weren't having any.

"Are you all right?" Pete asked. "If you're not ready—"

"No. It has to be now. The gossip in this town moves faster than the fighter jets."

He reached over and gave her hand a squeeze. "It's going to be fine. More than fine. From everything you've told me, Alayna loves you and is going to be thrilled to see you again."

"Until I tell her why I'm here."

"Even then. Besides, she'll understand your situation better than anyone."

"That's true and also the problem."

"I'm going to hang out next door with Luke so you guys can talk. Just give me a call when you're ready to go."

He grabbed her crutches out of the back seat, then helped her out before heading off. Jill got her balance on the crutches and started for the front door, happy that Pete wasn't going to stick around. That would just make her more nervous.

She'd thought about this for years—well, not exactly these circumstances, but seeing Alayna again. And even with all that thinking and ground-laying, she still had absolutely no idea what she was going to say.

She heard music playing inside and smiled. Alayna always played music while she cooked. She must be working on something for the restaurant. Taking a deep breath, she lifted her hand and knocked on the door. She heard pots clanking inside, and then the door swung open and a somewhat irritated-looking Alayna looked out.

Then her eyes widened and she gasped. "Jill? Oh my God! It's really you. And you're on crutches. What happened? Why are you here? Good Lord, get inside and sit down."

Then Alayna wrapped her arms around Jill and squeezed her tightly, preventing her from losing her balance. Her old friend was already laughing and crying when she released her, and Jill could feel the tears welling up in her eyes. She hadn't known just how much she'd missed Alayna until she'd opened the door. Now it was all rushing over her like a tidal wave.

Alayna motioned her into the living room. "Sit in the recliner. It's the most comfortable. Do you need ice? A pillow?"

"I wouldn't turn either down, but can I get some of that ice with water poured over it?"

Alayna laughed as she hurried into the kitchen. "I can probably do better than that."

Alayna returned with an ice pack and helped Jill take off the boot, then lifted her leg so that she could place a pillow underneath Jill's foot. Alayna winced as she took in the swollen, purple mass that used to be an ankle and gently placed a dish towel, then the ice pack on it.

"You're not driving with that, right? Did you take an Uber

here? I saw my friend Pete's Jeep in the driveway, but he must be next door."

"Actually, Pete brought me over."

"Huh? How do you know Pete?"

"It's a long story."

"Then let me get those drinks and you can tell me. I want to know everything."

Jill blew out a breath as Alayna hurried away. Somewhere between basics and everything was the problem. Bea already knew the whole truth, including Jill's alter ego, but Pete didn't. Somehow it seemed wrong for him to be the last to hear it given all that he'd done for her, but then she hadn't intended on anyone even knowing she was here besides Bea. And now, the whole island had probably already heard that she was back in town and that Drew had hit on her.

Jill had called Bea on the way back to the island to tell her that she'd been exposed. The older woman had just spoken with the sheriff as Detective Ward had advised him to make her a point of contact for Jill. He'd joined Detective Ward in stressing that sharing her situation with those close to her was a good idea. They were all stretched across the island and mainland during the day, with exposure to different people. It was possible that one of them would catch sight of Trevor before he located her.

Bea was completely on board with still keeping the Kate Coleson part of her story a secret, but she'd encouraged Jill to confess all to Alayna, who would understand better than anyone else what she was going through. And that had seemed perfectly logical when Bea had said it, but now that she was sitting here, in Alayna's living room, she had no idea where to start. With her other identity? With the stalker? It was all such a mess to untangle in a single conversation.

Alayna stepped back into the living room and placed a tray

on the coffee table. She handed Jill what looked like a straw-berry drink and Jill took the first sip and sighed.

"This is fresh strawberries and bananas. Just like high school."

Alayna smiled. "Your favorite."

"It still is—when you make them. I've tried, but I never get them as creamy."

"I have secrets, which I might be willing to share with you, just as soon as you tell me what's wrong. Because although that ankle looks bad, it's the least of your problems."

Jill sighed. "How did you know?"

Alayna reached over and squeezed her hand. "Honey, we might not have talked for years but I still know you, and I know that look. What going on? And what can I do to help?"

The simple, immediate offer from her old friend was all it took to send tears to Jill's eyes, then a second later, they welled over.

"I've missed you so much," Jill said. "I'm sorry I didn't stay in touch. Sorry I didn't contact you when everything was happening to you. But I didn't want you to think...you know..."

Alayna swiped away a tear from her own cheek with one hand, still clutching Jill's with the other.

"I've missed you too, but please don't apologize. I was equally guilty of letting our friendship drift away. We were both trying to get our adult lives started. It was a lot. And as crappy as it might be, sometimes it's all-consuming in order to make it work."

"God, isn't that the truth."

"So maybe let's start with you, and not what's going on now. You already know all about me from the nightly news, so no need to cover my drama. Go back in time. You can work up to the current problem, and then I'll have a better frame of refer-ence for understanding."

Jill felt some of the tension slip from her back. Alayna was right. This wasn't a novel. Starting with the inciting incident and then filtering in the backstory was just going to be confusing. Best to just lay it all out in linear fashion.

"Okay. So I'll start with college. There was an incident with my ex-boyfriend the last semester of college." She explained to Alayna what had happened and the subsequent name change and move across the country.

"That's awful," Alayna said when she'd finished. "I'm so glad you got away, although I cringe at the so-called penalties handed out. You can't be the first and won't be the last woman that man attacks."

Jill nodded. Her old friend had no idea how accurate she was.

"So you live in Oregon? And what do you do?"

"I started working for an insurance company after graduation."

Alayna frowned. "An insurance...marketing department?"

"No. Claims."

"I don't understand. You were always the creative one—I mean with words."

"Yes. But after Trevor, I just wanted to disappear somewhere that he'd never look for me. It paid well, good benefits."

"Paid? Past tense. So that's not what you do now?"

"It's what I tell everyone I do because my other identity is a secret."

Alayna's eyes widened. "That sounds a little too James Bond. What does this secret identity do?"

"She writes books. Books that sell well enough to allow me to quit that insurance job."

Alayna smiled. "Now, that's more like it! You were always writing in high school, and your stories were great. I'm not even remotely surprised that you're making a living with it. So given the ex, I assume you're writing under a pen name."

"Exactly. But it's not just the name that I changed. When I'm doing public appearances, I wear a wig, put on dark, dramatic makeup, dress differently—basically, I created a whole different persona so that no one would ever know who I really am."

Alayna's eyes widened. "Appearances. You're selling much more than 'well enough' if you're doing signings and interviews and such. What is this pen name?"

"Kate Coleson."

"Holy crap!" Alayna jumped up from her chair, staring at Jill in shock. "No way!"

She pulled out her cell phone and Jill assumed was googling pics of Kate. She looked back and forth from her phone to Jill, then dropped onto the couch again.

"I see it now. But I didn't before." She shook her head in obvious amazement. "I'm a huge fan. I've read everything you've written and loved every word. And I was your best friend. How could I not recognize you? Or your voice and style?"

"Kate looks nothing like me. She's polished and has that ultra-city look, which is intentional as I'm very girl-next-door. Hair and makeup can make everything look different. As for my voice and style, well, they've matured, refined, and gotten a heck of a lot better since high school."

"Yes, of course." Alayna shook her head. "I'm still trying to wrap my head around it. Wait—does Aunt Bea know?"

Crap. Hurdle number one.

The look on Jill's face must have given it away because Alayna frowned.

"She knows. Of course she knows. She encouraged you all those years."

"I'm sorry I didn't tell you. By the time things began to happen for me, we hadn't talked in so long. I knew through Bea that you were trying to make a go of it in New York, and I guess I didn't want to contact you out of the blue about it when you were still working your butt off to establish yourself."

"I would have been thrilled for you. You know that."

"I know. I wish I had a better reason. I just... I think everything that happened with Trevor changed me. I was always an introvert—you know that—but after college, I just retreated completely. No friends, no groups, no activities except things I could do alone and also be left alone while doing them."

"Don't blame yourself. Our losing touch was just as much my fault. More, actually, because I'm not an introvert, although my general tolerance for people has decreased the more time I spend around them."

Jill laughed. It was such an Alayna thing to say, and it had been far too long since she'd heard her painfully kind friend let loose her frustration with the decline of polite society.

Alayna smiled. "You're a big deal. A Really. Big. Deal. That is so incredibly cool. I have a famous person sitting on my couch, which is a far better thing than the infamous one who lives here."

Jill instantly sobered at the thought of all that her friend had endured and just weeks before. "I'm really sorry about how all of that went down. And then the aftermath that came as well. I know you're not an introvert, but all that negative attention must have been horrible for you to deal with."

"It was, which is why I recognize overwhelming signs of stress when I see them. So are you going to tell me why you're here? Because I'm guessing that has everything to do with why Bea is keeping secrets from me."

Jill was silent for a bit, trying to figure out how to present the situation. But then she decided that Alayna, of all people, would immediately understand.

"I have a stalker."

Alayna gasped and covered her mouth with one hand. "Tell me everything."

So Jill did. From the first card received to the attack on Wanda and her subsequent trip to Tempest Island to hide out in the lighthouse.

"Wait?" Alayna said, finally interrupting. "Aunt Bea owns the lighthouse?"

"Crap. I guess she hadn't told you."

"Seems there's a lot of things Bea hasn't told me."

"In her defense, I asked her to keep my being here quiet, and you've had more than a little on your plate. You know Bea will always err on the side of protecting you, and she's like a vault with a secret."

Alayna sighed. "I know. And I can't complain about it because the woman is a damned saint. I mean, not in the original sense because I think the church would take issue with some of her ideas and the things she says, but I've never known a better person."

Now Jill reached over and squeezed Alayna's hand. "I've known one other. And I'm sorry it took me so long to remember that. I desperately wanted to see you when I arrived. Sitting across the water from you, knowing that you were a short boat ride away was killing me, but I also didn't want to involve you in any of this, especially after everything you just went through."

"I get it. I don't have to like it, but I won't lie and say I don't understand. I did the same thing. I tried to shut Bea out because I didn't want to bring things down on her, but you know Bea. Then I did everything I could to ignore my attraction to Luke because I didn't want my problems dumped on him."

"I hear that worked out as well as avoiding Bea."

Alayna laughed. "Luke is just as determined as she is, and the truth is, I couldn't deny our connection. It was so present, you know?"

"I think I do."

"So your friend, Wanda, is she going to be all right?"

"Yes. Detective Ward said she's reopened her shop. I wish she wouldn't have but even if I could speak to her, I wouldn't be able to talk her out of it. On that front, Wanda reminds me a lot of Bea."

Alayna frowned. "So that stunt at the lighthouse with those two local idiots..."

"It was me. Scared me half to death. I thought Trevor had found me."

"Oh my God! I could just kill them. You must have been terrified."

"I won't lie—it probably took a year or two off my life."

"So does the sheriff know everything now?"

Jill nodded. "Detective Ward called him this morning. He knows everything except my Kate identity. Only Ward, Wanda, you, Bea, my agent and editor, my attorney, and my parents know that. But I guess it will get out when all this is over."

"When this is over, it won't matter any longer. So this Trevor—the cops think he's searching all your old stomping grounds?"

"That's what it looks like. We figured he'd come after me through my past, which is why my being here was so hush-hush. But then I injured my ankle and Bea talked me into letting Pete look at it because I didn't want to go to the hospital for an X-ray."

"Ah. So that's how you met Pete. This is all beginning to make sense. So I assume they finally talked you into telling me?"

Jill squirmed a bit. "Not really. Pete took me to get that X-ray this morning because my ankle wasn't getting better, and we wanted to be sure it wasn't a fracture. In a weird turn of events, the doctor turned out to be Isaac Nelson."

"Really? Isaac's a doctor? Good for him. He was always brutally smart. But I can't imagine seeing you was something he'd gossip about. Not Isaac."

"No, he wouldn't. But in an even weirder turn of events, I ran into Drew Alderman in the lobby."

"Oh no!"

"Yeah. It was like I was right back in high school. He gave me the all-body scan—I can tell he still thinks I should get breast implants—but he was happy with the look, and then proceeded to hit on me, pitching his new Mercedes convertible as bait."

"Ugh. He's so gross."

"Then he blamed you for cockblocking him in high school."

"What?!"

"Yeah, apparently, I couldn't possibly be uninterested. Then or now. The receptionist must have seen how uncomfortable I was because she went and got Isaac, who sent him on his way and called me back."

Alayna shook her head. "Well, I have to admit that I'm sort of happy your hand was forced and you had to tell me, but I'm really sorry it was Drew Alderman who did the forcing. I've only run into him once since I've been back and that was more than enough for me, but you'll never guess who I had a run-in with yesterday—Poppy."

"Holy crap! It's just not our week."

"Definitely not."

Jill listened as Alayna gave her a blow-by-blow of her exchange with Poppy.

"Why can't people grow up?" Jill asked when Alayna finished. "You being the exception. That comeback of yours would have never happened in high school."

"I was nicer then. I've met too many people like Poppy since, and it's taken my niceness down a few hundred notches. And almost dying tends to put a lot of things in perspective—the first one being taking crap from other people."

"Yeah, I can definitely see how it would."

"So your ankle... Is it okay?"

"A bad sprain. I got some prescription anti-inflammatories and that boot, so that should help."

"A hot doctor looking after you doesn't hurt either."

Jill felt her face redden. "It's not like that. Bea asked him as a favor."

"He must really like Bea then. I had no idea."

Jill laughed. "You know what I mean. He strikes me as one of those eternally nice guys."

"He is. But he's also hot. Don't tell me you haven't noticed because that red face of yours says differently."

"I mean, I'm not blind, so yeah, I'm attracted to him. He's hot and nice and smart and honorable. What's not to like? But I'm not in a position to act on that. Even if the stalker situation was over, I live across the country."

Alayna shrugged. "So move. You can work anywhere, so you can live anywhere, right?"

"You say that like it's so simple."

"It is and it's not. I know firsthand. Starting over is hard. But starting over here was both hard and easy. When I first came back, I felt like a failure...like I was a dog retreating with my tail tucked between my legs. But now, I can't imagine why I ever wanted to be anywhere else."

Jill smiled. "I'm so happy you found your place again, but I wish it hadn't come with such high costs."

"To get here, I had to go through all of that. And maybe when your situation is resolved, you'll feel the same way I do."

"The problem is I have no idea when my situation will be resolved. In the meantime, I'm in this horrible limbo."

"I get it. My situation was different in that the FBI kept saying I was in no danger, but I didn't believe that at all. I felt like nothing had been resolved, and it wasn't PTSD or guilt or any of that. It was this overwhelming feeling that something was coming. Then it was the feeling of being watched. Luke said we should never ignore those instincts because they save lives."

Jill let out a sigh of relief. "I thought it was just me. I mean, I know for certain that I am in danger and I am being stalked, but even coming here, I can't seem to relax. And there's no way to associate Kate Coleson with this place—or Jill Smith for that matter—but Jill Morgan is a different story. Trevor will eventually come here, and now that people have seen me, I think maybe I should leave."

"You don't want to put people at risk."

"No. He's already proven that he's willing to harm people, and if Wanda hadn't been on the phone when she screamed, he might have killed her. I can't have your and Bea's safety on my conscience."

"I understand what you're saying, but your logic is faulty."

"What do you mean?"

"People already know you're here, so the risk is already present. If you left, the stalker would simply assume we knew where you'd gone, or he could kidnap one of us to lure you back."

Jill sucked in a breath and cursed. "You'd think I'd know that. I write this stuff every day."

"It's easier to think clearer when it's not actually happening to you. It's time to stop running and take a stand. Until you do, you'll never be able to live a normal life."

"But now I've put you and Bea in the crosshairs."

"*You* didn't. He did. But you can't live like this forever."

Jill stared out the patio doors at the Gulf, wishing she had an argument for Alayna's comment. But she knew her friend was right. Wouldn't it be better to take a stand and be prepared rather than traipsing around hoping to put off the inevitable? And for what purpose? Short of leaving the country, changing her name yet again, and refusing any and all public appearances as Kate, there was no way for her to truly disappear. And did she want her life to be like that? Looking over her shoulder every day? Potentially for the rest of her life?

"You're right," she said finally. "I left home hoping the cops would catch him quickly and this would all be over, but that didn't happen. Maybe it's time to rethink my strategy."

"There is no better place for you to stand your ground than here. You have family here who cares about you and men who defend this country for a living and have connections with just about everyone you could possibly need. The local sheriff is a good guy, and he'll put out an alert to look for Trevor, warning that he's a threat. Everyone will be on the lookout. The island takes care of its own."

"But I'm not really an islander."

"Sure you are. Just ask. Well, ask anyone but Melody and Poppy."

Jill snorted. "Goes without saying."

"The locals don't need to know his intended target to report a bad guy, and these kinds of alerts don't happen often.

People will pay attention. So it's decided. You'll stay here for your showdown—that's what it's called, right?"

"Climax."

"That sounds too sexy, but okay. You'll stay for your climax and then when it's all over, you can reassess everything without the weight of this hanging over you. And you can start by going to dinner with me tonight."

Jill struggled to shift gears. "What? I don't know..."

"Luke has night training, so I was going to go snoop on this restaurant on the mainland—you know, checking out the competition—and I know Bea would be thrilled to get out of it. They have valet, so very limited walking. And you can spend the night here. I'll take the couch. Not like I haven't done it a million times before."

"But my clothes—"

"You can borrow some of mine."

Jill couldn't help smiling. "A sleepover and clothes borrowing. Just like old times."

And Lord, she wanted to do it. More than anything. Well, maybe not more than she wanted to kiss Pete again, but it was a close second.

"I don't think it's a good idea. What if he finds me here?"

"You're worried about what he might do to me?"

Jill nodded.

"Nothing," Alayna said. "He was in the bookstore the entire time you were upstairs with Wanda, right? Why didn't he do anything?"

Jill sighed. "Because he wants me alone."

"Exactly. He's waited all these years. He's not going to ruin it with an easy attempt on you. If that's what he wanted, you and Wanda would both be dead."

Jill knew Alayna was right. If Trevor or whoever spotted her at Alayna's house, he'd simply keep watching until she was alone and then make his move. And this time, there probably wouldn't be a card to alert her to his presence.

"Oh hell, why not," Jill said. "Maybe we'll see some people we know while we're out, and then at least my story about being here to visit you and Bea holds up."

"Exactly. I know this isn't what you wanted, but I'm glad you got outed. I've missed you."

Jill's eyes grew misty again. "I've missed you too."

CHAPTER EIGHTEEN

LUKE STARED AT PETE FOR SEVERAL LONG SILENT SECONDS, then shook his head. "Wow. That's a lot. No wonder she wanted it kept quiet."

"If it hadn't been for her ankle, she probably could have managed it, but running into old classmates pretty much blew the lid off any secrecy. I doubt the doctor will talk, but that idiot who was propositioning her in the waiting room has probably already told half the town."

Luke nodded. "I know the guy. I've gone to a couple business-related things with Alayna and Bea. He's a total ass. First time I went to one, I dropped them off at the door and went to park. I wasn't ten seconds behind them, but when I walked in, I saw him catch sight of Alayna and make a beeline for her. It was clear what his intentions were. You should have seen his face when she introduced me as her boyfriend."

"I would have loved that. I've run across him a couple times on the mainland. He's definitely a creep."

"Who thinks he's a player."

Pete shrugged. "As much as I hate to say it, we've known plenty of sailors with that same crap mentality about women, but it hasn't kept them from landing plenty. So as long as it keeps working..."

"Unfortunate but true. So now that Jill's had to come clean, are you going to work on that threshold-carrying situation?"

"We've never even had a date. And just because she's coming clean with Alayna doesn't mean anything's better. Honestly, if anything, I'm expecting her to decide to move on because of what happened to her friend. She's not looking for a repeat."

"Neither of them were expecting him to make a move. That's different now. Everyone around Jill will be on alert, and we have pictures of the likely suspect."

"Except what if it's not him?"

"I'm not saying it's not problematic, just that everyone around Jill will be watching and none of us are lightweights. I know Alayna. There's no way she's letting Jill leave, especially injured. And even if Jill could convince Alayna on that note, Bea is a much harder sell. She'll hold her car hostage if necessary."

Pete felt a bit of relief course through him. "That's true."

"So do I get to meet this woman who's managed to do what no other woman has before her?"

"I've carried plenty of women into buildings...battlefield, remember?"

Luke laughed. "I meant she caught your attention. As long as I've known you, I've never seen you thinking this hard on anyone."

"Maybe it's white knight syndrome."

"Dude, you spent years at war. There was no shortage of women who needed saving. But your mind was never locked on them after you patched them up."

Pete sighed. "I know. My luck, right? I finally have strong feelings for a woman and she's in absolutely no position to even consider a date, much less a relationship. And no way am I putting more pressure on her by asking questions she probably doesn't want to answer."

Luke nodded. "I understand. I felt the same way with Alayna. But it all worked out, and I have a feeling your situation will as well."

"I just want her safe, then I can think about everything else."

"Me too, buddy. Me too."

———

ALAYNA PULLED up in front of the historic building and jumped out to hand the keys to the valet. She hurried around to help Jill out of the car, but a second valet was already assisting her out of the seat and onto the crutches.

"Are you good?" Alayna asked.

Jill nodded. "Better than good, actually. Between the meds and the ice packs you kept rotating on and off, it feels 50 percent better."

"Well, let's not set you back. We're right on time, so we shouldn't have to wait to be seated."

They entered the restaurant and Jill gave it a critical eye. Given her lack of talent and interest in cooking, she'd been in her share of restaurants, and this one ranked up there for fancy. Unfortunately, it had slipped a bit past elegant and into snooty. Maybe if they changed the lighting and it wasn't quite so dark, or the furniture quite so heavy. Or maybe they just needed staff who didn't give people a critical eye when they walked through the door, as though assessing if they were actually worthy to eat there.

She had to assume the food was going to be awesome, but she already knew Alayna's restaurant would have this one beat except for those looking to put on a show of wealth. Her friend had shown her pictures of the space and all the finishings, furniture, and dishes she'd selected, and Jill was ready for it to open ASAP. Her friend's restaurant would be elegant but inviting and fit perfectly in the high-end coastal slot the island could use. And she had no doubt that Alayna would find and train her staff to be as welcoming as she was.

"Your table is ready, Ms. Scott," the hostess said. "Please follow me."

Alayna motioned for Jill to go first, and Jill worked her way through the tables to a two-top next to a window with a view of downtown. The server was immediately at their table with glasses of water. They both passed on drinks as Alayna was driving and Jill didn't want to mix alcohol with her medication. Alayna asked for the crab dip to start, and the server hurried off.

"Let me know what you're going to order, so I can get something different," Alayna said. "I'm probably also going to order soup and salad and multiple sides. I need to get as much tasting in as I can."

"Sounds like we're going to have some to-go containers."

"Luke won't complain. He won't finish up until early tomorrow morning, but he'll be starving when he gets home. I'll just leave the leftovers in his fridge."

Jill studied her friend's face, which seemed to light up whenever she mentioned Luke, and a small vein of jealousy ran through her. Not that she wasn't happy for her friend. She was thrilled, but the love, respect, happiness, and security Alayna had in her relationship was something that Jill had always wanted but didn't think existed.

Except in fiction.

Now she was looking at a woman who'd proven the fantasy was possible, even after a literal life-and-death situation. If

Alayna could come through everything she had and trust a man with her feelings again, then there was no reason Jill couldn't do the same. For years, she'd told herself and others that she was 'too busy' or 'just hadn't found the right match' or 'was not ready for a relationship at this juncture in my life,' but the reality was that what happened with Trevor had scared her so badly that she'd simply put a wall up where romantic relationships were concerned.

She hadn't trusted herself to make a good choice. After all, Trevor had fooled her for a long time before she saw his true colors. Or maybe she had ignored the signals. Looking back, she could recognize them now, but was that because she was more mature and knew the truth or because she'd stuck her head in the sand back then, not wanting to end things? For too long, she'd felt stupid and inept when it came to men. But Alayna had gone through the ultimate betrayal with her previous boyfriend—who'd fooled even his own family—not to mention the FBI agent who'd supposedly been tasked with protecting her.

Surely if Alayna could get past all of that, Jill could as well.

"You look deep in thought," Alayna said.

"How did you do it—trust someone again, I mean?"

Alayna blew out a breath. "I'm not sure I can explain it. I didn't want to. Was scared to death, actually. But no matter how hard I tried to pull away from Luke, I just couldn't. Of course, I worried that the situation had heightened all my feelings, and I thought when it was over, we'd both wonder what the heck we'd been thinking."

"But obviously, that wasn't the case."

"Not even for a second. Every day, I find more reasons to love Luke. More things to be thankful for."

She locked eyes with Jill. "You think you can't have this. That your situation means you're better off alone, but you're wrong. You can and *will* have this. You've just got to trust yourself. When you meet your person, you'll know. Because no matter how hard you try not to think of them or imagine a future with them, you can't stop. I have a feeling that's troubling you more than your stalker or your ankle."

Jill sighed. "I was never good at hiding things from you."

"Pete is a good man. As good a man as Luke. You have the advantage there because I can vouch for him. You're not coming in cold. And based on the way I saw him looking at you this afternoon when Luke came over to meet you, he's definitely feeling it too. You can have this, Jill. You just have to let down your wall. Or just give him the go-ahead. He's military. He can scale it."

Jill smiled. "I'll bet he can."

"Stop thinking about the logistics or the stalker, your house back in Oregon, your work...everything. All of that can be worked out. If I can have a do-over, then so can you."

"A do-over," Jill repeated. "That sounds lovely."

———

DINNER RAN two hours and Jill couldn't remember the last time she'd eaten so much at one sitting. Alayna had ordered so many different items, and Jill hadn't been able to resist tasting them all. She was glad Alayna had lent her clothes with stretchy fabric, because she felt as if she was testing its quality. And Luke had three big containers of leftovers to appreciate for breakfast and probably lunch as well.

They'd just stepped outside when Jill heard a familiar voice call her name. She turned around and saw Isaac on the sidewalk, standing next to a tall pleasant-looking woman with short, dark brown hair.

"Hi, Isaac," Jill said as he stepped toward them. "You remember Alayna."

"Of course," he said, and extended his hand. "This is Myra, my wife. Myra, this is Jill and Alayna. I went to high school with them."

"Oh! That's nice," Myra said, giving them both curious looks. "I figured with the crutches you were just another poor soul he was taking care of."

"Well, he's doing that as well," Jill said. "I'm here visiting and wasn't planning on messing up my ankle. But a friend got me in to see Isaac today and I think I'm on the mend. Your husband is the reason I passed calculus. He was a great tutor."

Myra nodded. "He pitches in when he has the time with some of my kids. I'm a social worker. Many of them have challenges with trying to get a good education given their home life, and that education is likely the only thing that's going to get them a better future."

"That has to be a frustrating job," Alayna said.

"It definitely can be," Myra agreed. "But it's also rewarding. You need a calling for it, though. Otherwise, the negativity would overwhelm you."

"I can see that," Alayna said.

"We were just headed to Bobby's Coffee Shop for a latte," Isaac said. "Would you like to join us?"

"Bobby's is still around?" Jill asked. "How cool. That was always the hangout when we were in school."

"That's because we didn't have a Starbucks yet," Isaac said. "The kids have shifted allegiance, but that's fine with us old fogies. We get Bobby's to ourselves, and the coffee is better anyway."

Alayna looked at Jill, obviously letting her make the call. Jill was tempted by the latte, which, if memory served, was stellar, but she was also getting tired. But thirty minutes wouldn't make a difference one way or another.

"Why not," Jill said. "I've been good about staying off my foot all afternoon. It won't hurt to sit in a coffee shop for a bit."

"And we'll prop it up and ice it again when we get home," Alayna said. "We'll meet you there."

Isaac gave them a nod as the valet pulled up in a new BMW sedan. Isaac opened the door for his wife, then gave them a wave as he climbed in and drove off.

"Nice ride," Jill said. "I'm so glad he's doing so well."

Alayna nodded. "Me too. I haven't run into him since I've been back, so I didn't even know he was a doctor here until you told me. Bea is woefully lacking in keeping me up to date on mainland gossip, or I could have avoided that whole scene with Poppy."

"For someone who never runs out of things to say, she really is tight-lipped over the good stuff."

They made the short drive to the coffee shop and headed inside where Isaac had already secured them a table in front of the big windows. Jill couldn't help feeling exposed when she sat but couldn't think of a viable reason to suggest another table without it sounding strange. Isaac returned with a tray of coffee and kicked off the chat.

"So your last name is different, Jill. Is there a Mr. Smith back home?"

"No. It didn't work out," Jill said, figuring a lie closest to the truth would be the easiest route. "I've thought about changing it back but never get around to it."

"I'm sorry to hear that," he said. "Myra and I are coming up on our three-year anniversary. I have to admit that I met her as a patient, but I promise I didn't ask her out until she was healed."

Myra smiled and shook her head. "You mean *I* didn't ask *you* out until I was healed. I figured he'd say no until then. He wears his sense of propriety like a shirt. I wish more people did."

"Isn't that the truth," Alayna said.

Myra gave her a curious look. "You're Alayna Scott, right? The chef?"

"That's me. I'm sure there's nothing I can tell you about myself that you haven't already read about online or seen on the news."

Myra frowned. "It was all quite horrible. There are so many evil people in the world. I see too much of it with what I do. If you know someone's childhood, it often explains why they become certain types of people as adults, but that's no consolation to victims."

"So you think evil is made, not born?" Jill asked.

"I think it's both," Myra said. "I think some are born with crossed wiring and others are so traumatized during development that the wiring gets damaged. In my experience, the latter are easier to spot. They have less control because their only goal was survival for so long. It's the ones born with bad wiring that quickly learn to mask their true feelings. Those are the most dangerous ones."

"I can attest to that," Alayna said. "My ex had everyone fooled—his parents, best friend, coworkers, investors, me—I still can't believe just how good he was at living a lie."

Myra shrugged. "I don't know that it is a lie. I think it's possible for them to have two different lives and be true to both. A lack of conscience makes things easier for them."

"That's a serious ability to compartmentalize," Jill said.

Myra nodded. "It's amazing what the mind can accomplish when it's not limited by ethics and morals. But enough negative talk. Alayna, is the new restaurant close to opening?"

"I hope to be open soon," Alayna said, crossing her fingers.

"I can't wait to try it," Myra said. "Will you still be here for the grand opening, Jill?"

"Oh, I'm not sure. I work remote, so my plans can be more flexible than most people's, but I'm still needed in person from time to time."

"Well, what do we have here? Keeping some late office hours for your patients, aren't you, Doc?"

Jill held in a sigh as she looked over and saw Drew Alderman headed their way. If being on Tempest Island meant she kept running into him, she might have to pull up stakes and leave. The stalker was starting to look like a better option. Isaac frowned as Drew approached the table, and Alayna outright scowled. Myra had apparently never had the pleasure but had clued in on the rest of the group's aggravation.

"My personal life is just that, Mr. Alderman," Isaac said. "If you need medical advice, then please call my office and make an appointment."

Drew grinned and rolled his shoulder. "Good as new, see? I've got a 9:00 a.m. tee time tomorrow."

Based on the way Isaac's jaw flexed, Jill assumed golfing so soon after his injury wasn't what Isaac advised, but she was glad he just gave Drew a nod and didn't say anything. If Drew wanted to make his shoulder worse, then let him. There was no point in arguing with him and especially not when Isaac was off from work.

"So Jill, I've got some free time tomorrow night. How about I show you my new car and all my other moves."

He gave her a smile and a wink that made her stomach roll and had her wanting to clock him at the same time.

"I can take you someplace fancier than this old coffee shop," he continued. "If it's all right with your warden, Alayna."

All of the aggravation and stress Jill felt, from Drew pressuring her in high school and subsequently causing her problems with others, to the abusive Trevor, then being stalked, instantly fused together and she felt something course through her that she'd never felt before.

Done.

She looked up at his smug face, and all the anger over the way men had tried to control and manipulate her from her father until now bubbled over. And for the first time in her life, she didn't stop herself from saying exactly what she thought.

"Drew, I'm not interested," she said. "Not tonight or tomorrow or ten years from now. Contrary to what you'd like to believe, I didn't date you in high school because I didn't like you then, and I see no evidence that you've changed. If anything, you're a bigger ass now. I want you to leave me alone."

His eyes widened and his jaw dropped, and for a moment, it was clear he had no idea what to say. Then a rush of red covered his face, and he gave her a murderous look.

"You'll regret that."

He whirled around and stalked out of the shop, slamming the door behind him as he went. Jill looked at Isaac, Myra, and Alayna, who were staring at her, almost as shocked as Drew had been, and felt a rush of regret.

"I'm sorry, Isaac...Myra," she said. "I've made a scene and probably cost you a patient."

"God, I hope so," Isaac said. "That would be the best favor anyone's ever done for me."

The statement was so unlike the kind, quiet boy she'd known that she stared at him for a moment, still unable to process what he'd said. Then it all registered, and she started laughing. Alayna joined in, then Myra and Isaac, and it took them a bit before they'd all caught their breath.

"That was a thing of beauty," Alayna said as she wiped her eyes with a napkin. "I don't think anyone has ever turned him down, much less like that."

Myra nodded. "It was obvious that he had it coming. Good for you, Jill."

Now Jill felt a bit of embarrassment creep in. "I don't know what came over me." She gave Myra an apologetic look. "I'm usually the person who says nothing and walks away."

"Some people don't respond to polite, and that seems to be getting worse," Myra said. "I've never met the man, but I recognize him from business ads and I've heard stories. None of them flattering. My guess is your response was the only way to rid yourself of him permanently."

"He was a bully in high school and never grew out of it," Isaac said. "He made me and my friends miserable with his taunting and far too many women uncomfortable with his persistent advances. I wasn't pleased to see him in my exam room today, but I had no basis for denying him service. I suppose now that he's threatened another patient, I do."

"Surely he won't be back to see you again after that," Myra said.

"It wouldn't surprise me," Alayna said. "Drew never could stand not getting his way."

Myra flashed a look of concern at Jill. "Do you think he'll attempt to cause you problems? Should you talk to the police about that threat?"

Jill shook her head. If only Myra knew just how insignificant Drew was in her current list of issues. "The worst thing he'll do is run his mouth, which is exactly what he did in high school."

"Are you sure?" Myra didn't look convinced. "He looked really angry."

"Don't worry," Alayna said. "Jill is staying with me and there are two very qualified sailors looking out for her. Drew wouldn't make it past the driveway if he attempted anything."

Myra raised her eyebrows. "Two sailors?"

"My boyfriend Luke and his best friend Pete," Alayna explained. "Luke was a SEAL and trains them now, and Pete is a Navy doctor. He's the one who convinced Jill to get an X-ray."

"Well, I know as capable, contemporary women we don't *need* to be taken care of, but I'm sure you appreciate having people who will do so, especially if Luke's friend is as handsome as he is." Myra gave Alayna a smile. "I saw him on that interview the two of you did with the local channel."

Jill felt a blush creep up her neck. "They are both attractive men, and nice. I'm fortunate to have such good friends."

Myra nodded. "Our wealth as humans is not our bank accounts but the people who love us."

"I agree," Alayna said. "But I think I need to get this asset home and get that foot propped up. Doctor's orders."

Isaac smiled. "Yes, that's correct. I'm glad it's already improving. You're walking much better now than this morning. I'm leaving for a conference tomorrow morning—a last-minute speaking request—but if you have any questions, Dr. Medford can help you. He's the other orthopedist in the practice."

"I think I'm on the road to recovery," Jill said, "but I really appreciate you working me into your schedule today. And thanks so much for the coffee. It was great catching up with you and meeting you, Myra."

"And taking out old trash," Alayna said, and they all laughed.

Jill nodded. "And that too."

They all headed out and Alayna looked over at Jill as she backed out of the parking lot. "You were incredible. Good Lord, it's like we've both been channeling Aunt Bea this week."

Jill laughed. "That's not necessarily a bad thing—not when it comes to Drew or Poppy."

"I guess not. But let's get you home before anyone else catches sight of you. I was hoping for a nice, quiet dinner so you could relax after everything that's going on, and here I walked you right into another confrontation."

"That wasn't you. That was all about small people who've never matured and never will. And dinner was great—not nearly as good as what you cook, though."

Alayna grinned. "That's what I was hoping you'd say."

CHAPTER NINETEEN

JILL'S CELL PHONE AWAKENED HER, AND SHE JERKED upright, a momentary wave of panic coursing through her when she didn't recognize her surroundings. Then she remembered she was at Alayna's cottage and reached for her phone, hoping it hadn't awakened Alayna as her watch was only showing 5:00 a.m.

Her back tightened when she saw Detective Ward's name in the display and she hurried to answer. It was only 3:00 a.m. in Oregon so if Ward was calling her now, something had happened. She answered in a rush.

"Did you find Trevor?"

"No. But we're close. We have him on a gas station camera three hours ago outside of Charleston."

"Charleston? He saw the alerts in Norfolk and left."

"It looks that way. I've already talked to law enforcement in Kings Bay, assuming he'll make a stop there, but I have to assume that he's headed your way. There are several options in Florida, so there's no way to guess how soon Tempest Island will be on his radar, but I think you need to consider relocating now, while you have time to get clear of the island before he arrives."

"No."

There was dead silence on the other end of the line for several seconds, then Detective Ward repeated her one-word answer.

"No?"

"I'm done running. This will never end until he's locked up or dead. And running and hiding out is no life. I've only been at it for a handful of days, and I'm already stressed beyond belief and miserable. I have people here who'll look out for me. Call in backup if you can, but this is where it all ends...one way or another."

"I don't like it, especially not with you injured."

"My ankle is improving quickly, and we know for sure nothing major is wrong. I have a gun and a location that's difficult to access. I'll head back to the lighthouse this morning and have Alayna spread the word that I had to cut my visit short and went home."

Ward blew out a breath. "It might work...if word spreads well enough."

"It will. Bea will help. All she has to do is mention it in front of the right people in her bookstore and everyone will be talking. Everything to do with Alayna has been a hot topic lately. Even my visit will be considered news."

"Remind me never to move back to a small town."

"Pros and cons, for sure."

"Okay, I'm going to notify the local PD around every Naval base in Florida. I'm headed to Kings Bay now to meet with the cops there and try to intercept him. We're going to get him."

"I believe you will."

"I'll call as soon as I have an update. Text me when you are back at the lighthouse."

Jill had just disconnected when she heard a tap on the bedroom door.

"Is everything okay?" Alayna asked as she poked her head in. "I heard talking."

Jill filled her in on Ward's status update and what she planned on doing.

"I don't like you out there alone, especially injured," Alayna said. "Let me go with you."

"Then our story wouldn't look legit. Locals already know someone was staying in the lighthouse. If someone catches sight of you out there, then they'll put two and two together. If you and Bea put out word that I've gone back home, then Trevor might watch long enough to determine that I'm not at your homes, but I don't see him taking it beyond that."

Alayna frowned. "I don't care if he comes after me thinking he's going to get information. I would especially love for him to approach me when Luke was around. He wouldn't fare any better with Aunt Bea."

"No. He wouldn't, but after thinking on it, I just don't think he'd take that risk. He would assume that even if I had no intention of going home when I left, I wouldn't tell you about it. And since it seems like he knows about the alerts, he'll also assume cops are watching you guys just like they did Wanda."

"You're probably right," Alayna said, but she still didn't look thrilled. "Your car is a problem, though. If he sees it in Bea's garage, then he'll know we're lying, and we have to assume he'll be watching. I'll have Luke take it to the base and park it in a restricted area."

"That would be perfect." Jill reached over and took her friend's hand. "I have to do this, or I'll never get a normal life. And there's no better place to make my stand than here. Besides, Ward is hot on Trevor's tail. There's a really good chance he'll catch him in Kings Bay, and the worst thing that will happen to me is I'll have locked myself away in the lighthouse for a few days. It's hardly a punishment."

Alayna gave her a small smile. "I get it. I don't like it, but I get it."

"I know you do. I want what you have, Alayna—the future wide open for whatever you want to pursue. Until coming here, I didn't realize how much I've let my past prevent me from living. I've closed myself off and I've lost all those years. I don't want to lose any more."

"I know. I don't want you to either."

"I need to get back out to the lighthouse this morning, before everyone is out and about and someone can spot me."

Alayna nodded. "I'll call Aunt Bea. But at least let me fix you pancakes before you go."

Jill perked up. "Do you have blueberries?"

"I just might."

———

AT BARELY 6:00 a.m. Jill carefully climbed into Bea's boat once again. Alayna had accosted Luke as he drove in from training and he was already on his way back to the base with Jill's car. Now her friend stood on the dock, biting her lower lip. She knew Alayna wanted to come with her, and she understood. If the situation were reversed, she'd feel the same way. But Alayna also knew the best way to keep Jill safe was for her to be alone. When Trevor reached Tempest Island, Alayna and Bea would be the first people he sought out.

She looked up at Alayna before she ducked into the cabin. "Thank you for everything."

"Call me," Alayna said. "Call me every hour if you need to.

Every half hour. I don't care. I'm not going to relax until this is over."

"That makes two of us. But I need you and Bea to go about your normal business. That's the only way Trevor will believe I left."

"At least I was already a nervous wreck over the restaurant," Alayna said. "That means I don't have to make an effort to look happy and carefree."

Jill laughed. "Yes. No one would expect a person doing construction to open a business to be Pollyanna. It's a good cover."

"Take care of yourself and call if you need anything. We can get it arranged."

"I've got this," Bea said. "Now, you get out of here and go pick up Luke before someone lays eyes on you at the dock. I'm going to stop off at Horseshoe Cove and catch some redfish before I head back in to get ready for work. Then I'll have my cover for anyone who saw me out in the boat this early."

Alayna gave Jill one last wave and hurried off to her car. Jill ducked into the cabin and closed the door behind her as Bea fired up the boat and pulled away from the dock. She could feel the shift between the calm waters of the Sound and the choppy waves of the Gulf as soon as the boat entered them. Bea called out to her and she stepped out of the cabin and onto the deck.

It was a beautiful morning. The sun was coming up bright and the water sparkled like diamonds. Birds flew overhead and dipped down, coming up with their breakfast before heading back for a place to perch and enjoy their meal. A fairly strong breeze from the south was the culprit creating the choppy water. Bea pointed out into the Gulf, frowning.

"Got a storm rolling in today," she said. "Looks like a big one on radar. There's a chance you could lose power."

"They don't call it Tempest Island for nothing," Jill said. "I remember the storms."

"Stuff is good in the refrigerator for a while, but if it's out for a day or better, you could get a bit hot in there, so crank the AC down as soon as you get inside to hedge your bets. There's flashlights and an LED lamp in the utility room closet. If it stays out too long, we'll figure out a way to get you out of here and into a hotel a town or two over. I still wish you would have gone for that option."

"Too many people and too easy for him to access. You know this is the best place for me."

"I can know it and still not be thrilled about it."

Bea guided the boat to the dock and helped Jill out. Between the anti-inflammatories, all the rest, and the walking boot, her mobility had vastly improved from the day before. She still used the crutches for balance and to prevent her from putting all of her weight on her ankle, but it barely stung as she walked. The sound of a motor carried across the water and Bea jerked her head up to look into the distance.

"Fishermen are headed out," she said. "Are you all right getting inside by yourself? I don't want them to spot my boat over here if we can help it."

Jill hefted her bag onto her shoulder. "I'm fine. My ankle is much better and it's a short, level walk. You go."

Bea didn't look happy about hurrying off, but they both knew it was the smartest thing to do. She backed away from the dock and Jill headed for the lighthouse. She quickly let herself in, then peeked out the front window and spotted Bea's boat headed for a known fishing reef spot not far away. She'd already stuck her rod in the holder on the back of her boat and waved at a fisherman as they crossed paths. Jill let out a breath of relief. Bea's plan had worked. She was safely tucked away in the lighthouse and no one was the wiser.

She headed to the south windows and peered out over the Gulf. The storm was building on the horizon and Bea was right —it looked like a big one. Well, she'd been through plenty of Gulf storms in her lifetime, and the lighthouse had been standing for a lot of decades. It wasn't likely to crumble today. She headed for the thermostat and cranked the AC down, then grabbed a blanket off the couch bed and plopped down on the recliner.

She was still full from breakfast and wasn't thirsty. Her laptop was right there in her bag and she needed to do some work, but what she really wanted to do was take a nap. Sleep had been hit-or-miss the night before and she'd awakened earlier than she preferred. Besides, she had all day to work, and once the storm rolled in, she probably wouldn't be able to sleep.

Right now, she felt safe. Even if he knew exactly where to find her, there was no way Trevor could have made it to Tempest Island yet. Now she could sleep without worry, and that's exactly what she needed to do.

Because she had no idea what the night might bring.

CHAPTER TWENTY

PETE STARED AT BEA, ATTEMPTING TO WRAP HIS MIND around what she'd just told him. Because he was certain that she hadn't said Jill had gone back to the lighthouse. Alone. He hadn't talked to Jill since he'd taken Luke over to meet her the day before. Every minute since he'd left, he wondered how she was doing, but calling, or worse, showing up at Alayna's cottage, seemed intrusive. Jill had his phone number and knew how to reach him. But he'd finally given up staring at his cell phone and headed to the bookstore. Asking Bea for an update seemed like a good compromise and didn't put Jill in the position of having to talk to him if she didn't feel like it.

"Don't give me that look," Bea said. "If you'd take half a second to get your heart out of the equation and think with your head, you'd know it was the right call. We don't have to like it, but we can't argue with her logic. And it's Jill's decision to make."

Pete felt the flush on his neck. "I *am* thinking with my head. She's injured and being stalked. What part of that suggests she's better off alone and isolated?"

Bea gave him a sympathetic look and placed one hand on

his arm and squeezed. "The part where her stalker will never find her there. I know you care about her. So do Alayna and I. But this is the smartest play. Alayna and I will spread the word that Jill has gone back home, and Luke moved her car to a secure area on the base. Hopefully, the police will catch Trevor before he even makes it here, but if not, he'll have no reason to stick around. When he takes a look in on Alayna and I, he's not going to see us doing anything out of the ordinary. He's certainly not going to see any sign of Jill."

Pete ran one hand over his head and blew out a breath. Yeah, it made sense, but it still made his chest clench. Which only proved Bea's point, of course. His emotions were overriding his brain.

"Okay," he said. "But I'm going to stick around the island today. If anything happens, you call me and I can be at the dock in minutes."

Bea nodded. "I will admit that does make me feel better. I know Luke is only a phone call away but they've been doing all those night trainings, so I'm never sure if he's gotten any sleep. But what about your work schedule? I thought you were on the early shift?"

"I'm off the next three days. We're trying a new four-three rotation."

"Seems like that would be a good quality of life move. But not if you're going to hang out on the island worrying all day. If you're going to stick around, at least take your board down to the beach. You'll still be close enough to help if you're needed."

"Yeah, okay, that sounds like a good idea." The combination of exercise and relaxation might be just what he needed.

"You're a good man, Pete. I hope when all this is over, Jill can see that."

He shrugged, a little embarrassed that his feelings were so

readily apparent. "I just want her safe. What she does after that is her call."

"Uh-huh. Well, you enjoy the beach. Looks like good surf today with that storm brewing offshore. Better get your waves in early before it hits."

"I will. Thanks, Bea."

"I'm the one who should be thanking you."

He nodded and headed out of the store, trying to convince himself that spending the morning surfing was going to calm his racing mind. But he knew it wouldn't. Right now, the only thing that would make him feel better was to have eyes on Jill, but clearly, that wasn't what she wanted. And this was all about her. He needed to deal with his own feelings and not try to make her responsible for them. If Jill needed him, she knew how to contact him, and he'd made it perfectly clear that he was happy to be contacted.

Hadn't he?

He shook his head as he directed his Jeep to Luke's cottage to pick up his board. That line of questioning was self-serving, and he needed to push it away. As soon as he hit the water, he'd have to focus on the ride or he wouldn't be upright for long. Maybe that's what he needed. Something that forced his thoughts into another direction.

Because right now, the only thing he was certain about was that he wasn't going to accomplish it on his own.

———

JILL STARED out at the Gulf and sighed. She'd managed to get a solid four hours of sleep, then spent some time watching television. Then she'd fixed a late lunch and eaten it at the counter while reading a book on her iPad, before shifting back to her recliner and ultimately finishing the book. And still, it was only late afternoon.

She'd briefly considered sitting outside for a bit before the storm approaching hit, but so many boats were still circling around that she didn't want to take the risk. All it took was someone who knew her to spot her, and Alayna's and Bea's claims that she'd returned home would be outed as lies, and that would have tongues wagging even more. As long as people believed she'd gone home, she wouldn't even cross their minds after a day or two.

Except perhaps Drew.

She shook her head as she recounted the scene at the coffeehouse the night before. What in the world had gotten into her? Maybe Alayna was right and they were both channeling Bea. But it was more likely that a tense situation had pushed her to the point she'd needed to be at all along—one where she didn't take crap from people, especially from men like Drew. It was high time she stopped letting bad men dictate her life. Which was the whole point of making her stand with Trevor now. The situation had already gone on for far too long.

And don't forget Pete.

She sighed again. As much as she'd like to claim that her decision to take her life back had nothing to do with her attraction to the good doctor, she'd be lying to herself. Regardless of the high stakes involved with catching Trevor and getting him out of her life for good, in the back of her mind, she was already thinking about what a future would look like if she moved to Tempest Island and did a reboot on everything.

If she took that next step with Pete.

Part of her worried that it would be jumping into things too soon—that the heightened emotional state because of what she was going through had convinced her that she had feelings that weren't real or not as strong as she believed. Alayna had moved into a relationship with Luke during a period of high trauma, but after seeing them together the day before, it was clear that they were as strong a couple as Jill had ever seen. It was as if they'd been special-ordered for each other.

Of course, that didn't mean Pete had been special-ordered for her, but she was having a hard time coming up with an image of someone who would be a better fit. He was everything she'd ever wanted but hadn't found. He was the kind of man she wrote as the hero in her books, but even better because he was real. He was strong and intelligent and incredibly kind. And the way her body tingled with even the slightest bit of his touch made her certain that they would burn as hot as jet fuel in bed.

You should call him.

The thought had only crept into her mind a hundred times since he'd left Alayna's cottage yesterday. But she had no reason to contact him. Alayna had promised that she and Bea would keep Luke and Pete in the loop on everything. Granted, Alayna had encouraged her to contact Pete herself, but when Jill had hesitated, her friend had jumped right in with the offer to do it for her.

And Jill, being a coward, had agreed.

But that didn't mean she couldn't also call him herself. Even just a chat would be nice. It was a frustrating and losing proposition, trying to make the hours go by more quickly. She'd briefly tried working, but had shoved her laptop back on the table after an hour of rewriting the same paragraph, only to delete the entire thing. And she was bored with television and reading. Nothing held her interest long enough to get her mind off wondering whether Detective Ward was closing in on Trevor.

She'd spent some time talking to Alayna earlier, but she couldn't keep her friend on the phone all day. Besides, Alayna had restaurant business to take care of if she was going to open on time. She picked up her phone, still trying to talk herself out of calling Pete, when it signaled an incoming call from Alayna. Given that she'd just talked to her friend an hour ago, she was worried about a call so soon.

"Alayna? Is everything all right?"

"No! I was at the restaurant going over things with my contractor and when I went to leave, I found a card on my windshield."

Jill sucked in a breath. "Not..."

"It looks like the ones you've been getting. I'm going to switch to FaceTime."

Jill waited for the signal and watched as her friend's worried face came into view. She was still sitting in her car and Jill could see the back of the bookstore building behind her. Alayna held up the envelope and Jill gasped.

"He's here," she said.

"I touched it already, obviously. I didn't know what it was because it was facedown, and I didn't see the writing on the front. I haven't opened it because I thought it would make the cops mad. What do I do?"

"Open it."

"Are you sure?"

"He's never left any evidence on the envelopes before, so it's highly unlikely he did now. I want to know what it says."

"Okay, I'm going to switch the phone around and prop it up here."

Jill watched as Alayna opened the envelope and slid out the card—the card that she'd seen many times before. Slowly, her friend opened the card and then gasped. Jill watched as she moved the card closer to the phone and understood Alayna's reaction.

Soon you'll be mine forever.

"Oh my God, Jill," Alayna said. "You have to leave. We have to get you away from Tempest Island."

"No! The card could be a ruse to flush me out of my hiding place. He'll be watching you and Bea to see if you come for me."

"Oh my God! What if he's watching me now?"

"That's very possible. Are there people around you?"

"Yes. My contractor is talking to two of his subs in the parking lot right across from me."

"Then start your car and get out of there before they leave."

"And do what? I can't just sit in public twenty-four hours a day, waiting for that detective to catch this psycho. He's made it all the way across the country without them putting hands on him."

"Take the card to the sheriff. You and Bea are spreading the word that I left. If he's watching and follows you, it will be clear that I'm not around. I'll call Detective Ward."

"Okay. That all makes sense. Good God, how are you so calm when I'm about to jump out of my skin?"

"I think it might be easier to be the target than to watch someone else be the target."

Alayna sighed. "Truer words."

"I'm so sorry he left the card for you to find. I didn't want to put you in the middle of this. I didn't want to put anyone in the middle of this."

"*You* didn't put me anywhere. This is all on the stalker. I'm headed out right now to the sheriff's department, so if that asshole is following me, he'll know I'm not leading him to you."

"Are there any cameras behind the bookstore?"

"No. But he's got a set of brass ones if he just strolled up and left that card in broad daylight."

"He's not brave. He's disturbed, which is worse."

"I'll call Bea on my way and get her to ask around and see if anyone else has spotted him. We're going to find him, Jill. He's not going to have a chance at even five minutes with you, much less forever."

"No, he's not."

"Call Ward. I'll call you back after I talk to the sheriff. And be careful. If you see or feel anything odd, call. Anything at all. Promise me."

The combined look of fear and desperation in her friend's expression made Jill's heart clench. "I promise," she said.

Jill disconnected, her hands shaking, and pressed Ward's name on her speed dial. But it went directly to voice mail. She said a silent prayer that the reason he couldn't answer was because he was apprehending Trevor, then left a message for him to call her. That it was urgent.

She clutched the phone, staring out at the storm that was quickly approaching. If she wanted to leave, she had to make that decision now, because asking anyone to come out in the storm wouldn't be fair. But she knew that wouldn't be the best call. She wasn't looking forward to riding out the storm on the lighthouse island, but Trevor had no experience with boats unless he'd gotten it after she left, so the storm would also be another deterrent, assuming he even figured out where she was.

Staying put is your best option.

She rose from her chair and hobbled over to the window, happy that her ankle barely ached as she walked, even though she wasn't using the scooter or the crutches. Granted, she'd only walked a handful of steps and was still wearing the boot, but that was still a big difference from the day before. The storm clouds were gathering in the distance, but the wind preceding them was already hitting the small island. Palm fronds and bushes swayed in the wind, occasionally whipping around in circles as strong gusts of crosswinds caught them. It looked as though it was going to be a doozy, as Bea would say.

She pulled her phone out of her pocket and checked the display. If Ward had called, it would have signaled, but her anxiety seemed to grow with every passing minute that he didn't return her call. What was going on? Had they caught Trevor? She prayed that was the case and that soon, she'd hear from Ward. Surely a takedown was in process and that was why he hadn't answered. She couldn't think of any other reason for his phone to be going directly to voice mail.

She stared out the window a bit longer and watched as the boats headed in from the Gulf. Being typical of local fishermen, they'd stayed as long as they dared, but the families who'd been fishing these waters for generations wouldn't risk being caught out in a storm like the one headed their way. Some were so severe they contained tropical storm—strength winds—nothing to be caught in out in a boat. She stood there for several minutes, and when there were no more boats in sight, she went to the front door and stepped outside.

A gust of wind hit her and she put one hand up against the outside wall of the lighthouse to maintain her balance. Her ankle was improved but she still didn't have the stability and strength needed to remain steady in the strong gusts. There was no good reason for her to be out here, risking a fall, but there was something about the magnificence of a storm sweeping across the Gulf that never failed to make her awestruck. It was as if the strength of the sea and the air had met in a clash of Titans, and it was breathtaking to watch as the dark clouds rolled toward the island.

In a matter of seconds, the light she'd been previously bathed in faded as if someone had turned a dimmer switch by half. She crossed her arms as a shiver ran through her, even though she wasn't the least bit cold.

Someone walking on your grave. That was the saying, right?

She gave the swirling sky one last glance before heading inside to double-check her gun. She wasn't ready for the grave just yet.

———

ALAYNA TAPPED her fingers on the armrest of the chair in Sheriff Maybank's office, frustrated and annoyed as he hung up his phone for the third time since she'd shown him the card and he'd tried to contact Detective Ward.

"It's still going directly to voice mail," he said. "That means he's in a situation where he can't afford for his phone to ring."

"That situation better be arresting Trevor."

"Given that he's across the country from his jurisdiction and can't be working another case, we have to assume that's the reason. I'm sure we'll hear from him as soon as he's able to pick up his messages. Did you check with Jill again?"

Alayna nodded. "Nothing on her end either."

"I know it's pointless to tell you this, but you shouldn't stress about the situation. Jill is in the best place possible. This Trevor doesn't know about the lighthouse, or he wouldn't have put that note on your car. He only knows about you and Bea, and neither of you are going to lead him to Jill."

"I know, but I can't help it."

He nodded. "I get it. But what I need you to do is watch *your* back since you're the one who's visible. And I think it's a good idea if you and Bea stick together until we hear from

Detective Ward. Trevor is no match for Luke, so maybe Bea could bunk with you for a bit?"

"Luke's on night trainings right now."

"Okay, then maybe you could stay at Bea's house tonight. It's not isolated like the cottage, and it would be harder for Trevor to navigate her neighborhood unnoticed."

"I can do that."

He nodded. "I'll put a deputy in an unmarked on her house as soon as you two are in residence. I have another who'll be patrolling the island and will do sweeps by the cottage, in case Trevor decides to head there."

"You're welcome to put someone inside the cottage. I want this guy caught."

Sheriff Maybank scrunched his brow. "This is a small force. and I've only got the two men to spare, but if you're okay with it, I can set up in your cottage myself."

"That would be a relief, actually. And I have leftovers from restaurant menu testing in my refrigerator. Help yourself to anything."

He smiled. "I was really hoping you'd say that. We're going to get this guy, Alayna."

She nodded but couldn't help feeling that everything was about to unravel.

Wipeout

"Thousands have lived without love, not one without the water." –
W.H. Auden

CHAPTER TWENTY-ONE

THE EYE OF THE STORM HIT THE ISLAND LIKE AN OPENING scene in a thriller. The dark clouds rolled in and completely blocked what was left of the sun from the sky. In an instant, the light vanished as if God had turned the dimmer switch completely off. An hour had passed since Jill left a message for Detective Ward, and she was starting to panic. What in the world could be keeping him? Had Trevor gotten away? Or worse, had he gotten the best of Ward? Surely her cowardly ex was no match for the detective, but then anyone could be ambushed.

She had worked herself up so much that when her phone rang, she jumped and lost her balance, barely regaining her footing by clutching the window frame where she'd been staring out at the storm. She yanked her phone from her pocket and relief swept through her when she saw Ward's number in the display.

"Did you catch him?" she answered.

"In a manner of speaking," Ward said. "He stopped for gas and beer at a Speed Track this afternoon and got into an argument with the clerk over the price of the beer. A truck driver broke it up and told him to pay the man and get out. Trevor waited for the truck driver outside and clocked him with the six-pack he'd just bought. It was a fatal mistake."

"Fatal?"

"That truck driver must be made of steel because he didn't even flinch. He turned around with a backfist and knocked Trevor into the wall. He cracked his head on the brick and was probably done with before he hit the ground. It's over, Jill."

Jill's mind raced. Trevor was dead. She supposed she should feel bad, but she couldn't quite work herself up to it. And something else was bothering her. Something she couldn't quite put her finger on. She put Ward's words on repeat, trying to figure out why that feeling of dread hadn't fled with Ward's declaration that Trevor could never bother her again.

And then it hit her. *Speed Track.*

"You said he got into a fight at a Speed Track, but those aren't in Florida."

"No. It was just outside of Savannah."

"Oh my God." Jill clutched the phone as a wave of dizziness passed over her. She staggered to the chair and dropped into it, her head pounding.

"Jill? Are you still there? What's wrong?"

She drew in a long breath and slowly blew it out. "You didn't get my message, did you?"

"I saw the message and the missed calls but haven't listened yet. I wanted to call you straightaway with the news. What's wrong?"

"It's not over."

———

PETE TUCKED his board under his arm and headed for his Jeep. He'd gotten in a couple hours of good rides and had sat on the beach and watched the storm roll in, but now it was time to pack up and get out of the potential lightning zone. Every year, he saw at least one soldier who'd been struck by lightning or was in or near water when it hit and suffered residual damage, so his observance of the storm definitely had an expiration time. When he saw the first lightning strike offshore, that was his cue.

He checked the time and realized it was barely 7:30 p.m. even though it looked as though it was well past 9:00. The bookstore and the ice cream shop would be closed by now, as well as the surf shop, but the pizza place and a couple other small eateries would remain open until 9:00. He could duck into one of those for dinner.

And then what?

Was he going to sleep in his Jeep tonight, just in case Jill needed him? He briefly considered checking with the motel to see if he could get a room, but he already knew it would be fully booked. It was high season and to be expected. Luke was training tonight, so he couldn't hang out at his house as an excuse to stick around. He knew his buddy would be happy to let him stay at his place, but Pete felt strange asking. It seemed too much like overkill given that the situation appeared to be under control.

After he'd dropped his board back at Luke's cottage, he climbed into his Jeep and sat there, still trying to decide. Maybe he should call Jill and check on her, especially since the storm looked like a big one. Granted, she'd lived on the island before and knew how storms were, but now she was isolated farther offshore and injured. Add all those variables to being stalked, and her anxiety had to be through the roof. His was, and he wasn't even the target.

She has your number.

He blew out a breath. And that was the bottom line, wasn't

it? If Jill wanted to speak to him, she could. Under normal circumstances, the fact that he hadn't heard from her would lead him to believe that she had no interest, but he simply didn't think that was the case. He hadn't imagined the heat between them. But he also knew that after what had happened to her friend in Portland, Jill was determined to keep the people she cared about out of the line of fire.

He'd spoken to Alayna that morning, after he'd talked to Bea, and although she'd agreed with her aunt that the light-house was the best place for Jill, he could tell she wasn't any happier than he was. Given what Alayna had just gone through, he imagined her stomach was in knots as well. Maybe he should give Alayna a call. See if she'd talked to Jill and could ease his mind. As he pulled his phone from his pocket, it signaled an incoming call from Alayna. He rushed to answer, hoping she had good news.

"Did they catch him?" he asked.

"Yes, but it doesn't matter, and I'm terrified, which is why I'm calling you."

He clutched the phone. "What happened?"

"Detective Ward caught up with Trevor outside of Savannah, where he was killed in a fight. He never made it here. But I found a card from Jill's stalker on my car this afternoon. Trevor wasn't the stalker. Or he wasn't the *only* stalker."

Shock coursed through him, and he cursed. Since Jill had told him about Trevor, his biggest fear was that the man would find her. His second biggest fear was that he would turn out not to be the stalker, and now it was staring him right in the face.

"Does Jill know?" he asked.

"Of course. She called me after she talked to Ward. I was still with the sheriff because I'd brought him the card, so we both talked to her."

"Where are you now?" He knew Luke was working night trainings, and Alayna's cottage was isolated and easily approached from multiple directions.

"I just got to Bea's house," Alayna said. "I'm going to stay here. There's a deputy in a car outside and another patrolling the island, including past my cottage. The sheriff is going to stake it out later tonight."

"Good. What about Jill?"

"She refuses to leave the lighthouse, and she won't let anyone come to her, either. She said he'll be watching Bea's boat and the sheriff and if anyone comes after her, we'd just lead him right to her. Plus, she doesn't want anyone risking going out in the storm because it's so bad out there right now. And as much as I hate it, she's right on both counts."

"There's one boat he won't be watching, and it will be out in the storm anyway." Pete started the Jeep and drove off much faster than the law allowed.

Alayna sucked in a breath. "Luke's training. He never gives me details, of course, but they're going to train in the storm, aren't they? Can he take you with them? I mean, without getting either of you into trouble?"

"I have clearance, if that's what you're asking, and technically, I'm off the next two days, so I'm not abandoning my duties."

"If you could get to her, protect her, that would mean everything. I can't stand the thought of her being out there alone."

Pete checked his watch. Luke wouldn't launch for another thirty minutes, which gave him barely enough time to get back to the base and onto the boat.

"I'm headed to Bea's now to get a key to the lighthouse. Just in case. I think I can make it back to the base before Luke leaves. I'll call Jill when I'm on the boat and tell her when I know for sure I'm coming."

"You can't. When the sheriff and I were talking to her, the call dropped and I haven't been able to connect with her again. The storm has knocked out communication."

Pete cursed again. Bad enough Jill was stranded on a spot of dirt in the middle of the Gulf during a massive storm. Add to it that she had no way to communicate and was injured to boot, and Pete was kicking himself for not forcing his presence on her this morning.

"This isn't your fault," Alayna said, immediately cluing in on the reason for his frustration. "So don't even go thinking you should have done something differently. If you'd headed out there this morning in Bea's boat, he could have followed you."

"But who the hell is he? And how did he find her here so quickly?"

"That's what we were starting to discuss with Jill when we got disconnected. Before Detective Ward locked on Trevor, Jill assumed it was someone who'd been stalking Kate and finally made the connection, but Sheriff Maybank thinks maybe we've been looking at it all wrong—that it wasn't someone stalking Kate but someone stalking Jill. She changed her last name after the situation with Trevor, but if he figured it out, someone else could have as well. Someone from even before Trevor."

Pete's head was spinning trying to keep up with what Alayna was saying, but none of it made sense. "What are you talking about? Who's Kate?"

"Oh crap! I forgot you didn't know, and now I've gone and said something I shouldn't have." She huffed. "You know what? To hell with it. When the cops take this guy down, the whole story is going to come out anyway. Jill is Kate Coleson, the famous thriller author."

Pete's jaw dropped. He'd read all of her books. Had seen her in interviews, but Kate looked nothing like Jill. He frowned. Or did she? The build and height were the same, as were the eye color and facial structure. The big difference was the hair and makeup. Well, she'd fooled him for sure, but it looked like the sheriff was right. She hadn't fooled everyone.

"Did you know?" he asked. "I mean, before Jill came here."

"No. Only Aunt Bea did."

Which explained why Jill had been so reticent to see Alayna. She'd been hiding her entire identity from her old friend.

He blew out a breath. "So the sheriff thinks it was someone she knew as Jill Morgan, but he couldn't find her because she'd changed her name to Smith. Then he recognized her as Kate and has been looking for her that way."

"And I'm afraid she came right to him."

———

JILL TURNED her phone on for the fifth time and saw zero bars again. She tossed the phone on the couch, cursing. Maybe if her stalker found her, she could throw it at him. That was about the only thing it was good for at the moment. Sheriff Maybank had just tossed a new theory out when her phone had gone dead. She'd tried to call them back so many times now, moving to every area of the lighthouse she could access, but with no success. She'd even briefly considered making the climb to the upstairs room, but she knew it wouldn't matter. The signal wouldn't return until the storm had passed.

Calm down.

She drew in a deep breath and slowly blew it out. Then she perched on the arm of the recliner, trying to follow her own advice. But she was still reeling from Detective Ward's revelation and Sheriff Maybank's comment. Clearly, Trevor wasn't the man who'd been hunting her for the past five years, but could the sheriff be right? Was it someone she'd known before —someone from her time on Tempest Island?

That thought sent her pulse back up into the stratosphere. She'd thought she'd be safe coming here, but what if she'd walked right into the lion's den? And who could it be? Jill had dated several boys while she'd lived here, but none of them had been great romances on either side.

Drew!

She sucked in a breath. Surely not. Drew had always made his pursuit of her clear—back then and now. So why would he hide behind mysterious cards?

Because you kept turning him down.

She ran her hands over the top of her head, trying to think. The card had only appeared on Alayna's car after she'd been seen in public. After she'd insulted Drew. Before that, he hadn't known she was there. Jill had always assumed Drew was into himself more than anyone else, but what if she was wrong? What if he'd been obsessed and had recognized her as Kate? But he'd been unable to find her because she'd changed her name after the problems with Trevor?

He was the first person she'd walked right into as soon as she'd gone out in public. Surely Alayna would think of Drew and tell the sheriff. He wouldn't be hard to find like Trevor. And she knew Alayna and Bea had spread the word about her departure. It would have gotten back to him already, and even if it hadn't, he'd be looking for her at Alayna's house, not at the lighthouse. Which made her feel worse because if it had been Drew all along, that put Alayna right in the crosshairs.

Calm down. Detective Ward is on his way. Alayna will tell the sheriff about Drew. They'll have him in custody by the time the storm rolls through and this five-year nightmare will finally be over.

She nodded even though no one was there to see it, but then, this entire mental exercise was about trying to convince herself. And she had. Sort of. All she had to do was sit here and wait for it all to be over. Which was just as well because it wasn't as if she could go anywhere anyway. Even if she wanted to leave and someone was willing to risk the storm to pick her up, she couldn't even call to ask. At least the power was still on.

And in an instant, that changed.

CHAPTER TWENTY-TWO

JILL CURSED AS SHE FUMBLED AROUND ON THE TABLE FOR THE flashlight she'd placed there earlier. Bea had stocked the lighthouse with everything she might need in the event of an outage. There were several flashlights as well as one battery-operated lantern. She'd put that on the kitchen counter, figuring it would cast a glow over everything she needed to access except the bathroom. Bea had said the lantern would run about twelve hours on a fully charged battery, so even if the power didn't come back on that night, she'd have light until sunup.

Of course, if the power wasn't back up the next day, she had no way to recharge it, but she was going to remain positive and believe that by the time her phone had a signal again, her stalker would be in jail. Then it wouldn't matter how long the power was off because she'd be back on Tempest Island and thinking about the redo of her entire life.

She rose, deciding that lighting the lantern was the right call, when she heard noise at the front door. The storm was still raging, so she knew whatever had made the sound was loud, otherwise she wouldn't have heard it. She grabbed her pistol and hurried behind the couch, then crouched down and aimed at the door. If anyone entered, she was in the perfect position to take them out. The seconds ticked by, and her legs started to cramp. A single bead of sweat ran from her forehead into her eye and she quickly brushed it away before clenching the pistol again.

Maybe something had blown against the door. She was just about to stand when she saw the door begin to open. She sucked in a breath and tried to force her shaking hands to steady. Her finger was firm against the trigger, just waiting for the door to open when suddenly, it flew open and banged against the exterior wall of the house. Jill tightened her finger on the trigger, about to squeeze off a round, when she heard a familiar voice.

Pete!

The breath she'd been holding rushed out of her as she put her gun down and grabbed the flashlight, turning it on the entry. Pete struggled with the door, trying to pull it shut against the wind, and finally got it closed and locked. He put one hand up to protect against the light, and she stuck the flashlight in the back couch cushions, facing up, where it cast a dim glow over the room. Relief flooded Pete's face when he caught sight of her, and he rushed over and gathered her in his arms.

Jill clutched him tightly, so overwhelmed that her legs buckled a bit, and he steadied her, pressing his body against hers. She looked up at him and he lowered his mouth to hers, drawing her into a light kiss that deepened, making her legs weak all over again. When he broke off the kiss, he reached up with one hand to brush the hair off her cheek.

"I'm so sorry," he said as he swiped one hand over his head and flung water off. "I've gotten you soaked, but you have no idea how relieved I am to find you here. When I saw the lights go out, I was afraid the stalker had beaten me here."

"A little water is the least of my problems. But I can't believe you came out here in the storm. Is Bea's boat going to be all right out there?"

"I didn't come in Bea's boat. Even with the storm, we were afraid someone would be watching. Luke's team is doing storm training and I hitched a ride with him. So the stalker couldn't have followed, even if he'd known to watch me. Before I used the key, I banged on the door as hard as I could and yelled. I didn't want to scare you."

"I heard a bang but never heard you yelling over the storm."

He nodded. "Alayna called and told me about Trevor, and with the storm and knowing you didn't have any way to contact us, I had to come. I know you didn't want people involved but—"

"I'm glad you came. I'm also glad I didn't shoot you. Again."

"Yeah. Your self-control has been a godsend for me."

"Have there been any updates?"

"Alayna wasn't sure when the call dropped. Did you hear the sheriff's theory before you lost signal?"

She nodded. "He thinks it could be someone I knew when I lived here. That's the last thing I heard."

"Right. So Alayna told him all about Drew Alderman, and the sheriff is going to check him out."

"Thank God. And Alayna and Bea?"

"They're both at Bea's house and a deputy is watching it. Another is patrolling the island. The sheriff is going to stake out Alayna's tonight in case he goes there looking for you, but he's going to try to run down Drew first."

Pete stared at her for a moment, his expression clouded

with indecision, then he gave her an apologetic look. "Alayna also told me about you being Kate. She didn't mean to, but it sort of rushed out when she was explaining about Trevor and the sheriff's theory."

Jill shook her head. "None of that matters. I'm sorry I didn't tell you myself. It's just that I've kept it a secret for so long. Before the stalker, only my parents, Bea, and a few business contacts knew."

"The fewer people who knew, the safer you were. I don't blame you for not telling me or anyone else. Besides, I can hardly take issue with not being told when Alayna didn't know either. It's not like you've known me long or that we have a relationship."

Jill's heart clenched a bit at his words, and she decided to throw caution into the raging storm outside. "That's true, but it's something I'd like to change. If you're interested, I mean. When all of this is over."

His eyes widened. "You're asking if I'm interested in having a relationship with you? Are you kidding me? I've barely thought of anything else since I met you."

Jill felt her heart pounding in her chest. "Really? Me too! I mean, obviously I've had other things occupying my mind, but you were always there. Always making me question my choices before and my options after this is over. But we barely know each other, so I figured... I don't know... It just seems like a big thing to hope for."

Pete raised a hand to her cheek. "When the stalker is locked up, we'll have all the time in the world to get to know each other. The only thing we have to commit to is giving it a try. There's no pressure for anything else."

She smiled at him. "So you're saying I should try you on for size?"

His eyes widened. "I'd be more than okay with that."

Jill stepped closer to him, pressing her body against his. "That's one thing that we don't have to put on hold. And it would solve that wet clothes problem."

He drew her in and lowered his mouth to hers, kissing her with a passion that she'd written about but never experienced. She groaned as he moved his lips from her mouth to her neck, trailing kisses down to her chest. Then in one fluid movement, he swept her off the ground and carried her around to the couch, which was still pulled out into a bed.

Handy, was all she could think before she allowed him to sweep her away.

———

ALAYNA SAT on the edge of the couch, staring at the television, and jumped at least a foot when Bea touched her shoulder.

"Good Lord, girl, you've got to calm down. Here, take my beer. I'll go grab another...and maybe a bottle of Xanax."

Alayna took the beer and downed a huge gulp. "You know you don't have any Xanax. You've never had anxiety problems."

Bea snorted as she walked back into the living room. "I've had plenty of anxiety. I raised you, didn't I? But not so much as I'd sit in a trance staring at a TV that's not even on."

Alayna looked at the TV and blinked. At some point, it had cut off, but she hadn't even noticed. "I can't stop thinking about it all. What's taking Sheriff Maybank so long? He should have Drew in custody by now."

"Could be Drew wasn't home. He might have headed out to carouse after work and decided to hole up in some club until the storm is over."

"I guess, but the sheriff has his cell phone number. He's not answering."

Bea raised one eyebrow. "Maybe he found a woman to hole up with."

Alayna huffed. "Lord knows, there's plenty of foolish ones who will buy his rich-guy lines. So why is he stalking Jill?"

"He had a girlfriend in high school, but that didn't stop him harassing her then, did it? A cad like Drew isn't going to act like a monk, even if he's fixated on one particular woman."

"Did you just say *cad*?"

"Go ahead. Make fun of my ancient vocabulary if it makes you feel better. So what's the new hip term for cad?"

"Hip?"

Bea waved a hand in dismissal.

Alayna smiled. "Creep still works."

"And it fits," Bea agreed. "Anyway, I'm sure we'll hear from him soon. It's only been a couple hours."

"You mean practically forever? Good God, Aunt Bea, how are you not losing your mind? Were you serious about that Xanax?"

Bea sat next to her niece and put her arms around her shoulders. "I'm just old and have had to worry more often, so know how to handle it better. I just got through a pretty intense round of worry over you, remember? I haven't quite packed the skill set away yet."

Alayna blew out a breath. "You'd think I'd be better at it, right? It's not like I don't know exactly what she's going through."

"My guess is that's why it's overwhelming you. What you went through was horrific and wasn't that long ago. Then we had that whole situation with Emma. I'd be more surprised if you didn't have a round of PTSD brewing, especially with this being about Jill, who was like a sister to you."

"You're probably right. Do you think I should see a therapist again?"

"Wouldn't hurt. Might help."

"Your optimism is overwhelming."

"My *realism* is overwhelming...to most people, anyway."

Alayna's cell phone rang, and she jumped again, grabbed her phone off the end table, dropped it, cursed, and finally retrieved it again.

"It's Sheriff Maybank," she said to Bea as she answered on speaker. "Did you get him?"

"No. He wasn't at his office or his home. There was an upstairs window open at his house, though, and the back door was unlocked. Given that the storm is moving through, I decided that was suspicious enough to warrant an entry. There's a room upstairs that's a...shrine, I guess you'd call it."

Alayna sucked in a breath and Bea put her hand over her heart.

"A shrine?"

"There are pictures of Jill everywhere. Pictures from high school, and I don't think she was aware that most of these were being taken. They're from a distance and she's not looking at the camera. There are also pictures she took for school and local stuff like clippings from the yearbook and the local newspaper. Then there's a wall of nothing but Kate—screenshots of her from pictures online, interviews she's done, and a couple from book signings that look like they were taken from behind shelves. I also found a stack of cards just like the ones she's been receiving. This is bad, Alayna. He's beyond obsessed."

"You have to find him!"

"I'm trying but there's another problem—a huge one. One of those clippings was my statement about the break-in at the lighthouse. Drew lives on a canal on the mainland. His boat is gone."

———

PETE LOOKED DOWN at the woman in his arms, her head lying on his chest, and marveled again at just how much his life had changed in a few short days. Feelings he'd never thought he would have had burst into his heart like a bullet, and he was still reeling from it all. And there was so much going on—so much outstanding, if you will—when it came to the future. But the only thing that mattered was that Jill had said she wanted to give a relationship with him a shot.

He'd agreed, naturally, and had promised her that if it didn't work, no harm no foul, but he already knew that Jill was the woman for him. If he couldn't make it work with her, there would be no other match. They were already a great fit in personality, and he'd figured they'd be fire in bed, and he hadn't been wrong. Jill was unlike any woman before her, and he had every intention of making sure she knew that.

She looked up at him and gave him a sexy, satisfied smile. "I knew we'd be good together. I've never had this level of attraction to anyone before, much less someone I just met."

He nodded. "I'm glad to know I'm not the only one. I've never met a woman like you."

She propped herself up on one elbow. "How's that?"

"No one has ever prompted me to think about things like waking up with them every day, cooking dinner together, doing mundane things like laundry and grocery shopping. But all of that flooded my mind after I met you. It was just different from anything before. Real. Permanent."

"I write about heroes and heroines connecting quickly under dire circumstances all the time, but I always figured it was fiction. That people didn't really develop those feelings that fast. But then I met you. At first, I dismissed it as being in a heightened emotional state and overwhelming sexual attraction—"

"I like the 'overwhelming' part."

She grinned. "Me too, but it didn't end there. When I talked to Alayna about her relationship, then saw her and Luke together, I realized their bond is undeniable, regardless of how they met. They fit as if they were carved out for each other."

"They do. And I'll admit that I've been a little jealous ever since I saw them together. I don't think I realized how much I wanted what they have before I saw them as a couple."

Jill sighed. "Me either. I started hiding from life so long ago that I think I forgot how to live it. At least a large part of it. I guess I didn't realize how much I was missing out on until I was forced out of the secure but isolated nest I'd built."

He kissed her lightly. "All of that is going to be unnecessary soon. But I'm afraid when this is over, your secret is going to be out. Everyone will know you're Kate."

"I know, and I'm okay with that. With Trevor gone, all I need is the stalker behind bars, and I'm good."

"They won't keep him there forever," he warned.

"But I'll know who he is. There's power in that."

Pete started to reply when he heard a noise. The storm had diminished a bit, but he knew this was just the first wave. A second, larger burst was not far behind the first. But the noise was definitely coming from outside. It sounded like someone calling out.

Jill pushed up. "Did you hear that?"

He nodded and jumped out of bed, tugging at his still-damp clothes. "It's coming from outside."

"But it was high-pitched, like a woman. Surely someone's not out in this storm."

"Could be tourists. Search-and-rescue have to go looking for tourists caught in storms every time one blows through.

They rent boats, then don't heed the warnings or don't believe them."

Jill shook her head. "Or they think the weather will change because 'I'm on vacation.' Can't tell you how many times I heard fools say that one when I lived here."

He nodded. "I have to go check. If someone is on shore, they didn't step off at the dock. I barely managed when I got here and had to make a good jump to do it."

"You think they fell off a boat?"

"Or worse. There could be other people out there."

Jill sat up and dressed as Pete checked his pistol and flashlight.

"Close the blinds on the back window," he said as he hurried to the entry. "Lock the door behind me. Do *not* open it for anyone else. And no matter what, don't come outside."

"But—"

"No matter what!"

Pete clutched his pistol in one hand and flashlight in the other and stepped out into the storm. Immediately, Jill closed and locked the door behind him, and he paused just outside the door, listening. It took a couple seconds, but then he heard the voice again, faint in the roar of the second wave of the storm moving in. But definitely human and definitely a woman in distress.

He turned his head one way, then another, and finally decided the noise had come from behind the house, not from the dock. He stepped out from behind the tiny entry wall and into the storm. The wind pummeled him straight on, and he bent forward and ducked his head to protect his face from blowing debris and sand. At least the rain had slowed to a mist, but he knew worse was coming. He had to find the woman before it hit. Keeping his flashlight trained on the ground, he swept it out from the path as he walked.

When he was almost to the back patio, he heard the voice again, and this time he could tell she was calling for help. It sounded like it was coming from just past the back deck. He hurried over and realized the voice was coming from underneath the deck, which was odd. But then, the back door was boarded up and she might have been trying to get out of the storm when the first wave came through. If she was injured, she might be unable to move again.

He followed the periodic calls until he got to a section of the deck with the largest gap between the structure and the ground. He shone his light under it and leaned over to see if he could locate the woman.

The instant he saw the cell phone, he knew it was a trap. But it was too late. The needle pierced the skin at the back of his neck, and everything went black.

———

JILL HURRIED to the kitchen counter and turned on the lamp, which cast a glow over most of the open area. Then she closed the blinds on the back window but remained standing there, lifting them every two seconds to peer outside. She'd seen Pete's flashlight going down the path toward the back deck, but she couldn't see the deck from this window. And with the back door boarded up, there was no other way to access the back of the house except walking around. Which she didn't need to do anyway, even if she were physically up to it.

Pete had told her to stay put, and it was the right call. Here, she could defend herself if something happened. Out there in the storm, she was much more vulnerable.

Like Pete.

She shook her head. Pete was a strong man with serious military training. But he was also a noble man, and the thought of leaving someone in distress out there wasn't something he could do. She understood because she was the same way, but if she was being honest, she wished he wasn't out there.

She lifted the blind slats to peer out again, and this time she saw the flashlight bouncing back down the path toward the front door. It was moving quickly given the storm, and she wondered if he'd located the sound of the voice. He was moving too fast to be aiding someone along, and probably not carrying someone with one arm available and at that speed in the storm.

What if she hadn't made it?

The thought ripped through her mind and her heart clenched. That would be a horrific way to go—drowning, alone in the storm—and with others potentially still at risk. She headed for the door and waited and finally, the knock came and Pete called out.

"Jill, it's Pete. Let me in."

She hurried to turn the dead bolt on the door and yanked it open, but the man staring at her was not Pete.

CHAPTER TWENTY-THREE

JILL STARED AT THE MAN IN THE DOORWAY WITH SHOCK AND confusion. "Isaac? What are you doing here? Where's Pete?"

He stepped inside and closed the door, then gave her a smile that made her feel like ice was coursing through her veins.

"I've come for you, Jill," he said. "It's time. I would have come before, but I couldn't find you. That day I opened the door to my waiting room and saw you sitting there, I knew it was fate that had brought you to me. We were always meant to be together."

"Where's Pete?"

"Pete doesn't matter. He was just another Drew and would have made you just as miserable. You don't belong with a man like that. I've loved you since the first time I saw you. But I had to prove myself worthy, so I became a doctor. But during that time, I lost you. I thought the fates had been wrong, that they'd taken you away. Then I saw you on television. You fooled everyone, Jill, but not me. I'd recognize you always. You belong to me."

Jill let out a strangled cry and backed away from the doorway, stumbling a bit as her boot connected with the edge of a table in the entry. This couldn't be happening. Isaac couldn't be the stalker. It was Drew.

But clearly, they'd been wrong. Again.

Isaac stared at her with his dark eyes—snake eyes—and that horror movie smile, and she let go of the table and shifted her hand to her back, reaching for her pistol. But it wasn't there. Panic coursed through her when she realized that in her rush to open the door for Pete, she'd left it on the windowsill across the room.

"Isaac, you're married," she said, attempting to reason with him as she inched toward the other window. "And my life is in another state. I'm leaving as soon as the storm has passed."

He shook his head. "Did you know people don't trust men who haven't been married? Especially women. Certain professions benefit from the picture-perfect family image, and doctors are one of them. That's what my wife is—a prop. I chose her because she'd had uterine cancer as a teen, and I knew she couldn't have kids."

Jill took another step back, reeling from the cold delivery of those statements. "She was your patient, so you had her medical history."

He nodded. "Fate delivered her to me as well. Just like he did my mother. I never cared anything about her theater nonsense, but she forced me to learn anyway. I've stood right in front of you and got a book signed and you didn't even know who I was."

"You made your voice sound like Pete," Jill said, holding back tears. Had Isaac killed Pete? She didn't see a weapon and hadn't heard a gunshot, and Isaac certainly couldn't have overpowered Pete, but obviously he'd done something to him because otherwise, Pete would be here.

"I'm good at voices."

"You're good at a lot of things, but I don't love you, Isaac. Even if you don't want to remain married, you've built a good life here with your practice. But it's not the life for me."

"Oh, I would never stay here. Did you know my grandparents had money? Tons of money, actually. I had no idea because they were always so secretive, and they never lived big. I had to take out loans for medical school, so when they died in a boating accident while I was doing my internship, imagine my shock to find out they'd left me a house and cars and millions in the bank. Myra knows about the house and cars because we're using them, but she never knew about the money."

He smiled again. "I've already bought us a new place in the mountains. It's remote. So remote it takes a full day to drive there. No one will ever bother us, and we'll live together forever, the way we were always meant to."

A wave of dizziness coursed through Jill and her mind raced with scenarios, all of them bad. Ultimately, her choices filtered down to one option. Isaac was crazy and if you couldn't escape crazy, the only chance you had to beat it was to face it straight on. She was injured and had no transport off the island. And Pete was out there somewhere, and she had to get to him. She'd rather die here than disappear and have people looking for her the rest of their lives.

"I'm not going anywhere with you," she said. "You'll have to kill me."

"Oh, Jill. I'm a doctor. A little sedative is all it takes, and if we run into anyone, I'll flash my credentials. No one will blink at a doctor transporting an unconscious woman. You underestimate me. You always did, but that's okay. You have the rest of your life to understand just how much I love you and what I'm willing to do to make you mine."

"If you think holding me captive will make me love you, you're wrong. You're not stable, Isaac. You're a doctor. You know better."

He slowly shook his head, his expression one of a parent exhibiting infinite patience with an ignorant child. "You just haven't had a chance to understand it all."

"I'm in love with another man!" Jill yelled, hoping to jolt Isaac out of his trance.

He stiffened and blinked, then reached into his pocket and pulled out a needle. "You're confused. But don't worry—I can heal you."

Terror coursed through her. That must have been what happened to Pete. But was he unconscious or dead?

Isaac stepped closer to her, and she spun around as quickly as she could and ran for the window, praying that she could grab her pistol before he jammed that needle into her. But she only made it a couple steps before he grabbed her arm and yanked her back around to face him. He lifted the needle, ready to plunge it into her arm when the door flew open.

They both started and Jill jerked her head around, praying that it was Pete, but they both stared in surprise as Myra stepped inside, a pistol leveled at them.

"Myra?" Isaac said, looking as shocked as Jill. "What are you doing here?"

"I'm saving you," she said. "Did you really think I didn't know about your little obsession? Or the house you purchased? I've had a tracker in your travel bags for years now. I know where you've really been when you claimed to be at those conferences."

Myra shook her head. "I have to say, for a doctor, you're not very observant. I followed you on several of those trips and you never noticed."

Isaac looked genuinely puzzled. "Why?"

Myra laughed. "What a silly question. Because I love you, of course. Because I've wanted you the first time I laid eyes on you in the coffee shop."

Isaac shook his head. "That's not right. We met at my practice."

"I injured myself just to get an appointment with you, and it worked exactly as I thought it would. But I've always known you were holding back in some way. I just could never figure out why. Then I found your storage unit. All those pictures and clippings of *her*. What a waste. She doesn't love you. She just used you in high school so that she could pass her class, and she's using you now to fix her ankle. *I* love you, which is why I fixed everything."

Isaac frowned. "What are you talking about?"

"I took all that stuff from your storage unit and put it in Drew Alderman's house. After that scene with Jill in the coffee shop, everyone will think he's the stalker. I'll even put some of her blood in his boat before I take it back. You'll have to take our boat back yourself, of course. Then no one will ever know we were here."

"What did you do to Drew?" Jill asked.

Myra snorted. "Don't worry—he's still alive. For now. But as soon as I'm done cleaning up Isaac's little mess, Drew will be so overwrought by what *he* did to you that he'll overdose. The police will consider the case of Kate Coleson's stalker closed with a tragic ending for poor Kate. But a happy ending for Isaac and me."

"You can't do this, Myra," Isaac said, clearly starting to panic.

"Of course I can. You won't even try to prevent it, or I'll tell everyone that you're the real stalker and that you killed Jill because you couldn't have her. And before you consider taking me out to save yourself, my attorney has a sealed envelope with all the proof—pictures, video, rental statements for the storage unit, travel logs for all those work conferences you claimed to be at—with orders to bring it to the cops in the event of my arrest or death."

"What is the point?" Isaac raged. "I don't want you, Myra. I never did."

"And I don't want you," Jill said.

Isaac's jaw dropped as the reality of the situation finally started to take hold.

"See," Myra said. "She'll never be happy with you, and then you'll never be happy. But if she was gone, you'd still have me, and Drew would go down for all of it. We could start over. Fresh. With no distractions."

Myra leveled the gun at Jill's chest. "All I have to do is squeeze off one little round."

———

PETE GROANED as the rain pelted his face, and he clutched his head as he tried to pull himself into a sitting position. Whatever he'd been dosed with was strong, but not strong enough. Likely it had been meant for Jill, which was all the more frightening. Certainly Drew didn't have any medical training, and people could easily kill someone if they didn't know what they were doing. Was that the end game? Was he going to kill Jill, or was the injection meant to sedate her so he could haul her off the island to God knew where?

That thought terrified him so much that he ignored his pounding head and weak body and forced himself to stand. The wind was blowing a gale, making his already compromised balance even worse, but he had to get inside. He had to rescue

Jill before Drew injected her. He didn't even want to imagine Drew getting her off the island. The man had the resources to hide and his obsession with Jill was unlikely to provide a good ending.

He had another moment of panic as he reached for his gun, but it was still safely tucked at his waist. Drew had made a mistake not taking it, and it was a mistake Pete hoped to capitalize on. If he wasn't already too late.

He recovered his flashlight on the ground where he fell but couldn't risk using it, nor could he risk the potential noise of using the side of the house to guide him around. He stumbled as he went, huge gusts of wind almost knocking him over as the rain pelted his skin so hard it stung. Each time he staggered, he caught himself just before slamming into the house. With the sedative still coursing through his body, each step was an excruciating and slow process, and no matter how hard he tried to go faster, he simply couldn't.

When he reached the edge of the house, he peered around the side, but it was impossible to see more than a couple feet given the minimal moonlight and the blinding rain. But if he couldn't see Drew then Drew couldn't see him, so he stepped around the corner and headed for the front door. As he stumbled toward it, he thought he heard voices inside, but it was impossible to discern them with the noise from the storm. He was halfway to the front door, but his options were severely limited.

The door was the only viable way into the lighthouse, but there was no cover once he entered, and Pete's reaction time was significantly delayed. If Drew was near Jill, he could use her as a shield or a hostage, but Pete didn't really see another option besides bursting in and hoping he could get off a clean shot.

He readied his weapon in his right hand and said a quick

prayer that his training would be enough to overcome the drug coursing through his system. Then he took a deep breath before starting to close the gap to the front door.

That's when he heard the first shot.

CHAPTER TWENTY-FOUR

JILL SAW MYRA'S FINGER WHITENING, AND WHEN THE OTHER woman smiled, she knew this was it. She gathered all her strength to launch, praying she could make it behind the couch and maybe, with a miracle, over to the windowsill for her gun. If she didn't make it out of here, at least she could try to make sure Myra and Isaac didn't either. If Pete wasn't already gone, then it would give him a chance.

The instant she dived, she felt Isaac shove her, giving her momentum and lift to dodge the bullet that Myra fired. As she hit the floor, Jill heard Isaac gasp and Myra scream and realized Isaac must have taken the bullet meant for her. Myra screamed again—this time in anger, not horror—and she started to unload her gun into the couch. Jill flattened herself on the floor and pushed herself toward the window. She had the slimmest of chances of getting the gun and shooting Myra before one of Myra's shots hit her, but she had no chance at all if she didn't try.

She stuck her boot against the couch and gave a good shove, unable to stifle a cry as pain tore through her ankle. But the kick had advanced her to the edge of the couch. All that was left was to get up and leap for the gun. Myra had stopped firing, which probably meant she was walking toward her. She was out of time.

Gathering her body and her courage, she shoved herself off the ground, the pain in her ankle completely forgotten. She managed to grab the windowsill with one hand, but her balance was so off that she fell, knocking the pistol onto the floor as she went.

"Don't move," Myra's voice sounded above her.

Jill twisted her head around and looked up to see a furious Myra standing above her with her pistol trained at Jill's head. Jill's gun was just out of her reach, and there was absolutely no way she could make a grab for it before Myra could fire.

"You stupid bitch," Myra said. "You've ruined everything. Why did you have to come back here? Of all the places to hide, you came to the one place where *my* husband was. And my perfect plan is ruined. Now I have to kill both of you and play the victimized widow who had no idea her husband was a stalker."

Myra's finger tightened on the trigger, and Jill clenched her eyes shut. When she heard the gun fire, she braced herself, waiting for the bullet to tear through her body and for everything to go black.

But that moment never came.

Myra gasped and the pistol slid from her grasp. Jill stared as the woman clutched her throat, blood spilling between her fingers before she staggered backward and dropped. Jill jerked her head around and saw Pete limping in the doorway, one arm still lifted with his pistol pointed at Myra. Jill was so overcome with relief at seeing him alive that she almost passed out, but then she saw Isaac's leg move and scrambled to grab her own gun.

"Are you all right?" Pete asked as he grabbed the back of the recliner to steady himself.

Jill looked up at him and nodded. "I think she shot Isaac, but his leg just moved. I don't know if he has a gun."

She pushed herself to the edge of the couch and tried to pull herself up, but the pain in her ankle was too much to handle. A second later, Pete gathered her in his arms and helped her rise and sit on the edge of the sofa bed, then he kissed her softly. She could feel his body trembling as he held her.

"Isaac?" she asked when he pulled away.

He shook his head. "The movement was just nerves. She got him right in the heart."

Her entire body slumped with relief. It was over. "Are you all right?" she asked.

He pulled the end table over and sat on it. "The woman's voice was his phone. He must have seen us through the window and lured me out. He got me with a needle when I looked under the deck. The dosage must have been meant for you, which is why it didn't completely take me out. But my body is definitely running at a deficit."

"It was running well enough." She reached over and put one hand on his face. "I thought I'd lost you. I thought I'd lost myself. I can't believe it's over. Thank you for saving me."

"I couldn't imagine my life if I hadn't."

——————

THE ER DOCTOR looked up in surprise as Alayna burst into the room. A nurse yelled behind her, but she completely ignored them both and ran straight to Jill and threw her arms around her.

"Luke called, but I couldn't wait. I had to see you." Alayna looked her up and down. "Are you all right? Are you injured?"

The doctor waved off the frustrated nurse, who shook her head and backed out of the room.

"I'm going to grab a new boot," the doctor said and exited.

"I torqued my ankle again, but I'm fine," Jill said.

Pete, in a genius move, had gone to the top of the lighthouse and used a spotlight to flash an SOS signal into the night. Luke was still out with his trainees and had responded. Pete had insisted on staying on-site until the sheriff could get there and document everything, so Luke and his crew had hauled Jill back to the mainland where she was transported to the hospital. He'd gotten the rundown of what had happened from Jill and informed the sheriff and the Coast Guard.

"I can't believe it was Isaac," Alayna said.

"I know. I'm still trying to wrap my head around it. And Myra. Good God. It's so messed up."

"Did you know he had a thing for you in high school?"

"No idea! He was nice but kinda shy. In a million years, I would have never guessed any of this. Have they found Drew yet?"

"Yes," Bea said as she walked into the room. "Sheriff Maybank called as Alayna and I were pulling in, so I stayed in the lobby to talk to him. After talking to Luke, he headed back to Drew's print shop and broke in. He found Drew in the storeroom unconscious. The paramedics are already there, and he was starting to come around."

"Thank God. Now if the paramedics could just get out to Pete."

"The Coast Guard is already there," Alayna reassured her. "They have medic training and supplies, and Pete is a doctor. He's going to be fine."

Jill nodded. Of course, Alayna was right, but she still felt so overwhelmed by it all.

"He refused to leave with the bodies there and all," she said. "Oh, Bea, I'm so sorry! Your beautiful house and now—"

"Don't you dare apologize," Bea cut her off. "Stuff can be replaced. People can't. I'm just thankful that you and Pete are all right."

Jill teared up. "If it wasn't for Pete, I'd be dead. I wouldn't have let Isaac take me. I wouldn't want the people I loved living with not knowing. Pete saved my life."

Alayna wrapped her arms around Jill again. "And for that alone, I will love him forever."

"Yeah. I might have to do the same."

Alayna gave her another squeeze. "I'm kinda hoping your love for Pete is a little different than mine."

Bea snorted. "You two sure do require grand gestures from your men."

Alayna smiled. "Thank God we have the kind of men who are into making them."

Jill nodded, too overwhelmed to speak. Now that she knew for certain everyone was safe and being attended to, the adrenaline she'd been storing for so long was finally leaving her body. That fuel that had kept her running was about to expire, and she had no doubt that she'd be left exhausted and overwrought.

The doctor stepped back in with the new boot. "The Coast Guard just called. The storm is breaking. They're sending Dr. McCord by helicopter along with the other syringe so that we can identify the sedative used and formulate the best treatment for both him and Mr. Alderman. Dr. McCord is lucid and already gaining strength. He's going to be fine."

Jill's shoulders slumped and she started to cry. Alayna held her close.

It was finally over.

CHAPTER TWENTY-FIVE

ONE WEEK LATER

JILL STEPPED out onto the tiny porch of Pete's apartment and handed him a beer. He smiled as he took the drink with his left hand as his right was busy flipping steaks on the small grill in the corner. She sat in one of the two chairs tucked into the opposite corner and stared out over the Naval base while she stroked Gus's head and marveled at how much her life had changed in such a short time.

"Sheriff Maybank showed me the documents delivered to him by Myra's attorney," Jill said. "It laid out everything that Isaac had done. All the claims of medical conventions when he was stalking me at signings. The trips to try to discover where I lived. And he kept logs. He was the one who attacked Wanda in her bookstore."

"We figured that."

"Yes. I guess I was still thinking there was a slim chance it was Trevor. Not sure why it matters. They were both insane and evil. But Myra's documentation closed up all the gaps in the investigation. She laid it all out, even her own role."

Pete shook his head. "It's hard to understand how someone can be so methodical and yet so incredibly unchecked from reality."

"They both were. The difference is Isaac never saw it in Myra, but then he probably never looked at her that hard. She was just a prop, which is so incredibly wrong. Obviously, I'm not saying what she did was okay. It absolutely wasn't, but I can see where his actions could send an already unhinged mind into overdrive. The look on his face when he told Myra he didn't want her and I said the same thing to him still haunts me. I don't think he ever got just how far he had gone. Not until that moment."

"It's too bad he didn't realize it before it cost two people their lives. They might have been able to salvage their futures with some serious therapy."

"I wish they would have gone that route. Sheriff Maybank had to tell Isaac's parents what happened. He said it was the worst thing he'd ever had to do. He said Isaac's mother collapsed. I feel so bad for them."

Pete nodded. "I can't imagine living with that. And Isaac being their only child, them thinking they had done a good job. He was a respected doctor, married to a woman doing a thankless job for the community for practically no pay. I hate to say it, but I wonder if they'll ever get over it."

"I don't even know where they'd start."

"I think if it was me, the first thing I'd do is move. I don't think I could face people here every day, knowing what they were saying about Isaac. And worse, knowing it was justified. Seems like it would be a constant reminder."

"A change of scenery has served me well in the past."

"Speaking of which, has Detective Ward gotten any more information on Trevor?"

"Not much. According to some bar regulars who knew him, he'd been ranting lately about how his life had been ruined ever since I put him away. That I was a lying whore and the reason everything had gone wrong ever since."

"So he was on a revenge trip."

"Seems like it. Amazing how he blamed me for all his poor choices. It's not like I was the only woman he abused."

"People like Trevor don't take accountability or understand that actions have consequences. What happened to him was inevitable. At some point, bullies run up against someone bigger and badder and angrier than them."

"Speaking of actions and consequences, I also talked to Drew today. He was back at his print shop and I stopped by."

"What? Why?"

She shrugged. "I've been feeling bad about everything that happened. Drew's a creep, but no one deserves to be drugged so they can be set up to take a murder rap and then killed."

"True. Although you have nothing to feel bad about. So what did he have to say?"

"He actually apologized for the way he treated me, now and back in high school. He said that all of this had made him aware of just how different things can be for women and he didn't ever want to be considered remotely similar to Isaac. He still seems pretty shell-shocked."

Pete nodded. "I would be too. He was set up to lose everything, even his life."

"And his parents, instead of Isaac's, would have been left with the fallout and the guilt forever. It would have ruined a lot of people's lives. I don't think we'll ever be friends, but I think he's reconsidering how he treats people, so maybe one good thing came out of all of this."

UNDERTOW

Pete gave her a look of dismay so comical that she laughed.

"Okay, more than one," she said. "But technically, I'd call you an incredible, awesome, spectacular thing."

"That's better. How is Wanda doing?"

Before stepping out on the patio, Jill had been on the phone with her friend—again. Wanda had called several times a day ever since Jill left the hospital.

"She still wants to talk me out of moving, but then she says she looks at the pic I sent her of us and stops herself. I'll miss her, but Wanda is the only thing that I'll really miss about Oregon. My house there is beautiful but it was never home. No place ever has been, really, except Tempest Island."

"We'll find a place there, and then Wanda can come visit as often as she wants."

Jill grinned. "It might be that I've already found one."

"What? Where? When? You've been here all afternoon, and you spent your morning talking to Alayna, the sheriff, and Drew. How many more people could you have fit in?"

"I have a phone, and more importantly, I have real estate connections."

"You've been talking to Bea. What else does she own that I don't know about?"

"Probably plenty, but in this case, it's something we're aware of and that's she's willing to part with for me. We've just got to wait until Alayna and Luke finish construction on their cottage and move out of the other."

Pete's face lit up. "Bea's going to sell the beach cottage?"

"Yes. She said Alayna and I were always sisters in heart, and after everything we'd all been through, she couldn't think of anything that would make her happier than us living right next to each other."

Pete set the spatula down and let out a woot before grabbing her up and twirling her around, as much as he could twirl in the limited space.

"That is incredible!" he said. "I wanted a place on Tempest Island even before I transferred here, but never did I imagine getting a place at the beach. But you're not paying for this. I'm in for half. I'll get a loan for it because I can't imagine it's going to come cheap, even with Bea as the seller."

Jill shook her head. "I own my Oregon home outright. It will easily cover the cottage, even at market price, which I'm insisting on paying with a small discount that Bea insisted on."

"And since I know that whole rich uncle was a cover story, I know you also paid for your home in Oregon yourself. I've been saving money for a home. I can do my share."

"What if you used the money for improvements instead?"

"What kind of improvements?"

"I was thinking we might want to go the route of Alayna and Luke and add a couple rooms and another bathroom before we move in. That is, if you can handle sharing your apartment with me for a while longer."

He gave her a soft kiss that made her sigh. "I love having you to myself in small spaces," he whispered.

"Good. Can you handle dealing with the construction part as well? It's not my thing."

"It's a deal. I'm so excited. I already have some ideas about expansion. The cottage is already awesome, but there's plenty of room to add another couple rooms and a bath off the west side of the living room. Speaking of construction, did Bea say anything about the lighthouse?"

"It's been cleared by Sheriff Maybank and Detective Ward, so she can get people in to address everything. She said she's not selling it, but she's not going to rent it either."

"No? Then what's she planning to do with it?"

"She might have said that a certain writer and her incredible man are free to use it as often as we'd like."

Pete smiled. "She's going to keep it for family."

More Tempest Island stories of love, strength, and courage coming next year. To receive information on new releases, sign up for Jana's newsletter.

MISS FORTUNE SERIES

If you're a fan of humorous, fast-paced mysteries, give the New York Times, USA Today, and Wall Street Journal bestselling Miss Fortune Series a try. The first book in the series, LOUISIANA LONGSHOT, is free.

It was a hell of a longshot...

CIA Assassin Fortune Redding is about to undertake her most difficult mission ever—in Sinful, Louisiana.

With a leak at the CIA and a price on her head by one of the world's largest arms dealers, Fortune has to go off grid, but she never expected to be this far out of her element. Posing as a former beauty queen turned librarian in a small, bayou town seems worse than death to Fortune, but she's determined to fly below the radar until her boss finds the leak and puts the arms dealer out of play.

Unfortunately, she hasn't even unpacked a suitcase before her newly-inherited dog digs up a human bone in her backyard. Thrust into the middle of a bayou murder mystery, Fortune teams up with a couple of seemingly-sweet old ladies whose looks completely belie their hold on the little town. To top things off, the handsome local deputy is asking her too many questions. If she's not careful, this investigation may blow her cover and get her killed.

Armed with her considerable skills and a group of old ladies referred to by locals as The Geritol Mafia, Fortune has no choice but to solve the murder before it's too late.

Made in the USA
Coppell, TX
20 October 2023

23120516R00168